He wasn't going to do this

Jude could read the expression on Tess's face. She wanted him. More than that, *he wanted her*. Wanted to see where comfort took them.

But no. He wasn't even going to *think about* doing this.

It probably would have been much, much smarter to let Tess go on believing he was a married man, a picked peach with a helpless infant depending on him. Because they wouldn't be lovers, tonight or ever.

He'd felt the years of deprivation in her body, more skin-and-bones than slender. He'd felt the terrible, lifelong isolation that left her shocked that anyone was willing to catch her when she fell.

And he felt the hunger, far deeper than a lack of food. A chronic lack of love that made intimacy frighten her so much she fought it even when she was unconscious.

But no. He had sworn off wounded birds. And this beautiful little sparrow was as broken as they came.

Dear Reader,

When I started writing The Sisters of Bell River Ranch series, I knew I wanted to include at least one sister who came to the family by an indirect route. I've known so many loving, loyal families who bring each other great comfort and happiness— but who weren't "born" to one another the old fashioned way. I wanted, somehow, to honor those wonderful bonds.

The heroine of *The Secrets of Bell River,* Tess Spencer, is illegitimate—her very existence one of the biggest secrets of all. She's a half sister to some, no blood relation at all to others, and yet she finds her way straight into their hearts.

In the end, sisterhood is not just blood, or even growing up in the same house. It's about sharing tears and dumb jokes, and circling the wagons against common enemies. It's about seeing the world the same way. I'm lucky enough to have had a sister in the conventional method, but through the years life also granted me friends who were such kindred spirits that they claimed a sisterhood of the heart. One came to me as a childhood friend, but another I found much later in life— something I hadn't imagined was possible. All of them are gifts beyond measure, and I know I'm not the only one who has what I call "like sisters"—the women who have, indeed, become "like" sisters. It makes for a rich life, indeed.

In fact, the only thing a woman needs after that is...a hero of her very own. And that's where the gorgeous, wounded Silverdell carpenter, Jude Calhoun, comes in.

I hope you enjoy their story! And if you, too, have sisters and "like sisters," I hope you'll hug them today.

Warmly,

Kathleen O'Brien

P.S.—Stop by and say hi at www.facebook.com/KathleenOBrienAuthor, or visit me at www.kathleenobrien.com!

O'BRIEN

—

The Secrets of Bell River

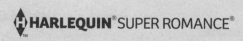

Recycling programs
for this product may
not exist in your area.

ISBN-13: 978-0-373-60844-7

THE SECRETS OF BELL RIVER

Copyright © 2014 by Kathleen O'Brien

www.Harlequin.com

Printed in U.S.A.

ABOUT THE AUTHOR

Kathleen O'Brien was a feature writer and TV critic before marrying a fellow journalist. Motherhood, which followed soon after, was so marvelous she turned to writing novels, which could be done at home. She believes the true friend is the one you trust with your secrets—even if it's just that embarrassing thing about popcorn and reality TV. The *best* friends are the ones who love you because of those secrets, not in spite of them.

Books by Kathleen O'Brien

HARLEQUIN SUPERROMANCE

*Four Seasons in Firefly Glen
**The Heroes of Heyday
#The Sisters of Bell River Ranch

HARLEQUIN SINGLE TITLE

MYSTERIES OF LOST ANGEL INN
"The Edge of Memory"

Other titles by this author available in ebook format.

To Chaela, Celie, Ann...and, of course, Renie.
My "sisters" of the heart, whether you like it or not.

CHAPTER ONE

IN TWENTY-SEVEN YEARS, Tess Spencer hadn't ever felt like she truly belonged anywhere, and it took only one look at the snow-covered perfection of Bell River Ranch to know she didn't belong here, either.

So what if the women who owned it were technically her "family"? She didn't know them—hadn't even heard of them until two months ago, when, on her deathbed, her mother had dropped the bombshell about Tess's paternity.

The Wright sisters didn't know Tess, either. Not even that she existed.

And they probably never would.

She'd left Los Angeles, where she'd lived all her life, and she'd come to Silverdell thinking she might, just *might,* tell them. That had been her mother's dying wish—to leave a safety net for the only child she was leaving too soon. In Tess's imagination, introducing herself to Rowena, Brianna and Penelope Wright had seemed possible. Terrifying, but possible.

But now that Tess saw the beautiful ranch, nestled in its rolling winter landscape like a warm brown egg in a silver-white fairy nest…

How could she tell these elegant, successful strangers—her "sisters"—anything? According to Tess's mother, the three women seemed to be decent people. They'd known plenty of heartache as well as privilege. They probably wouldn't even be terribly shocked to learn about Tess. Their dad, Johnny Wright, had done a lot worse in his life than take a mistress and father one secret illegitimate baby.

Eighteen years ago, he had killed his wife. Their mother.

Tragic, but…still. Soaring Greek tragedy and low, dirty squalor weren't the same problems. Tess Spencer and the legitimate Wright sisters didn't speak the same language. One was a struggling, divorced massage therapist who had lived in crummy apartments all her life, hand to mouth—and that was on a good day. On bad days, she went hungry. The Wrights were landowners, Colorado heiresses who, in spite of their childhood calamity, had always possessed every tree, rock, building and animal they could see.

The gap between their worlds was as wide as the gap between earthlings and martians.

Besides, though they might not be shocked to meet a secret sister, they would undoubtedly be dismayed. Obviously Bell River Ranch was working very hard to leave its scandalous past behind. Nothing proclaimed *civilized* and *unsullied* more than this well-kept, orderly cluster of buildings with sweet blue smoke curling out of chimneys and sunshine sparkling off pristine windows.

"Sorry, Mom," Tess muttered as she parked the car beside the charming wood-and-glass building that housed the spa. "A bastard of Johnny Wright would be about as welcome here as a hole in a lifeboat."

She killed the engine and regrouped. Okay, no thrilled surprise family reunion. She'd always known that was greeting-card schlock, anyhow, not real life.

But that didn't mean she couldn't work here. Work was something Tess knew how to do—and she desperately needed a good job. Her mother's illness had cleaned her out emotionally, and the divorce from Craig had done the same financially.

All the Wright sisters had to do was hire her. That shouldn't be hard to pull off. She was a damn good massage therapist with extensive training, enthusiastic recommendations and five years of experience. Hire her, pay her, maybe appreciate her talents a little, and she wouldn't ask for anything more.

Well, she admitted as she got out of the car, she'd satisfy her curiosity about her birth father at the same time, of course. But that wouldn't cost anyone anything.

"Hi," she said as she opened the door to the spa. She was greeted by soft harp music, and the aroma of expensive lotions mixing with the sharp, piney scent of new construction. The spa had obviously been added quite recently, no expenses spared.

"Good morning," the young blonde goddess behind the streamlined wooden reception desk said. She gave Tess the official "serenity" smile known to any spa employee. Cool, unflappable, full of grace.

You can be a goddess, too, the look was designed to whisper to the client. A few procedures, a small fee...

Tess felt like applauding. A fabulous, incredibly subtle sales pitch. But all wasted. The goddess obviously hadn't yet figured out that Tess wasn't a paying client.

A real client, a late-middle-aged woman in crisp navy blue pants and starched white shirt, sat in the waiting room, perched on the edge of one of the stylish armchairs. She'd been reading a celebrity magazine, but glanced up sharply when Tess entered.

"You haven't forgotten *me,* have you? My appointment was five minutes ago." The woman's voice was as crisp as her clothes, but held an undercurrent of chronic dissatisfaction. Her frown had been so immediate, and the vertical lines between her eyebrows were so firmly grooved, that Tess had to assume scowling was her instinctive reaction to almost anything.

A fussbudget. Tess smiled—her own inner spa employee taking over—though she didn't expect the scowl to go away, and it didn't. She'd encountered clients like this, and she knew how hopeless it was. These people wouldn't ever relax, not if massaged for a week with angel feathers.

"Of course not, Mrs. Fillmore," the goddess purred, unfazed. "How could we ever forget you?"

Tess glanced at the goddess/receptionist. Was she imagining things, or did Blondie's placid voice have an undercurrent of irony?

"I'm Tess Spencer," Tess said. "I have an appointment with Rowena Wright."

"Ah." The young woman looked relieved behind that perfect smile. She wasn't quite as cool and impenetrable as Tess had first thought. She actually said a lot with those blue eyes. "Good to meet you, Tess. I'm Bree. I'm sure Rowena will be here any minute, but—"

"Cancel the search-and-rescue team. I'm here!" Behind Tess, the door blew open with a swoosh of clean, frosty air. "I'm so sorry I'm late, Bree. Don't shoot me. It's insane at the house. Absolutely insane!"

Tess turned to see a willowy young woman

shaking snow from a tangle of long, black hair. The flakes fell to the floor, adding to the crusty crystals left by the tread of her expensive boots. When she finished, she raked back her hair with one hand and lifted her face.

Tess stopped breathing for a second—not because the newcomer was beautiful, though she was absolutely that. When you worked with a pampered, well-heeled clientele, you got accustomed to physical beauty. This woman took Tess's breath away with her sheer radiating vitality. And those green eyes—they seemed lit from behind, alive in an almost otherworldly way, like a forest animal, or a fairy.

It had to be Rowena. Or at least one of the other Wright sisters, since the blonde was Bree. *Brianna,* the middle sister.

Yes, this new woman was Rowena—and she was maybe seven months pregnant, her belly the one rounded spot on an otherwise lean, athletic frame.

Tess had done her homework. Most of the stories she'd found had been either archived ones about Johnny Wright's murder case, in which most papers had been too delicate to print photos of the motherless daughters, or business stories about the opening of Bell River Ranch and its implications for Silverdell's economy, also short on pictures.

She hadn't been surprised. Why should women

who had been through a public scandal at such a tender age seek publicity?

Still, she knew the basic facts. Rowena was the eldest, and the only one with gypsy-black hair. The youngest was Penelope, and the one picture of her as a child showed a honey-brown fall of hair half-hiding a sweet, timid face.

Rowena was obviously the pack leader. Her air of authority was unmistakable. It showed in her indifference to how she tracked slush into the pristine space, in her willingness to bluster into Serenity Central and never be cowed for a second.

Rowena was living proof that everything Tess had been thinking was true. Tess Spencer, the hard-scrabbling itinerant employee with a chip on her shoulder the size of Colorado, had nothing in common with the poised, ebullient Wright sisters.

"You must be Tess!" Rowena turned the amazing green eyes toward her, and her smile deepened, projecting warmth in spite of the chill that still clung to her gold sweater and cords. "I'm Rowena! I'm so sorry I'm late. Gawd, why do I keep saying that? I couldn't help it, really I couldn't. Some meddling fool called the health inspector, and now I'm going to have to dance him around, proving we're not serving ptomaine every night for dinner."

"Ro." Bree pursed her lips, though her eyes had an inner light that hinted at repressed laughter.

"You know you're saying this stuff out loud, right? And everyone can hear you?"

"I can't hear her," a male voice called out from behind the reception area. "And I'm not planning a lawsuit as we speak."

Rowena and Brianna burst into laughter. "You'd better not be, Jude," Rowena said merrily, raising her voice a little to be sure the invisible man could hear her. "What would be the point? You know firsthand how broke we are. In fact, if you get paid this week, you'll be lucky!"

"Ro." Bree shook her head, giving the starchy client a meaningful glance. "Again. You said that out loud."

Ro gave the woman a look of her own. "Oh, we don't have any secrets at Bell River. Silverdell's too small a town for secrets, isn't it, Mrs. Fillmore?"

Tess raised her eyebrows. Again, the subtext of irony. These two didn't like Mrs. Fillmore one bit. She wondered if the feeling was mutual, but the scowl on Mrs. Fillmore's face was too firmly entrenched to be sure it meant anything.

"Indeed," the woman said, pinching her nose with a sniff. "Too small, and sadly too addicted to petty gossiping." She twisted her wrist to look at her watch. "Rowena, my masseuse is ten minutes late."

Tess bristled. No one said *masseuse* anymore. It

had been used too often as a substitute for activities a lot less professional.

"Your massage therapist is Ashley today, Mrs. Fillmore."

One point for Rowena, who had corrected Mrs. Fillmore without making an issue of it.

"And?" Mrs. Fillmore seemed to find Rowena's explanation inadequate.

"You know Ashley always gives everyone a little extra attention if they need it." Rowena smiled warmly. "That's why you always ask for her, I'm sure."

Another sniff. Mrs. Fillmore looked down without answering, turning the pages of her magazine, as if intensely interested in the paparazzi photo spread.

How exactly that differed from petty gossip, Tess couldn't say. But she didn't have the job yet, and she couldn't be snarky with the clients. Luckily, she rarely wanted to. Once she got her hands on a person, even a person like Mrs. Fillmore—

Tess was a tactile person. She thought, and heard, and spoke, and even learned, through her hands. It was her talent. Really, her only talent. If she'd had a choice, she would have chosen something far more lucrative, like computer programming or rocket science.

But she hadn't had a choice. All she had was the ability to learn about a person by touching their skin, working their body. By hearing the tension in their muscles and the strain in their joints. By knowing which pressure points they responded to, what made their blood flow more easily, what drained the unhappiness from their faces.

Once she worked on someone, she understood them in a new way, and the urge to judge, or mock, or take down a peg simply vanished.

"I'm not worried about the health inspector, really," Rowena went on, indicating to both Brianna and Tess in her explanation. "There's nothing to find, so he can dig away. Whoever phoned is just causing trouble for the fun of it. The real problem is that I will have to dance him around, which means I won't be available for the working massage, Tess. We'll have to find someone else for you to work on."

Rowena turned a hopeful gaze toward her sister, who shook her head implacably. "Sorry," Bree said. "Much as I'd love to let someone work out these kinks, I've got nine eight-year-olds waiting to take a sleigh ride to see Santa in downtown Silverdell."

Rowena made a raspberry of annoyance. "Drat. Forgot about that. Really, next year we are going to have to close from Thanksgiving to New Year's, like we planned. Won't that be heavenly? I'll sleep the whole time." She gave Tess a rueful glance. "This year, we can't afford to close a single minute.

Which is why we're interviewing four days before Christmas, in case you thought that was nuts."

Tess smiled neutrally. She had been part of start-ups before, and she knew the first couple of years were insane, and very touch-and-go, financially. Rowena might be optimistic to think they'd be on solid footing in twelve months.

Besides, Tess couldn't bring herself to think about Christmas this year. Her mother had died two months ago, and the jingling bells and twin-kling lights all over town were a jarring reminder of what she'd lost.

She didn't intend to celebrate any holidays for a while. The only toast she'd raise this year was to a new beginning and an entirely new life.

"I'm glad you were," she said, "since four days before Christmas just happened to be when I was looking for a job."

Rowena accepted that logic with a nod, then turned to Bree. "What about Becky? Can't she take over?"

"Nope. She's leading Pilates. We'd have a mu-tiny if we canceled Pilates."

"Mark? He's good with kids!"

"Good with kids?" Brianna laughed. "Are you kidding? Mark threatened to tie Alec to a tree yes-terday if he didn't stop putting snowballs down Ellen's back."

"So?" Rowena grinned. "I threaten to tie Alec to a tree every day."

"Well, you're his stepmother. I think it's written in the job description."

"Hey," Tess interrupted, finally realizing that if she waited for an opening she'd be here all day. "It's okay. Really. I can come back tomorrow."

Rowena shook her head. "No, that's silly. I need you to *start* tomorrow, if everything works out. With Devon leaving in a week, there's hardly any time to get you up to speed."

Rowena chewed on her lower lip, narrowing her eyes with fierce determination. "There has to be a way…there must be someone." Her eyes opened wide. "Mrs. Fillmore! Is there any chance you would be willing to let Tess do your massage today? She has excellent credentials, and we need some feedback on a working massage, so that—"

"No." The older woman folded her magazine tightly, the paper crackling under the force of her fingers.

Rowena frowned. "Of course it would be a complimentary session, as you'd be doing us a favor. And if for any reason it wasn't satisfactory, we could ask Ashley to—"

"No." For a minute it seemed Mrs. Fillmore wasn't going to elaborate, and would let the rejection hang there like a slap in the face. But apparently she realized how rude it sounded and bent a little.

"My sciatica is acting up today. Ashley is the only one who knows how to give me any relief. I'm sorry, but I just can't take chances with a…" She paused, wrinkling her nose slightly. "A beginner."

Heat flooded Tess's face. *Beginner* was insulting enough, given that she had three degrees and five years of experience. But she had, in her intuitive way, "heard" all the other words that Mrs. Fillmore had considered saying. A *nobody.* A *stranger.* A *loser.* An *urchin.* A *child.*

It struck a nerve. Tess was always being taken for younger than she was. She was only five-three. She'd always been too thin, the kind of thin that broadcast the years of going to bed hungry when her mother got laid off. The kind of thin that made her breasts look ridiculous.

And she wasn't one bit glamorous, didn't possess an ounce of the confident gloss that rich, well-tended women acquired. She had a small chip out one of her front teeth that should have been repaired long ago, but there'd never been enough money. She worried off her lipstick and couldn't be bothered applying mascara.

Her only real asset, a mass of curly brown hair that bounced and shone without spending a fortune on it, had to be pinned back ruthlessly when she worked. No one wanted the massage therapist's curls tickling their bare back.

The compliment she'd heard most often from kind-hearted clients was that she had a *sweet* face. She knew that was shorthand for "not ugly, of course, a perfectly nice-looking girl, but…"

"Beginner? Beginner?" Rowena's high cheekbones were tipped with red. "Tess isn't a beginner, I assure you, Mrs. Fillmore. In fact, we're quite lucky to get her. Her last job was at the—"

"It's okay," Tess said, wondering about Rowena's temper. There was zero chance that Mrs. Fillmore would have heard of the Pink Roses Salon, the luxury spa where Tess had worked a year before her mother's death. Impressing Mrs. Fillmore was impossible. "Really," Tess added firmly. "Mrs. Fillmore is right. Sciatica can be debilitating. She should have the massage therapist she trusts."

And Tess should have a fair judge of her talents. A woman bullied into accepting an unwanted massage didn't look like the most impartial critic.

To her credit, Rowena seemed suddenly to get that. "Oh. Right." She took a deep breath, clearly tamping down the irritation with the older lady. "Of course."

Bree, who clearly either didn't have a temper or knew how to hide it, smiled. "I know. What about Jude?"

"What about Jude?" The man's amused voice

came from behind the wall, and was followed by a rustling sound, then the appearance of a large body.

For a minute, Tess wasn't sure he was real. Surely people that exquisite, that drop-dead gorgeous, didn't just emerge from behind walls on command. Not even here, at the fairy-tale Bell River Ranch.

Tumbling black waves of hair. Eyes bluer than cornflowers. Lips, jaw, cheekbones, forehead— all chiseled Michelangelo perfect. Tall, lean, perfectly proportioned.

The beautiful creature was dressed as a laborer. A carpenter, probably, judging from the leather apron slung low on his trim hips, like a gunslinger's belt. His weapons appeared to be screwdrivers, wrenches and other tools she was too ignorant to name.

She almost laughed. If he'd been sent to a movie set by central casting, the director would have rejected him instantly, on the grounds that no real person, carpenter or king, ever looked like this.

"Jude, this is Tess Spencer. She's applying for Devon's job." Rowena spoke, but neither she nor Bree seemed surprised at the appearance of Adonis. "Tess, this is Jude Calhoun. Our carpenter and general woodworking genius. He's single-handedly responsible for building the spa. And about half the other buildings at the ranch, too."

Jude came forward, brushing his palms lightly

across his back pockets, as if to remove sawdust. Then he held out his right hand to Tess. "She's exaggerating, of course. Rowena doesn't do anything by half measures, including compliments."

Tess put her hand out, too, rather numbly.

His shake was warm and firm. "Nice to meet you, Tess."

Rowena checked her watch. "I don't mean to put you on the spot, Jude, but I've got to meet the inspector. Would you mind letting Tess do her working massage on you? You've gotta need one, after being on that ladder all day."

Inexplicably, Tess felt her cheeks flushing, but she couldn't demur about this recruit, too, not after rushing to rule out Mrs. Fillmore. She might look as if she were afraid to do the working massage.

At least this guy didn't seem as if he'd be bitchy about it.

"Well…" He smiled at Tess, his cheeks dimpling about an inch from the corners of his lips. Of course. If he'd been a computer-generated image, the dimples couldn't have been placed more effectively. "It's a terrible imposition, being blindsided like this, and asked to accept a free massage. But I suppose I can take one for the team."

TEN MINUTES LATER, Tess was ready. She'd received the quickie tour of the facilities from Bree, essentially killing time while Jude had a shower.

As they went through the spa, Tess noted again that the Wrights had spared no expense, and she congratulated their taste. One of the indefinables that characterized any successful retreat was a soothing, almost spiritual feeling. This one had it.

The cream-and-taupe marble was peaceful, and Tess recognized top-of-the-line products everywhere. But the real magic was the location. The spa had been brilliantly designed in a *V* shape, obviously to provide all the main rooms with a view of a waterfall mere yards from the building.

The small waterfall had frozen in this unnaturally cold December, and it sparkled like white crystal ribbons in the sun. Tess could only imagine how transcendent the view would be when the water spilled liquid diamonds in the summer.

"That's Little Bell Falls," Bree said. "It's pretty, isn't it? You should see it during wildflower season."

Interestingly, Bree's placid face didn't register the same delight Tess felt, but she didn't comment further. Was there a problem? Perhaps proximity to water presented a dampness concern? Had there been a debate about where to build the spa?

Tess was surprised to realize how curious she was to know everything about the Wrights and Bell River. Should a secret blood connection she'd discovered only three months ago, and which had been no part of her life for twenty-seven years, affect her so profoundly?

In the end, these people were strangers, and probably would never be more to Tess than amiable employers. And not even that, if she didn't nail this massage.

"Sorry you can't work in one of the cozier single rooms," Bree said as she led Tess into a large space that obviously was set aside for couples massage. Two tables, a hot tub, its own nail station. "But we have just the two singles. Chelsea is using the Taupe Room, and Ashley's got Mrs. Fillmore in the Blue Room."

Mrs. Fillmore. Another nuance Tess would have loved to explore. Another detail that was none of her business.

"I don't mind at all," she said honestly. The frills—the decor, the candles, the music, the lighting—were mostly for the clients' benefit. When Tess worked, she went into a zone and didn't register anything except the body under her hands.

Bree seemed ready to leave Tess, but she paused about halfway to the door. She glanced down the hall, toward the faint, distant hiss of water where Jude had disappeared to "wash the work off."

"You know, there's nothing to be nervous about," Bree said, turning to Tess with a disconcertingly sharp gaze. "He's a nice man, very down-to-earth. Not an ounce of arrogance in him, amazingly."

"It hadn't occurred—"

"No?" Bree smiled. "Come on. We grew up with him. He's always been around—he and Mitch, Rowena's brother-in-law, are best friends, so he's practically like a brother to us all. And yet sometimes even we can't believe how good-looking he is."

Tess shrugged. "I've lived in L.A. all my life. Even before I went to work for Pink Roses, I'd seen some amazing things."

"Oh? I didn't know that. That'll give you something in common, then. Jude spent a little more than six years in Hollywood."

"Really?"

"Yeah." Bree's elegant brow pinched a fraction. "Not that I'd mention it. It wasn't an entirely happy experience for him."

Tess tried not to bristle. Massage therapists weren't priests, but discretion was definitely desirable. "I don't tend to chitchat while I'm working. I need to concentrate, and the clients usually prefer to relax. Even if they talk, I mostly listen."

"Good. Well, I guess that's everything." Bree fidgeted with her earring, clearly a bit uncertain about leaving Tess without supervision. "Except… I probably should mention that—"

"I'm fine." Tess hoped her voice didn't sound too tight. The hovering was a little annoying. Five years, remember? She'd worked her way up to some of the most demanding spas in the country, spas that catered to people who expected perfection, even in their massage therapists.

Yet Bree acted as if she were leaving a kid at kindergarten on the first day.

Tess forced a smile. "Really. I'll be fine."

Nodding, Bree turned, practically running into Jude, who stood in the doorway, wearing a white terry robe monogrammed with the initials BRR across the breast.

"There you are!" She patted his chest casually. "Okay, then, if you guys are both set, I'd better run. Remember, if you need anything, both Chelsea and Ashley are a shout away."

"Thanks," Tess said.

And then she and Jude were alone. For an awkward minute, she was ridiculously tongue-tied, forgetting her protocols as if she really were the newbie that Mrs. Fillmore and Bree took her for.

His coloring and perfect features had been striking enough, even in his work clothes, but like this, half-dressed, tousled and damp from the shower…

It was impossible not to have a purely female reaction. The robe hugged the lean contour of his hips, ending just above the knees. Long, trimly muscled legs extended bare beneath the hem. The casually knotted belt nipped the robe in at his narrow waist, but above that his chest and shoulders tugged the cloth apart, exposing golden skin and a light dusting of dark hair.

Pull yourself together, girl! She never did this. *Never.*

Once clients lay on the table, they ceased to be "people" in that way—they weren't male or female, young or old, beautiful or homely. They certainly weren't sexual.

They were simply exquisitely complex interlacings of muscle, tendon, nerves and needs. They were…well, it sounded silly but she sometimes thought of their bodies as works of art entrusted to her care. Art that had been damaged somehow. Misaligned. Knotted. Twisted, overtightened or blocked. Her job was to find the parts that had been disturbed and restore them to harmony.

Perhaps Jude was the *most* artful of all the works she'd ever been asked to restore. But so what? In her experience, athletes and body-builders and actors—all the physical perfectionists who populated Los Angeles—needed her help more than most.

They punished their bodies to take them to those heights of performance, and, once they relaxed, they proved to be masses of knotty pain and foreshortened tendons.

"Are there any injuries I should know about? Anything you'd particularly like addressed today?" She was glad to hear that her voice was normal.

He shook his head. "Nothing serious. I've got an ankle sprain that bugs me now and then, but massage helps, as a rule."

Internally, she noted that.

"Okay, then. Good. There's a sheet on the first table, and a light blanket, in case it feels a little cold to you. Make yourself comfortable, and I'll be right back."

Her crisp, competent tone made her feel less nervous, and Jude's easy smile helped, too. "Sure thing," he said.

She stayed away longer than was strictly necessary, giving him plenty of time to get covered, and giving herself plenty of time to get calm. Finally, she gathered the supplies she had chosen earlier, took a deep breath and moved down the hall, too.

He'd left the door open, so she walked in— slowly enough to alert him, and speaking as she entered. "Sorry. I don't know where everything is, so it took me a minute to find it all."

No response.

She moved to the counter nearest the massage table, where he lay on his stomach, his head not in the padded opening, but turned to one side, so that he presented his elegant profile. He was completely still.

"Mr. Calhoun?"

Tilting her head, she looked closer. He was so completely motionless he might have been dead…

except that as she drew near he shifted once, sighed deeply and let out a low rumble that was...

Instinctively, she smiled. Yes, it was a snore. In the dim lighting, made more soothing with the addition of a few candles, with a Chopin Prelude playing on the sound system and the perfume of clean sheets and lavender oils floating in the air, he had fallen asleep.

She fiddled with her supplies, not banging things around, but not attempting to be particularly quiet. If he woke on his own, it would be much less awkward.

He didn't. He wasn't snoring anymore, but he remained utterly still, his eyes shut and his beautifully bowed lips slightly apart, glistening in the candlelight.

She allowed herself the indulgence of studying him. It wasn't voyeurism. As a therapist, she could learn a lot by how he held himself, whether his shoulders relaxed into symmetry when he slept, whether his body twitched in those little ways that spoke of tension that dissipated only when the conscious mind shut down.

A couple of seconds passed before she could stop staring at his face, but when she finally transferred her gaze to his shoulders and back, she inhaled sharply.

The perfection stopped there. On either side of his spine, starting just below the neck and running down between the shoulder blades for at least five inches, were the unmistakable thin, thready scars left by a set of human fingernails.

She'd seen similar scars before, once or twice. But Jude's were deeper than the average remnant of exuberant passion. These were more like...an attack.

"I suppose this is what Bree meant," he said, "when she said she should probably warn you."

Tess's gaze flew to Jude's face. His eyes were open, and he was smiling. She tamped down her momentary embarrassment and reached for her lotion.

She didn't see any point in pretending she hadn't been staring at the scars. His body was her business, right now.

"No need for a warning," she said calmly. "I don't think the scars present any special concern. They are clearly fully healed. Are they sensitive?"

"No." He raised himself on his elbows and rubbed his thumbs across his eyelids, as if to scrape away the sleepiness. "I'm sorry I passed out. I was up all night with the baby, and I guess it caught up with me the minute I lay down."

The baby?

The word surprised her. He didn't look...

He didn't look what? Like a father? How absurd was that? There was no "father" look. But then she realized that, on some subconscious level, she'd already observed that he didn't wear a wedding ring.

Equally absurd. Her subconscious shouldn't be registering such things in the first place, and, in the second place, wedding rings weren't required in the baby-making process.

"No problem," she assured him as placidly as she could. "You wouldn't be the first client I've had who slept through a massage." She warmed some lotion in her hands. "Though usually they do wait until I've begun, at least."

As he chuckled, she touched gently between his shoulder blades. He automatically dropped down, as if he knew the drill well.

"Might make it tricky to rate your technique, though," he said, his voice muffled by the cushion of the face support. He seemed about to speak, but the word dissolved into a contented "mmm" as she began to massage the lotion into his skin.

From then on, he didn't utter a sound. She didn't worry that his silence meant a lack of appreciation, or that he'd fallen asleep. He was her favorite kind of client, the kind who understood that the body spoke for itself.

When a tight muscle began to relax under her fingers, she didn't need a murmur of bliss to tell her about it. And when she encountered a knot of pain, she didn't need a wince to alert her. She read the ridges, valleys, ribbons and rocks of his body as if he were a story written in braille. Any decent massage therapist could do the same.

The irregular embossing of the scars was harder to read. They weren't sexual in nature, she felt sure of that. The gouges had been too deep, caused by true violence, whether intentional or accidental. And they had been painful.

She thought she might, with time, be able to break down some of the collagen build-up and reduce the scars, but that wasn't her mission today. She'd been asked to demonstrate a Swedish massage, the kind that felt great and left the client purring.

Besides, Jude might not have any interest in having his scars worked on. He didn't seem to be a bit self-conscious about them. She could tell when she hit a client's sensitive spot, either physically or emotionally. Some vibration under the skin, through the nerves and muscles, changed slightly, hitting a new note like a string on a guitar. His vibration didn't alter an iota when her fingers skimmed along the scars.

She found plenty of tender spots. The external abdominal obliques, especially, were too tight. His job… He probably didn't stretch enough after a tough day. And warmth pooled in the small of his back…sometimes that meant there was a gait problem, though she hadn't noticed one while he walked.

The time vanished, as it often did. She always set a timer to buzz in her pocket as she needed to switch through the phases of the massage, because she knew she'd lose track of the hour if she didn't. Today, though, she must have failed to do it. She worked on his back, then on the front, alternating long strokes and detail work on the pressure points.

She was lost—she couldn't have said how long— in exploring the pressure points on the face and scalp when a light rap sounded on the door.

"So sorry, guys." Chelsea's throaty voice was soft as she cracked the door open. Tess recognized it instantly. Chelsea, the spa's director, had put her through an extensive telephone interview before this working massage. No point bringing in Tess at all, unless she passed that initial phase.

Jude rose onto his elbows, stretching his neck slowly. "Time's up already?"

"Yeah, sorry." Chelsea waved two fingers at Tess. "I wouldn't disturb you, except that we've got the Ardens out there, and they're not the patient type."

"No, of course." Tess was annoyed with herself for letting the session run long. She liked to end with a short head massage, which seemed to make the transition to real life smoother. She began wiping her hands on a clean towel. "We were just about finished, anyhow."

Chelsea nodded and ducked out. Jude sat up,

keeping the sheet around his hips, and let out a long, satisfied sigh.

"Nice," he said with feeling. He tested his shoulders, stretching out his obliques. "Oh, yeah. *Very* nice. Maybe the best I've ever had." He grinned. "And that's saying something, because I get a lot of massages."

She smiled, but something in her eyes must have registered surprise, because he laughed. "I'm the official guinea pig around here. Ro always says she wants to check out new hires, but in reality she's too busy. So…" He yawned and ran his hand through his hair, mussing it. Somehow the disheveled look suited him. "As I said, tough work, but someone has to do it."

"Thanks," she said, glancing away. Did that mean there was a high turnover of therapists at the ranch? She couldn't ask, of course. "I'm glad you feel relaxed."

She gathered her supplies and hurried toward the door. Behind her, she heard the soft whisper as the sheet fell to the floor.

Out by the front counter, the serenity had been jangled a bit. Rowena had returned, and was helping Mrs. Fillmore set up her next appointment. If the woman's massage had relaxed her, she didn't show it. She leaned over Rowena's appointment book, as if challenging something, and reiterated in a brittle voice that she would accept Ashley and only Ashley.

In the waiting room, a long-limbed couple straight from the pages of *Beautiful People Magazine* were tapping manicured fingers against thousand-dollar boots and giving off restless vibes.

In that moment, Tess could easily imagine why there was high turnover of therapists at Bell River Ranch. It had positioned itself at the high end, and the clients were the entitled type, demanding and finicky. In Tess's experience, these well-heeled clients often could be iffy, looking for any excuse to avoid tipping. Difficult clients, high turnover, possibly disappointing income...

That was three strikes....

But it didn't matter. As she returned the lotions to the elegant chrome shelves, and listened to Rowena wryly but deftly handling Mrs. Fillmore, Tess realized the truth. She wanted to be a part of Bell River, even if only temporarily. Even if her true relationship were never revealed.

If she got the chance, *nothing* would prevent her from taking this job.

CHAPTER TWO

JUDE SWALLOWED HIS last delicious mouthful of Marianne Donovan's prime rib, dropped a ketchup-bottle cap onto the café table with a flourish, then tilted his chair on its back legs, though Marianne, who owned the café, would kill him if she saw him.

"And there you go—that's nine in a row. You might as well go home, grandpa. It's not your night."

Old Grayson Harper snorted, glaring at the tic-tac-toe grid they'd made out of straws and the ketchup caps from every bottle on the adjoining tables. He knew Jude had beaten him, but was, as usual, refusing to admit defeat gracefully.

He lifted his piercing blue eyes and tried to impale Jude with them. "You're cheating, you young skunk, and if I could prove it, I'd have you arrested."

Jude smiled, then yawned loudly. He hadn't slept again last night and didn't have the energy for the customary verbal sparring that Harper loved so much.

"Yeah," he said, scratching at his chin. He'd forgotten to shave this morning, though he'd showered twice, right before and right after the baby barfed on his shirt. "I'm cheating at tic-tac-toe. Hey, look. Dallas is sitting right over there. Tell him."

"I ought to."

"Sheriff!" He called loudly enough to be heard where Dallas and his deputy were sitting, though it elicited a scowl from Esther Fillmore, who sat with Alton, her mousy husband, in the corner booth. "I'm a tic-tac-toe desperado. I'd like to turn myself in."

"Shut up, Jude." Dallas rolled his eyes. He'd known Jude too well and too long to pay any attention, so he went back to his own steak dinner. "No one cares."

Jude chuckled, and winked at Esther to annoy her. He brought his chair back onto all fours, finished his tea, then wiped his mouth one last time.

"I've gotta head home," he said with a sigh. It had started to snow, and he'd rather just lean his head against the café's green wall and take a nap. "Half the time, Molly forgets to eat unless I stand over her."

Harper's gaze softened. "She's no better?"

Jude shrugged and reached for his coat. He didn't gossip much about his little sister's depression, but everyone knew it was a problem. "Physically, yeah, I think she's improving. But emotionally…"

"Hey, don't you even think about leaving before I fix up some chicken soup for Molly." Marianne appeared at the edge of their table, her red curls piled up in a big, adorable mess on her head and topped with a sprig of holly and a couple of silver bells. With Christmas a couple of days away, the Kelly green of the restaurant needed only a few red ribbons to be fully decorated.

"Besides," Marianne said, grinning as she made her bells ring, "I want to hear about the new hire at the spa. I heard from Barton that the wheels are coming off over there. Word is Chelsea ran off to get married, and Devon's leaving, and Ashley can't take over as the director because she's getting her master's, so Ro might offer the position to the new gal, who thought she was just applying for a part-time job and is staying at the motel over at the west end. He said Ro said you said she's good, and she's going mostly on your word alone." She rested her hip against the table. "So, come on. Tell me everything about her."

Jude held up his palms, trying not to laugh. *He said Ro said you said...*

"Mari, there is clearly nothing about Silverdell or its inhabitants that anyone could tell you. I'm not actually one of the family out there, you know. I hadn't even heard Chelsea was leaving."

"The heck you're not family. Give me a break." She waved her hand impatiently. "Forget about Chelsea. I want to know about the new one...Jess? That her name?"

"Tess."

"Right, Tess. So? What's she like? Is she pretty? Is she nice? Is she going to fit in?"

"How would I know that?"

"Oh, don't be such a male." Marianne clicked her tongue against her teeth impatiently. "Barton didn't even lay eyes on her. But you should know. She gave you a massage, right?"

"Right."

"Well? You couldn't tell anything about her?"

He exchanged a resigned glance with Harper, who looked sympathetic but shook his head, as if to say Jude was on his own. Harper was already pulling out his wallet.

Jude turned his gaze to Marianne. "I could tell she was a good massage therapist," he said slowly. "But I get the feeling that's not what you're asking."

Marianne drummed her Christmas pencil against her order pad. "Oh, just forget it. I'll call Ro later. But don't you move an inch until I bring that soup, you hear?"

"Yes, ma'am." Jude resisted the urge to salute.

Harper seized his chance and jumped up in Marianne's wake, dropping a ten on the table and making his way to the checkout station to pay his bill. Jude didn't blame him. No one ought to get dominated in tic-tac-toe and interrogated by Marianne Donovan in the same night.

Not that Marianne was your typical small-town

gossip. Actually, she didn't have a nasty bone in her body. She just had an insatiable curiosity and a deep love for their little town. Maybe it was some kind of thwarted affection or something, though Jude wasn't big on psychoanalysis. Still, she'd been left a tragically young widow last winter, and had no kids.

Whatever the reason, she represented everything Jude loved about Silverdell. And the opposite of everything he hated about Los Angeles.

As the door opened, the four beginning notes of "Danny Boy" rang out. On the first day, at the first meal served at the grand opening, when the door chimes sounded, the customers had spontaneously joined together to finish the line by singing out, "The pipes, the pipes are calling!"

It had been the birth of a beloved tradition. Mari had tried in vain to break the habit, which could really be annoying during the dinner rush. She'd even threatened to disable the entry alert. But the truth was, everyone loved the instant camaraderie those few notes created, and no one could imagine Donovan's Dream without it.

She'd considered changing the tune to "Jingle Bells" during the holidays, but the customers had threatened a boycott, so she left it alone.

Many customers didn't even look up as they sang, it had become so automatic. But for some reason Jude did glance toward the door, as the gust of snowy wind blew in. Tess Spencer stood there, looking bewildered by the musical greeting.

A few curious glances stayed on her—but Silverdell had enough new tourist spots these days that strangers weren't the oddity they once were. Most people went back to their conversations and their dinner.

Jude was one of the few who kept staring, surprised at how different Tess looked from the woman who had massaged him two days ago. Then, she'd been working hard to downplay any sexuality, as a good massage therapist would, naturally. Hair scraped back, no makeup, loose-fitting clothes. His main impression had been that she was petite— shortish, thin and vaguely fragile. He knew that a massage didn't have to be bruising to be effective, but even so he'd noted how delicate she seemed and wondered whether she was up to the job.

She had been. She was a darn good therapist. And that was what he'd noticed.

But now...

She wasn't dressed up or anything, but apparently as soon as she stopped repressing her femininity it busted out all over. She wore only lipstick, but the pink of it drew attention to the perfect, slightly pouting bow of her mouth. Her shining brown hair fell over her delicate shoulders in lush waves that curled just above her elbows. As she shrugged off a nice blue wool coat, her jeans and sweater hugged curves that were designed to make a man's palms itch.

She still hesitated in the doorway, as she scanned the room for an empty table. She didn't look nervous, just patient…and yet, inexplicably, Jude had a sudden impression of her as terribly alone.

Impulsively, he waved at her and called her over. He did need to get home. But at least he could say hi, maybe introduce her to a couple of people. And she could have his table.

To his surprise, she flushed when she saw him. But, after a slight hesitation, she moved toward him, her coat over her arm.

"Hi," she said. "Nice to see you. Don't let me… I mean, don't let me interrupt your dinner."

"You're not," he said. "I just finished. Besides, I was hoping we'd run into each other. I wanted to tell you how much better my back is feeling."

She smiled. "Good. I'm glad to hear that." She hugged her coat awkwardly and looked around once more, as if hoping an empty table would magically appear. Instead, her gaze stopped as she recognized Esther Fillmore. Jude saw the older woman give Tess the evil eye, apparently for being new in town. Alton shook his head subtly, as if trying to calm his wife. But Alton was no match for the crotchety old broad, and she didn't even blink.

"Don't mind Esther," Jude said, quietly conspiratorial. "Her face always looks like she sucked a lemon. I first saw that expression when I was seven and sneaked a soda into the library."

Tess glanced at him, as if uncertain whether she ought to laugh. "She's Silverdell's librarian?"

"Yep. But don't worry. Silverdell has a bookstore, too. Fanny Bronson owns it, and she's much easier to get along with."

"Then I guess I'll be buying my books while I'm here." Tess smiled, finally. "If I get the job, that is."

"I wouldn't be surprised if you do," he said. He didn't want to raise her hopes, but judging from what Mari had said, it seemed a shoo-in. And he had this ridiculous sense that she needed cheering.

"Really? Have you heard something?"

"No. But word is you got a wildly enthusiastic recommendation for your working massage."

She flushed again. "Thank you. That was very nice of you. But really, I mustn't keep you. I thought I'd get dinner, but obviously they're packed. Maybe I'll grab something and take it back to my hotel."

"No. Stay." Jude heard the words come out before he could stop them. "Donovan's has great food, and it would be a shame not to eat it warm from the oven. It would be half frozen if you tried to take it across town in this weather. I could—"

At the last minute, he pulled himself from the brink. What was he thinking? He couldn't keep Tess company, no matter how "alone" he imagined her to be.

He had obligations at home. Molly always got depressed come sundown, especially if she'd been alone with the baby all day. Or if Garth had called, trying to get her to come home. When it snowed she was even worse. Like a form of cabin fever, Jude sometimes thought, though the doctor had a fancier term: postpartum depression.

But it didn't leave much room for Jude to have a life, did it? And right now, when he was standing at the most important fork in the road he'd ever faced…

A shimmer of frustration passed through him—followed immediately by a wave of disgust with himself for being so selfish. Molly hadn't timed her illness, or her marital problems, to annoy him. She couldn't help that Garth was an abusive bum, or that her post-baby chemistry had gone out of whack.

"Here's the soup!" Marianne bustled out of the kitchen. She didn't see Tess at first, concentrating on wrestling a large biodegradable to-go bowl into a paper bag. "If this doesn't perk Molly up, nothing will."

She extended the bag. But as she looked up and noticed that he wasn't alone, her eyes widened.

"Hi, there," she said warmly, her gaze sweeping over Tess like a computer scan, missing nothing. "Welcome to Donovan's! I'm sorry…shall I get this table cleared off, or are you here to pick up Jude?"

Tess hesitated, obviously still undecided about whether she'd stay, but the alternative, that she'd come to pick Jude up, was equally untrue.

Jude took the soup and stood. "Mari, this is Tess Spencer. I told her she could have my table, but she said she might order takeout."

"Oh, no! On a night like this?" As she spoke, Marianne flicked one quick look toward Jude that asked the important question—*the* Tess?—and received her answer in a fraction of a second. Satisfied, she reached for a bright green menu and handed it to Tess. Then she deftly began piling dishes and debris onto a tray.

"I do hope I can talk you into staying. We have some wonderful comfort food, perfect for a cold December night."

Her tray full, she balanced it with one hand and pulled out a chair for Tess with the other. "Sit while you look at the menu. Jude can tell you what's good."

Tess sat, draping her coat across her lap. But she remained on the edge of the seat, back erect, as if unready to commit to staying. Across from her, the companion chair seemed conspicuously empty, like a question spoken aloud. Was he going to join her, or not?

Well, was he?

He wanted to. In fact, he was surprised how strong the urge to sit was. It felt like a magnetic pull. He'd love to talk to her, to find out more about her, and at the same time provide a buffer between her and the avid curiosity radiating from the Dellians around the room.

But why did he think she needed a buffer? The curiosity was mostly a result of him talking to her. He knew all too well how much gossip he'd caused by coming home, and how many people speculated on what had happened between him and Haley in Los Angeles.

If he wanted Tess to be less conspicuous, the best thing he could do was leave. No one here was going to accost her. He took inventory. None of the more rambunctious young men of Silverdell were here, and none of the unhappily married drinkers, either. In fact, the only unhappily married man in the room was Alton Fillmore, and if he ever got mad enough to hassle a woman, surely it would be his witchy wife.

Besides, Dallas was the sheriff, and he'd make sure everyone behaved. Tess was hardly in danger of anything but an hour or two of loneliness.

This alone thing was probably entirely a figment of his imagination. She'd entered the restaurant with the express intent of eating by herself. Maybe she'd even been looking forward to some privacy.

He studied her, wondering whether the pink on

her cheekbones meant she hoped he'd stay—or was praying he'd go.

As if she felt his gaze, she looked up from the menu. "So…what's good?"

"Everything," he said. Molly would just have to wait a few more minutes. "And that's not an exaggeration. In fact…"

He had just scraped the chair back from the table, as if to sit, when his cell phone chirped softly in his pocket. For a split second, he considered ignoring it.

But he didn't, of course. Even if it were only another pseudo-emergency, it was real to Molly, and Jude was all she had. He darn sure didn't want her crawling back to a man who beat her, just to get some comfort and support.

"Sorry," he said, as he dug out the phone. He clicked Answer without even looking.

"Molly, sweetheart, I'm about to leave Donovan's—"

A trill of musical laughter flowed through his ear and into his gut. "It's not Molly, Jude."

"Haley?" The name came out on an exhale of shock, and within an instant he knew what a mistake that had been. At least two people were sitting close enough to have heard him. And those two people would tell two people, who would also tell two people…

In fact, behind him, he could already hear someone whispering, "It's Haley. Haley Hawthorne."

"Hold on." His voice was hard and gruff, but *damn it*. They'd agreed she would leave him alone, entirely alone, for six full months, before she tried to talk him into returning to L.A.—and to her.

It had been only four months since he'd come home. He had actually begun to hope she'd accepted the inevitable and moved on. Every time he heard about her partying with some celebrity, he crossed his fingers.

So why was she calling now? Why tonight? Did she have some kind of radar that warned her he was about to sit down with a very pretty stranger?

And why did he mind so much? One way or another, he would have to leave. He wasn't footloose enough to sit around flirting with the new massage therapist, no matter how adorable she was.

He put his hand over the speaker and turned to Tess. "I'm sorry. I have to go."

ALMOST AN HOUR LATER, Tess pulled through the open iron gates of Bell River Ranch as twilight lowered a blue wing over the landscape. She loved this time of day anywhere, even in smoggy Los Angeles, but here, on this rolling land bordered by ancient trees and snowy mountains, the beauty almost took her breath away.

Or maybe her heart was beating so rapidly she couldn't get enough oxygen.

She worked at taking slow breaths. She wanted

to be calm and professional for this meeting, but it wasn't easy. Ever since Rowena had called and asked Tess to come by the ranch to discuss the job, her nerves had been tingling with anticipation.

She'd asked twice…did Rowena mean for Tess to come to the main house? Not the spa's office, as she had on Monday? Rowena had been offhanded, but definite. Yes, she wanted Tess to meet the others, and it was easiest to do that at home.

The others. Rowena said it so casually, as, of course, she would. She took her network of connections for granted. *At home.* She took that for granted, too.

They were going to offer her the job, surely. Why else would they invite her here? And she would get her first glimpse of the house her biological father built.

As she neared the house, a large, open wagon drawn by two horses rumbled past. Loaded with hay and about a dozen laughing children, and spangled with colored lights, it was clearly a holiday adventure offered to the guests. What a fun vacation Bell River must be—sleigh rides on Monday, hay rides on Wednesday…

The kids waved as they passed her car, though they had no idea who she was. Through her closed windows she could hear giggling and singing, and happy shouts of "Goodbye, goodbye!"

She couldn't resist waving. She parked, climbed

out and pulled her coat around her more tightly against the clear, sweet cold. After a lifetime of warm Los Angeles holidays, this certainly was a change.

Good. There was nothing left in California for her anymore. A change was what she desperately needed.

Someone must have seen her pull up, because before she could ring the bell the door opened, the Christmas wreath chiming merrily with small bells. Rowena stood in the bright rectangle of light, smiling.

"I'm so glad you were nearby," Rowena said. "Marianne's food is fabulous, isn't it? Here, come in and get warm."

Tess had imagined this moment a hundred times since deciding to apply for the job. So much to absorb, so many people and things she wanted to see. Her mother had obliterated all traces of Johnny Wright from her life, and had very little to share when she was ready to confide in Tess.

They'd apparently been lovers only briefly, having met when he had a meeting with her boss over a real estate deal he was considering in Denver. Her mother had lived there, though Tess had never known.

She hadn't realized Johnny was married until she told him of the pregnancy. Whatever his reaction had been, it had frightened her mother enough that she left Colorado entirely. She bore her daughter in Los Angeles, raised her there and never spoke of him until she lay on her deathbed.

So the picture of Johnny Wright and his family was no more than a blank silhouette in Tess's mind. She'd met Bree and Rowena. But Penny, the third sister…would she be here? Would Tess meet the men who had married the Wright daughters? Did they have children?

But now that the moment had arrived she felt flustered and could hardly take in a single detail. Rowena ushered her past the beautiful holiday decorations of the entry and into a large parlor room teeming with people. It took several minutes to get through the introductions, and even then, when she sat on a comfortable armchair, Tess wasn't sure who was who.

Bree, of course, she recognized. But except for Rowena and Bree, Tess found herself staring at a room full of ridiculously good-looking men, from late twenties to eighty, so Penny must not be here.

Tess worked to get the men straight. The oldest one was the ranch manager, Barton James. Then there was Dallas, Rowena's husband, and a gorgeous blond named Gray, who apparently was married to Bree. The dark-haired guy was Max, Penny's husband, even though Penny herself was nowhere to be seen.

The youngest of the group, who had a rascal's

smile, freckles and every bit as much sex appeal as the older guys, was Dallas's little brother, Mitch.

Whew. She thought that was all. It was certainly enough.

"Did Rowena even give you enough time to finish eating?" Dallas turned his shockingly blue eyes toward her from his perch on the piano stool. "If you had to give short shrift to Marianne's prime rib, that's a crime."

Oh, yes, that's why this one looked familiar. He had been in Donovan's tonight, too. He'd been in a sheriff's uniform, and he'd left right after Jude did.

"A crime? You planning to arrest me, Sheriff?" Rowena, who was passing him, bonked him on the head with a sheaf of papers she carried. "You know we're desperate here. I couldn't put prime rib ahead of Bell River."

"You don't put *anything* ahead of Bell River." He grabbed Rowena around her waist and drew her in with a chuckle. He put his lips against her stomach. "You hear that, Hatchling? You'll have to come to Daddy if you need anything, because Mamma's got a one-track mind."

Rowena shook her head in mock exasperation, but she ruffled her husband's hair affectionately before pulling away and coming to sit near Tess.

"I guess you've figured out that we want to offer you a job," she said.

"Yes." Tess glanced around the room, finally noticing the elegant pencil-thin tree in the corner and the mistletoe dangling from the chandelier. "This does seem like a big crowd to bring in to tell me thanks but no thanks."

Rowena nodded. "Exactly. And I'm sure you've realized it's a big crowd to bring in to offer you just a part-time massage therapist job, too. The truth is, we're hoping you'll accept a position that's a little more important than that."

Tess folded her hands in her lap. Her heart had begun thrumming again. "What position is that?"

"Well…" Rowena took a breath. Then she handed over the papers. "Spa director."

Tess wasn't sure how to react. She accepted the papers automatically, but her brain was still processing those two words. *Spa director.* That was a full-time position. It would undoubtedly come with a contract, a good salary and possibly upgraded living quarters. It was about fifty steps up from the job she'd applied for.

And that brought with it all kinds of complications. When she'd decided to come here, she'd imagined spending a few months in Silverdell, at the most. The pay was good, and all full-time Bell River jobs also offered on-site housing, dormitory style, which would make it easier for her to rebuild her bank balance.

She hadn't expected to be more than a run-of-the-mill employee—the kind of massage therapist who could stay a short while, do a good job, but not leave a big hole in the operation when she left. She certainly didn't want to cause Bell River any harm while she satisfied her curiosity about her birth father.

"I'm sorry," she said after a minute, "but I have to ask. Why me?"

"Like I just said, we're desperate."

Bree groaned. "Ro, sometimes you're just too tactless, you know that?"

"What? We *are* desperate."

Shaking her head, Bree turned toward Tess. "What she *meant to say* is that we're well aware you weren't necessarily looking for this much responsibility or this big a commitment. We understand that you hardly know us—and we hardly know you—and therefore this is undoubtedly quite a surprise. But we've had an unexpected vacancy, and your references and experience are so stellar that we hoped maybe you'd consider helping us out."

Rowena laughed. "Yeah. That's absolutely what I meant to say. See? That's why Bree is the sweet-talking social director, and I'm the blunt-force sledgehammer who gets things done." She leaned forward. "And honestly, Tess, we are desperate. Our director is gone. Like already. Tonight, right now, just plain *gone*. We think you might be able to save our skins here, if you say yes."

Her self-effacing manner was so warm and engaging that Tess couldn't help smiling. "It's a very flattering offer. And I don't want to sound ungrateful, but there's something I probably should ask."

Rowena sat back, obviously encouraged that Tess hadn't rejected the idea outright. "Anything," she said. "It's all there. Salary, accommodations, bonuses, hours. You'd get the same contract Chelsea had."

"It's not that. I mean, those details would come later, but before I'd even consider it, I'd need to know…" Tess considered her words carefully. "It's unusual for a director to bolt like that. Was there anything…?"

"She fell in love." Bree stated the fact baldly. "With a guest. He left for Greece tonight, and she went, too. We had no idea. We have a strict policy against dating the guests, so obviously she didn't mention it to anyone. He was here only a week."

"Yeah, but he was dreamy," Rowena said. "So a week was probably plenty."

"Hey!" Dallas's protest was gruff, but he didn't exactly look threatened.

"Anyhow," Rowena went on, as if he hadn't interrupted, "the bottom line is that Chelsea didn't leave because conditions were oppressive, or because of any mistreatment. We're still in our first year of operation, so I won't pretend we don't have to budget carefully, or that sometimes things aren't pretty lean, but I think we can promise you at least a year's employment. Of course, we're hoping all goes well, and the job could be permanent."

A year. Tess definitely hadn't imagined staying at Bell River that long. She was deeply curious about the Wright sisters, and she wanted to know more about her biological father, but could she really afford to invest that much time?

She needed to return to a real city soon, somewhere she could put down roots and build a clientele. With any kind of luck, eventually she'd save enough to open her own practice and create a life for herself.

Repeat clients, a steady income, a home base. Independence and security. Those were her only goals, now that both her mother and ex-husband, Craig, were gone.

And yet, she remembered how she'd felt after the working massage. She remembered that inner tug, that feeling that she wanted to take the job, no matter what.

The tug was stronger than ever now. And there was something else, too. Something that felt like excitement. She smothered it instinctively. Excitement was dangerous. It made you do stupid things, things you hadn't thought through....

"You don't have to answer tonight," Bree said gently, as if she sensed Tess's inner conflict. "Why don't you take the contract home and look it over?

Then tomorrow we can meet again to answer any questions."

"That's a good idea." Tess grasped the chance to escape. All these strangers watching her, all these hopes hanging on her answer, felt like a hot, heavy cloak thrown over her shoulders.

And they *were* strangers, she thought on an unexpected wave of vertigo. Complete strangers. She didn't look like these women—not even a whisper of kinship showed in their faces. She didn't think like them, or live like them.

Merely being here, in this fancy home where everyone belonged but her, was depressing. She felt an overwhelming exhaustion, realizing that she'd spent a lifetime trying to find a connection with someone, *anyone*…and failing.

Even with her own husband.

The parlor was big, but there wasn't enough air in it. Cinnamon and pine were thick in the air, and she feared she might be sick. She wished she hadn't eaten so much at Donovan's. It had tasted great, and Marianne had been so welcoming.…

But now, the food began to roil oddly in her stomach.

When Tess didn't speak, Rowena looked disappointed. She opened her mouth, but then she exchanged a look with Bree. Something must have passed between them, because Rowena closed her lips.

Eager to leave, Tess was trying to stuff the papers into her purse—which was far too small to hold them—when a commotion in the doorway made her look up. A boy, maybe eleven or twelve, stood in the doorway, his hands on his hips.

"There's a big problem," he announced dramatically. "But it's not my fault, honest!"

"Of course it's your fault." With a sigh, Mitch rose, shaking his head. "When was it ever not your fault?"

"You don't even know what it is!" The boy tucked his head back, indignant.

"I still know it's your fault." Mitch smiled at Dallas as he passed. "I'll take care of it."

"Not you, Uncle Mitch!" The boy held out his hands. "It's Isamar—and she wants Ro. She says the ghost is on the stairs again, and won't let her pass with the vacuum. Plus, she's scaring Becky, who was trying to dust, and they look like they're going to scream any minute. And that'd be worse than having me interrupt." He looked around for confirmation. "Right? That'd be *a lot* worse."

Rowena groaned, but she stood immediately, as if there were no denying the summons.

"Maybe it's just as well somebody mentioned this now," she said in a strangely flat, resigned voice. She looked at Bree. "I'll handle the maids. You'll tell Tess?"

Bree nodded, her face utterly expressionless. "I'll tell her."

For a moment after Rowena and the boy departed, no one spoke. They all looked uncomfortably at the empty doorway. It was only when a weak, high-pitched shriek wafted from the floor above that Bree cleared her throat, squared her shoulders and turned to face Tess.

"Okay. So. There's one thing you should know about Bell River. The house has a history. And, at least according to this particular housekeeper, we also have a ghost."

MITCH GARWOOD, whose nickname had always been *mischief* and whose favorite word had always been *yes*, found himself craving peace these days. Like some tired old codger, he was happiest when he could sit quietly in the handmade rocking chair in Jude Calhoun's workshop and watch his friend turn wood.

He wondered whether that meant he was getting old. Not by the calendar, of course. That relentless numeric ticker still said he was a few years shy of thirty. But maybe he was getting old when measured by the heart, which seemed to count age in buoyancy...or lack thereof.

And it had been months since he'd felt anything that came even close to buoyant.

Not since that September morning when he'd

opened his eyes and discovered that the other side of his bed was empty. Bonnie was gone. Bonnie. His lover…his friend. His future and his life.

That was the day his heart turned to lead.

At home, back at Bell River, he put on a pretty good show. But it was exhausting. That's why he liked to be here. The twirling lathe and Jude's spindle gouge made a soothing white noise, and it took away any pressure to talk.

Jude gave off utterly peaceful vibes, too. He belonged in here, with the sawdust and the scent of fresh wood. Back when they were boys together, Mitch had understood that Jude's one dream was to be a carpenter, like his father. When Mr. Calhoun dropped dead of a heart attack, Jude was only fifteen. Maybe that's why he always projected such calm in here, in the workshop full of his dad's memory, and his dad's lovingly tended tools.

It had probably half killed Jude when Haley talked him into leaving all this behind for Hollywood. For the hundredth time, Mitch wondered why on earth Jude had said yes.

Of course, Mitch would have left Silverdell, Bell River, everyone and everything, for Bonnie. He had done exactly that, in fact. Bonnie had come to work for Bell River, literally out of nowhere, with no past and no promises that she'd stay. She'd been there only a few months, but during those months he'd fallen in love. When Bonnie told him one day that she needed to run away from Silverdell, he'd chosen to go with her, no questions asked.

But Haley and Bonnie were two entirely different kettles of fish.

At least he hoped they were. Because in the end, what did he really know about who Bonnie was?

To distract himself, he picked up a couple of magazines from the nearby table and leafed through them. Molly must have left them here. He couldn't imagine Jude reading *Behind the Screen* or *Hair Today*.

He flipped through the hair magazine first, hoping he'd see something ridiculous enough to spark a joke or two. And sure enough, he saw women paying big bucks to look like poodles, and San Quentin convicts, and bristlecone pines, but none of it seemed very funny. It made him think about Bonnie again, and that tantalizing glimpse of golden-red sunshine that sometimes had peeked out at the roots right before she touched up the dye on her hair.

Why hadn't she ever told him the reason she had to hide her real color? Why hadn't she trusted him enough to tell him what she was running from? Why hadn't she ever told him...*anything?* He'd been her lover. He'd been by her side for nine whole months, and he'd kept his promise...no questions.

But why should he have had to ask? He loved

her. She loved him. Shouldn't that have given him the right to know what they were fleeing from?

"Just for the record," he said, "love is a giant sucking, stinking sinkhole."

Jude raised his head, lifting his gouge from the spindle he'd been turning. "Very poetic, Shakespeare."

"No. I'm serious. And I'm not just talking about me. What about Molly and that phlegm-head husband of hers? And what about…yeah, I'm going to say it, buddy. What about you and round-heeled Haley Hawthorne?"

Mitch was pushing his luck. Jude had made it clear when he got back from Los Angeles that he didn't intend to discuss the romance with Haley, his accident or his years in Hollywood. Not with anyone. The Dellians who were dying of curiosity could just die, for all he cared. He even stonewalled Mitch most of the time. But once or twice, late at night like this, Jude had let enough slip that Mitch understood how crappy the whole thing had been.

Jude's blue eyes glittered, hard marbles in the bright light over the lathe, and for a minute Mitch thought he was about to get blasted. Weirdly, he almost welcomed it. A bruising, pissed-off fistfight would at least be a sign that he was still alive.

But Jude blinked and his shoulders relaxed. "Okay, but what about Rowena and Dallas? What about Bree and Gray? What about Penny and Max?"

Mitch rolled his eyes. "They don't count. There's gotta be something in the water over at Bell River, some kind of love potion that makes everyone go gaga."

Jude turned to his lathe. "So drink some, for God's sake, and quit whining. The cure for one woman is another woman. You've known that since you were ten."

Maybe. But that particular "cure" worked *only* when you were ten. It worked only when all girls were identical bundles of hormones wrapped up in slightly different packages. It didn't work when...

It didn't work when you grew up. It didn't work when you fell in love.

But he didn't say any of that out loud. Even he was ashamed to whine that bad.

He dropped *Hair Today* on the table and opened *Behind the Screen*. He turned two or three pages. And then, out of nowhere, there she was, the biggest picture on a page full of starlets, right under a headline that read, Faces to Watch. Beautiful, pouty-lipped, slutty-eyed Haley Hawthorne.

"Oh, *brother*." Without realizing it, Mitch made the disgusted sound out loud.

In the corner, the lathe slowed again. Without turning, Jude spoke tersely. "Don't waste your time reading trash, Mitch."

"You saw this?" He held up the magazine, but Jude still didn't turn around.

"Of course. Molly eats that crap up. But even if she hadn't shown me, at least six people in town did."

"Nice." Mitch felt like spitting onto the picture, though that would be pretty juvenile, and not anywhere nearly as rewarding as spitting in Haley's actual face. Now *that* might make him feel fairly buoyant for a minute or two.

"Gossips are saying she called you, earlier today," he said carefully.

Jude didn't respond.

"Well, did she? Dang it, Jude. Why are you such a clam about it? I thought she'd promised not to bother you for six months. I thought she had given you that long to heal and—" he chose his words judiciously "—to decide what you really want."

Jude's mouth tilted up at one corner. "And Haley always keeps her promises. She's famous for her patience."

"Don't go all sarcastic on me. What did she want?"

"What she always wants—me to come back."

"You told her you aren't going to, though, right?" Mitch knew Jude must have done so. Jude had told Haley no for months now, but the delusional brat was so spoiled she didn't believe it. She always thought she could cast a spell on anyone, and get exactly what she wanted, sooner or later.

"You told her no. *Right?*" Mitch wasn't sure why he even asked, except that he lived in fear that one day Haley might prove that she hadn't been delusional—that Jude was still under her spell and she could dance him straight back to Hollywood.

"Of course I told her," Jude said softly, his tone indicating his refusal to be drawn into melodrama. "But you know how she is. She cries, apologizes for rushing me and vows not to ask again until the six months are up. She thinks I just need time to—" he looked at the piece of wood he held "—get over what happened."

What happened. Mitch had heard only bits and pieces, but that was enough.

"I don't know how you stand it, Jude," Mitch said, his voice surprising him with its husky anger. But damn it. He and Haley and Jude had been kids together here. Jude had straight-up saved her life, no two ways about it. For her to treat him that way, as if he were a meal ticket, a sugar daddy, a stepping stone on her way to stardom...

Well, it chaffed Mitch big-time. And if she were pretending to be singing another tune now, he hoped Jude was smart enough not to fall for it.

"I don't know how you listen to everyone carry

on about her, 'such a sweetheart, such a beauty, such a credit to Silverdell'…and never say a word."

Without answering, Jude angled his gouge and put another scroll in the wood. Frustrated, Mitch stared at his friend's back, thinking of the scars beneath his ratty sweater, and the limp that showed up at odd moments, when he stepped wrong on that bum ankle.

"I don't know how you do it," he repeated harshly. "And frankly I don't know *why* you do it."

There was one explanation, of course, and it chilled Mitch to consider it. Maybe Jude protected Haley's reputation because he still loved her. Maybe, in spite of everything, he was still the guy who had, once upon a time, faced dragons to protect her, gone hungry so she could eat.

Maybe Jude and Mitch weren't that different, after all. Both of them still in love with women who no longer existed.

It made him sick. Jude deserved a hell of a lot better than Haley Hawthorne. And if he didn't find someone soon, he'd be that much more vulnerable to Haley's siren call. She might be a skank, but she was hot.

"Hey," he said, suddenly inspired. "I hear you met the new hire, Tess, when she came to interview. I hear you were the guinea pig again."

"Yep."

"So what did you think?"

"She's good."

"Yeah. But I mean what did you *think?*"

Jude chuckled. "What is it with everyone? I think she seems very nice. She's pleasant. She seems to have walking-around sense. She's talented. She's fine."

Mitch let a second's silence pass. "Not bad-looking, either."

"You think so?" Jude lifted a shoulder. "Then good. Ask her out. Maybe she'll take your mind off Bonnie for a while."

"No. Not me." Mitch had a feeling Jude was being deliberately dense. But he didn't want to come right out and say that Tess's fragile vulnerability seemed like it might be right up Jude's alley. Mitch had only seen her for twenty minutes or so, but somehow she looked like the kind of gal who could use a knight in shining armor.

And, to put a spin on Jude's advice to him, the only cure for one damsel in distress was another damsel in distress....

"I was thinking about *you,* numbskull. I was thinking *you* might ask her out. She's kind of interesting. When they offered her the job earlier tonight, I thought she was going to turn it down. But then, at the last minute, she said yes. And you know what's weird? It was almost as if the clincher, the thing that made her decide to take it, was learning about the ghost."

Jude turned at that comment. "No way."

"Yes. They had to tell her, because Isamar had one of her visions. You know, she thinks she sees Moira floating on the staircase."

"I know. What I don't know is whether Isamar is loony or just putting everyone on. Or—" Jude smiled "—maybe she has the occasional nip of brandy. I've heard that enhances one's ability to detect paranormal activity."

Mitch laughed. Everyone knew Isamar was one of those sweet but superstitious types who secretly wanted life to be a lot more exciting than it was. She "saw" Moira, sure, but she also saw the ghosts of her favorite characters in books, and even once insisted that the ghost of Brad Pitt had come to her room asking for milk and cookies.

"Yeah, well, anyhow, she usually keeps her visions to herself, so as not to scare the guests. But this time 'smart' Alec came in blurting it out. We all figured that cooked the goose, for sure, but instead Tess seemed positively fascinated, and—"

Before he could finish the sentence, the baby monitor, which sat on Jude's workbench, never more than a foot or two from him, crackled to life. The static was followed by the sound of a baby's cries. And then came his sister's voice, weighed down by the threat of imminent tears.

"Hush, Beeba, hush. Please. *Please*. Can't you sleep? Just one night? Can't you—"

In an instant, Jude was heading toward the house. "Sorry, Mitch," he said as he reached the door. "If anyone is going to ask Tess out, it'll have to be you. My life has way too many females in it already."

CHAPTER THREE

JUST TWO DAYS. Tess had been on the job for two days when the first crisis hit. They'd been closed on Christmas Eve and Christmas day, so she'd had only Saturday and Sunday to get her feet steady under her. She'd stayed focused, though, and made real progress. She'd begun to believe she could handle it, begun to relax enough to start enjoying herself.

Naturally. That was the kind of cockiness that made Fate itch to bring you down a peg or two.

And so, on the Monday after Christmas, both Darlene, the college kid who was the regular receptionist, and Ashley, the massage therapist, called in sick. Tess had been interviewing as fast as she could. The part-time job she had applied for still needed to be filled. But she hadn't brought anyone on board yet.

Now, with Ashley and Darlene out, Tess would have to run the spa, do all her own appointments and pick up Ashley's, too.

She left a voice message for Rowena—to give her a heads-up, not to ask for help. She knew Rowena was far too busy this week between Christmas and New Year's to pitch in. Everyone was slammed.

They'd all done the best they could to get Tess up to speed. Ashley had taken on extra hours to train Tess about spa services, equipment and clients. Rowena came into the facility at dawn each day so that she could steal a couple of hours to explain bookkeeping procedures and policies. Bree stopped by now and then with supplies, maps, instruction manuals for the various electronic devices. Even the ranch manager, Barton James, visited at lunchtime with salads and sandwiches from the kitchen, and cookies for moral support.

But other than that Tess had hardly seen any of the family these past two days. It had been like jumping into a war midbattle—as a five-star general. And, if the truth were told, Tess had found it thrilling.

Until today. Today was going to be a mess.

She started calling Ashley's clients to be sure they were all right with a substitute therapist. And wouldn't you know it…the first name on the list was Esther Fillmore. Lucky lady got a weekly massage, and she was still so grumpy? Maybe her poor husband encouraged the expenditure, in the hopes that someday she'd chill out and be a little easier to live with.

No one answered, so Tess left a message and moved on to the next name. Everyone she reached was friendly and contented either with a new appointment, or with the idea of Tess taking over for Ashley. At eight o'clock, the nail tech showed up and went straight to work. So far, so good.

At 8:05 a.m., Esther Fillmore walked in.

She didn't look surprised to see Tess behind the counter, wearing the official blue Bell River uniform, so the grapevine had obviously done its work well. She didn't smile or say hello, of course—she maintained her natural sour frown that seemed to mean almost nothing.

"Good morning, Mrs. Fillmore," Tess said, with an extra dose of sunshine in her voice, hoping that perhaps being recognized would stroke the woman's vanity enough to smooth the moment. "I'm so sorry I wasn't able to reach you before you made the trip over. I called your contact number, but I didn't get an answer."

The woman froze in the act of removing her coat. "Why were you trying to call me?"

"I wanted to let you know in advance that Ashley isn't here today. I'm happy to fill in for her, but I know you prefer your usual therapist whenever possible."

"I *insist* on it," Mrs. Fillmore said flatly, as if, hearing that, Tess would somehow be able to produce Ashley out of thin air.

"Then perhaps you'd like to make another

appointment? Ashley will be in again right after New Year's."

"After *New Year's?*" The older woman lifted her chin. "You expect me to suffer with my sciatica until then? With my nieces and nephews at the house? With family meals to cook, and to clean up after?"

"I can understand how difficult that would be," Tess said sympathetically. "I'd be happy to do what I can to help. I've worked with many clients suffering from sciatica, and—"

"Sciatica is not one-size-fits-all, like the common cold," Mrs. Fillmore interrupted tersely, as if Tess had insulted her.

Tess took a deep breath, reminding herself that sciatica often caused profound pain. Maybe that accounted for Mrs. Fillmore's nasty manner. Chronic pain could suck the joy out of life.

"Perhaps, if you told me in detail what procedures Ashley uses, and what you find most effective, we could bring you some relief. Although I know it wouldn't be the same, maybe it would be better than nothing. And, of course, there would be no charge for the service today."

As she said that, Tess had to quell a few butterflies, remembering how close to the bone Bell River was operating this first winter season. Rowena was candid about money, which Tess appreciated, because it helped her to know where she stood. Even if they all stood pretty close to the edge.

Still, surely keeping a repeat client happy—especially one who would freely broadcast her dissatisfaction to the whole town—was worth the price of a massage.

If Tess had to, she'd take it out of her own pay. Heaven knew she was making more as director than she'd ever expected to as a part-time therapist.

To her surprise, though, Esther appeared to have lost interest in the conversation. Instead, she seemed to be staring with narrowed eyes at Tess's necklace. Or was she staring at her chest? Tess's hand went instinctively up to cover herself, though her uniform was hardly low-cut or revealing.

"Is everything all right, Mrs. Fillmore?"

"I…" The woman dragged her gaze up to Tess's. "Yes. I was just…I was admiring your pendant. Where did you get it?"

Her tone made Tess uncomfortable, and for a minute she didn't want to answer. Stupid, but she felt reluctant to even speak of her mother to such a nasty woman.

Besides, surely that wasn't really what Mrs. Fillmore had been about to say. Her pendant was pretty, but not ostentatious or, surely, unique.

Tess didn't ordinarily wear jewelry while working, but this modest necklace was special to her, and she liked having it on. She always tucked it inside her shirt, but it must have slipped out.

"It was a gift from my mother," she said, and tucked the pendant beneath her top.

Not the whole truth, but close enough. She'd found it among her mother's things after her death. She wondered why her mother had never worn it. The workmanship was lovely—it was a small teardrop-shaped ruby that formed the bud of a rose, its setting designed like a slim gold stem and two curving gold petals.

Maybe, she thought, her mother had never worn it because she suspected that one day she'd have to sell it. Who knew how many other gold pieces might have been stashed away in that jewelry box, but sold off, one by one, to make ends meet?

"Your *mother?*" Esther frowned, obviously surprised by the answer—and not pleasantly so. "Are you sure?"

"Of course." Tess was frowning now, too. She wondered what answer the woman had been expecting. A boyfriend, perhaps? But why would she care?

"The necklace belonged to my mother," Tess reiterated blandly. "Now. Would you like me to take over for Ashley, or would you like to rebook?"

"Neither," Esther said coldly. "My husband tells me the new resort at Silverdell Hills will have a spa. You people at Bell River might do well to remember that. You won't be the only game in town anymore."

Tess bit her lip briefly, then smiled the best she could. "I'm very sorry we can't help you, Mrs. Fillmore, but I certainly understand your need—"

The polite words were wasted. The older woman had already turned her back and, buttoning her coat as she walked, was heading briskly toward the door.

Though she knew it was irrational, Tess felt deflated by the failure. It would have been so rewarding to overcome the woman's strange hostility. But oh, well. Let her go home and be her unfortunate husband's problem for a while.

Tess took a couple of moments to calm herself, then dove into making the calls. The minutes flew, and when the alarm on her phone trilled she was surprised to see it was time to get ready for her first appointment of the day.

She was also surprised to see that Craig had called. Eight times. The divorce had been final for two weeks now, and he'd promised to leave her alone. But she'd become a challenge to his pride, no doubt. He didn't like failing. He used to be a high school–football star, and he still thought of everything in terms of wins and losses. He despised losses.

Craig was a smooth-talking, self-indulgent former jock who had made it to middle management in her mother's insurance agency. Their six years of marriage had been a mistake from the start—a rebellion on her part against an upbringing that had been overly strict, big on rules and short on fun.

She knew now, of course, why her mother had been so stringent, so fearful that her daughter might repeat her own mistakes. But back then, her insistence on no freedom, no car, no boys in the house, no broken curfews—nothing that could encourage sex before marriage—had left Tess eager, at twenty, to marry the first man who made her laugh and gave her presents.

She sometimes wondered why he'd been willing to marry her. Probably because, otherwise, she wouldn't have sex with him. She should have. If she had, she would have realized what an insensitive egoist he was, or else he would have checked "Conquer Tess" off his list and moved safely on. If only her mother hadn't…

No. She stopped herself right there. Her mother had always insisted on honesty, and the truth was it wasn't her mother's fault she'd married Craig. It was her own. She'd fallen for him because he was handsome and a little older, which seemed glamorous, and he gave her nice things. He told her she was pretty. He told her she was smart.

Looking back, she realized she had sold herself far too cheaply. She should have held out for love.

Twenty had been plenty old enough to recognize a louse, if she'd been looking hard enough.

She slid her phone into her pocket quickly as she heard Jean, the manicure technician, coming out of her room. Jean, who had been at Bell River only about two weeks longer than Tess, led out her client, made a new appointment for the woman, smiled at Tess, then started to head back to clean her area.

"Jean? You don't recognize this client's name, do you?" Tess pointed to the line on the computer screen for eleven-thirty. *Marley Baker.* "I'm not even sure whether it's male or female."

Jean, who was short and curvy and extremely savvy, twitched her nose, as if that might help her remember. "Nope," she said finally. "I think I took the appointment over the phone, but I can't really remember anything about it. It has been a little nuts around here this week."

Tess chuckled. "A little. Oh, well, it doesn't matter."

"Sorry," Jean said as she disappeared into the supply room.

Tess wasn't too worried about the client's gender. She never used particularly flowery scents anyhow, so most of her products would please anyone. What did worry her was that Baker was about ten minutes late. Ordinarily it wasn't an issue, but today…

As she waited, Tess checked on the Blue Room, which was in perfect shape, opened a box of toners that had been delivered this morning, made a couple of notes in her personal client log and then did some deep breathing, to keep herself from pacing.

Fifteen minutes later, she was about to call the contact number for Baker when she heard a soft trill of chimes, and the spa door opened on a swirl of cold air and an odd smell of motor oil. A small, wiry man entered, reeking of aftershave and putting his crooked teeth on display in something he probably thought was a smile.

"Mr. Baker?"

His smile widened, the pink of his gums glistening. "In the flesh," he said.

"Good morning," she forced herself to say pleasantly. A frisson of distaste moved down her back as their gazes met, but she steadfastly ignored it. She had worked on unpleasant physical specimens before. Everyone, even people who weren't as clean as they should be, even people who smiled like that, deserved to have their aches and pains soothed.

"Are you Tess?" He glanced down, and this time she was darned sure he wasn't looking at her pendant. Either he had a slight twitch, or the man had actually wiggled his eyebrows in some kind of secret salacious joke with himself.

Was he one of *those?* A few men—thankfully

very few—seemed to believe their therapists owed them what they lewdly referred to as a "happy ending."

Well, if he were one of those, she knew how to make him see his mistake without embarrassing anyone.

And if he were one of the really terrible ones—the dangerous, violent ones, who were only legend for her, so far, thank God—well, she knew how to deal with that, too. Her very first mentor had taught her a couple of moves that would make it unlikely that Marley Baker would be thinking such thoughts, or going to the bathroom on his own, for at least a week.

"Yes, I'm Tess. I'll show you to the room, if you're ready."

As if to compensate for thinking such thoughts based on nothing but her own bias against his type, she gave the man an extra warm smile. Immediately, when he smiled back with that strange, oddly feral curve of his thin lips, she regretted it.

"Oh, I'm always ready," he said.

Again, she bristled at his tone. She toyed with telling him there had been an emergency. She'd have to cancel. Every instinct was warning her not to end up alone in a room with him. But how would she explain herself to the Wrights? Two days on the job, and she was turning away badly needed clients? She couldn't. It was unprofessional, and it was unfair.

And he hadn't actually said a single word out of line. He just wasn't as well-to-do as most of the clients, and his tone was rough around the edges. So what? She'd been poor most of her life. She had seen her friends' parents eyeing her cheap sneakers and secondhand clothes, assuming a low bank balance meant a poverty of morals, intelligence and breeding.

"This way." She led him to the Blue Room and showed him where to put his clothes, made sure one more time that the towels and sheets were all folded back and ready, then left him to prepare.

She chose her lotions carefully. She wasn't stalling. She was simply being extra careful. She'd use an herbal muscle calmer, probably. Chamomile and aloe vera, since those wiry muscles seemed to indicate he did manual labor, and probably didn't take care to stretch or take anti-inflammatory supplements. *Calm, calm, calm.* That's what she needed to be with this one. He might not be aggressive or dangerous, but he was without question oddly revved, full of some unhealthy tensions. Her instincts couldn't be that wrong.

She decided to leave the door open and double-checked that her phone alarm was set and safely in her pocket. She added gloves to her supplies and, squaring her shoulders, headed to the Blue Room.

She knocked on the door, but just as with Jude Calhoun, she heard no response. A wriggle of discomfort made its way into her midsection. She didn't like the unnatural quiet. Jude had been different. No way a man humming with nerves like this guy could have actually fallen asleep. She hoped to God Baker wasn't playing games, pretending not to hear her so that he could be "caught" with his nakedness uncovered.

Suddenly, she wasn't nervous anymore. She was annoyed. To heck with him. She wasn't a debutante who would run shrieking at the mysterious horror of a man's naked body. She was a professional therapist. She was also a lot tougher than she looked, and she was having a bad day. If he got cute, she'd hustle his puny self out so fast he wouldn't know what hit him.

"Mr. Baker." She knocked again, loudly enough to wake the dead, and then she shoved the door open, ready for anything.

To her surprise, the room appeared to be empty. The man was nowhere in sight.

"Mr. Baker?" It was a simple room, without a lot of hidey-holes, but she checked every spot she could imagine a man's body would fit into. Cupboards, the closet, even under the massage table, though she felt a pure fool doing so.

She straightened, her hands on her hips, and

stared at the windows, which let in a soft light through their muslin shades.

Marley Baker was gone. And, now that she had a chance to think through the details, she had to wonder whether he'd ever intended to stay. The sheets on the table hadn't been touched, hadn't been wrinkled or shifted by a fraction of an inch.

Even more mystifying—how had he managed to leave without her realizing it? It made her skin crawl to think he might have tiptoed inches behind her as she picked out lotions and powders, and headed surreptitiously for the front door.

Her nerves prickling, she stopped by the nail tech room, where Jean was now giving a pedicure to a middle-aged woman talking volubly on her cell phone.

Tess signaled to Jean, who excused herself and came to the door.

"You didn't happen to see a man walk by in the past few minutes, did you? Dark-haired? Kind of short and wiry?"

"No." Jean frowned. "Is anything wrong?"

"I don't think so." Tess shrugged, keeping her tone light. "My client left unexpectedly. I guess he got a call or something."

Jean's frown deepened, but she returned to her post.

Tess did the same. The phone was ringing. Plus, she had another client coming in half an hour, and she had to change the sheets, in case Marley Baker had touched them, however briefly.

She tried not to dwell on the unpleasant morning, concentrating instead on her afternoon clients. Her massages were therapy for her, too. And, as usual, turning her attention to other people helped. By the end of the day, she was exhausted, but in a good way, and utterly relaxed.

And maybe a little proud of herself. She'd pulled off another miracle, and kept the spa humming almost single-handedly.

Marley Baker was the furthest thing from her mind. At least…until she was leaving and noticed a tiny rectangle of paper tucked inside the chic plaque that read Bell River Ranch.

Though it could have been left by anyone, for a dozen perfectly innocent reasons, she felt her hair follicles rise. With her clumsy gloved fingers, she pried the paper out and awkwardly unfolded it.

Two short words were scrawled there. Just a dozen bright red, simple block letters, more like a random shout from a passing car than a true message. But for a minute, though she stood with snow fluttering down the collar of her coat, then melting disagreeably against her neck, she couldn't move, couldn't take her eyes off the angry, red words.

DIRTY, it said.

And then on the next line, *BITCHES.*

OVER THE PAST couple of days, while Tess had been wearing blinders that prevented her from seeing anything but the spa's most immediate needs, she'd almost forgotten about all the other holiday festivities going on elsewhere on the ranch.

The ugly note she held in her hand felt even more obscene here, as she stood at the front door of the main house, which was framed in pine-scented garland and sparkling with fairy lights. She wished she could turn around and go back to the hotel. She was extraordinarily tired, suddenly. She needed to get off her feet. She needed something to eat. She needed—

The door opened. One of the men she'd met the night they offered her the job—she thought this one was Gray, Bree's husband—stood there, smiling.

"Hey, Tess," he said easily, as if she'd worked there for years. If she hadn't been paying close attention, she might have missed the subtle surprise in his eyes. "Everything okay?"

"Yes." Too late, she wondered whether uniformed employees were supposed to use the rear entrance. "I think so," she amended. "But there is something I should talk to Rowena about, if she's free."

"Well, Ro isn't ever *really* free, but I think we can snag her. Come on in." He stepped back from the door, and through the garland-swagged foyer Tess could see that the living room was in shadows.

The only lights came from a twinkling Christmas tree by the windows, and a projector's beam hitting a big screen at the front. A crowd of people perched on folding chairs, and they seemed to be watching a slide presentation.

"Oh. I've come at a bad time."

"Not at all." Gray smiled. "On Monday night, Penny shares the nature shots taken during her photography classes. Ro isn't a part of that. She's in the great room dealing with a totally different minicrisis. Barton has a sing-along starting in about half an hour in there, but right now we're all trying to get Alec off the wall without breaking anything."

Tess frowned, wondering if he was kidding. "The…the wall?"

He gave her a wry look over his shoulder. "Yeah. It's okay, though. He can't hold on much longer, so he'll be down in the next couple of minutes, dead or alive."

They had reached the entrance to the lovely great room, with its cathedral ceiling, huge fireplace trimmed in red candles and green fir, and impressive river-rock surround.

The room was full of people. In front of the fireplace, Bree, Mitch, Barton and Max, Penny's husband, stood in a perfect square, holding the corners of a thick blanket above a layer of sofa cushions and quilts, as if they were making a safety net of sorts.

Their faces tilted toward the ceiling. Tess followed their gazes, and to her horror spotted Alec a foot or two from the upper edge of the river rock. From this distance, he looked small, skinny and awkward, his arms and legs splayed like a superhero as he tried to hold on to the lumpy rock.

Tess glanced around, wondering how everyone was maintaining such calm. Over at the end of the room near the kitchen, Dallas and a young man in a Bell River uniform were rapidly assembling an articulating ladder. An ordinary stepladder would never reach high enough.

"Where's the damn mattress?" Dallas glanced toward the foyer doorway once, then refocused on the ladder.

"Isamar and Carrie are bringing it now," Rowena said.

"I'll go help." Gray touched Tess's arm. "Hang on. Ro will be free soon."

Tess felt her mouth hanging open slightly. Her stupid anonymous note seemed absurdly trivial. The boy was at least twelve feet in the air. If he fell…

She shivered. He probably wouldn't die, not with the people below, and the pillows, and the blanket. But he might miss. Even a partial miss could be catastrophic. He might well break half a dozen bones.

And he must be scared to death.

"Dang it," the little boy said, his voice and words a touching echo of his father's. He sounded very far away, but was full of bluster, clearly reluctant to reveal fear. "Too bad Jude's not here. A stunt man would know what to do. My hands are getting sweaty."

A little girl piped up from the corner. "I *told* you it wouldn't be as easy to come down as it was to go up."

Max gave the girl a hard look. "Really? You think this is the right time to say *I told you so?*"

She blushed and hung her head, but didn't say another word.

Two seconds later, Gray showed up, the large, thick mattress, which must have weighed a ton, carried over his head as if it were light as a feather.

"Coming through," he called, and plopped his burden as near the safety net as he could. Then he dropped to a squat and muscled the mattress until it lay directly under the blanket. A couple of Bell River staffers rearranged the pillows and quilts on top of the mattress with lightning speed.

"This'll be faster than the ladder, Dallas," Gray said, putting his hand on Dallas's shoulder. "And just as safe. Tell him to let go."

Dallas glanced at the pile of cushioning, the outstretched blanket and his team of helpers. He looked up at his son, then down, clearly calculating the geometry of the placement. And then he nodded.

"Keep going," he said quietly to his assistant beside the ladder. "Just in case."

Then he moved closer to the fireplace. "Okay, buddy. Time to give those arms a rest. We've got you covered. Let go, and try to fall on your rump, okay?"

The little boy was silent for a moment. He twisted his neck for one second, trying to get a look at his dad, but swiveled it back quickly, as if the motion scared him.

"Come on, Alec." Dallas's voice was utterly calm. "It's all good. You'll be fine."

A tiny voice floated to them. "You sure?"

Tess found herself holding her breath, and the room spun a little, as if she might faint, which surprised her, because she wasn't the fainting type.

"Yep," Dallas said, projecting complete confidence. "I'm sure."

"Well, then. Okay."

As though someone had pulled a lever, the boy dropped from the wall. Tess's knees seemed to liquefy. She touched the wall for support. As if in slow motion, the blanket dipped as his scrawny form hit it, rump first, just as his father had requested, and then bounced up.

Thank God. Alec's smiling face emerged from over the edge of the blanket, beaming and laughing, as if it were all a grand game.

Strangers and staffers who apparently had been

watching from the margins of the room broke out in scattered applause, which then tapered off as Dallas glared, obviously not wanting them to encourage the boy.

The four people who had held the blanket's corners moved toward each other, letting their weighted cloth sag until it came to rest against the mattress. Alec bounced once on the springs, as if it were a trampoline, then rolled off and onto the carpet.

Rowena grabbed him the minute his feet hit the floor and gathered him in for a tight, half-suffocating hug.

"Idiot," she said raggedly, burying her face in his hair. "You impossible, ridiculous, infuriating *idiot.*"

"Well, Ellen dared me." He pulled free and began stuffing his shirt into his jeans. "She double-dog dared me," he repeated, as if that were an absolute defense.

"I did *not,*" the little girl countered, scowling fiercely at Alec.

"Enough." Dallas's voice had taken on a completely different quality now, carrying the unmistakable authority of an angry dad. "Upstairs, both of you. I'll be up later to let you know whether we've decided to toss you to the wolves or eat you for dinner."

The kids scurried away. As they exited, though, they could be heard giggling, which drained the moment of its drama. A relieved chatter rose from the room's occupants, and life seemed to resume.

Now that the commotion was over, Tess felt dizzier than ever and miserably uncomfortable. She felt out of place and conspicuous, like the interloper she was. This was obviously not the time to bring a new problem to Rowena's door.

But to her surprise, Rowena walked calmly toward her. "Hey," she said. "So sorry about the chaos."

"No, no. I'm the one who is sorry, for intruding on—"

"Don't be silly." As Dallas walked past, Rowena squeezed his hand. "Just your average Monday night at Bell River Ranch, right, Sheriff?"

"Yep." He shook his head, grinning. "We should have let him break something, you know. Not his neck maybe, but a finger? A toe? If he keeps escaping unscathed, he'll never learn anything important."

"Sure he will." Rowena put her hand against her husband's cheek. "He'll learn his family is always here to catch him when he falls. What's more important than that?"

The heat of tears stung Tess's eyes, and, though it seemed weak, she had to look away. This moment was private, in spite of the guests and the staff and the whole circus aura of the moment. She should not be here. She should *not* be here.

"Anyhow, sorry to keep you waiting." Rowena returned her attention to Tess. "Gray said you needed to talk to me?"

Suddenly drained by the whole wretched day, Tess found herself eager to get it over with. She plucked the folded note from her uniform pocket. "It's nothing serious. I just…I found this slipped in behind the door plaque as I closed up tonight."

Rowena frowned as soon as she saw the paper, and Tess knew instantly. This wasn't the first anonymous note they had received.

"Oh, hell," Rowena said under her breath. She unfolded the paper and read the red words written there. "I'm sorry. We should have warned you. We get these from time to time. There are people in Silverdell, it seems, who can't let the past go."

Tess wondered exactly what that meant. Who exactly were the *dirty bitches?* The three Wright daughters? They had told Tess the whole story the night they hired her—not realizing that, of course, she already knew it. Tess couldn't help wondering whether they would have mentioned it, if the ghost-whisperer maid hadn't run into Moira Wright's ghost that night.

Maybe they would have. This didn't seem to be a family that played things close to the vest. Perhaps years ago they'd learned that secrets were dangerous…or maybe they'd learned that it was impossible to keep secrets for long.

Either way, they'd explained the basic facts: Johnny had been convicted of deliberately pushing their mother down the staircase, and Moira had been exposed as an unfaithful wife, who had been carrying another man's baby. But both of the principal players in the melodrama were dead now, long gone. Surely it was a little Victorian to continue to punish the daughters for the sins of the parents.

And...*dirty?* Odd choice of insults. Tess hadn't met Penny yet—though she'd seen her petite, shadowy outline in the living room, standing in the projector's beam as she pointed to something on a photo. But Rowena and Bree were about as far from dirty or bitchy as two women could get.

Rowena must have sensed Tess's confusion. "Some people simply believe we had a bad gene pool. They keep waiting for us to turn into nymphomaniacs, or kill each other, or something."

She laughed when she said it, but Tess heard an undercurrent of pain beneath the mirth. Rowena acted tough, but perhaps something softer lay beneath?

"Not *they,*" Dallas corrected gently. "It's probably just one person. You know most of Silverdell is on our side."

Tess could imagine how unsettling it must be to walk the streets of Silverdell, wondering whether every face might be the face of this anonymous enemy. "Do you know who it is?"

Rowena shook her head. "No. There are a few likely suspects, sourpusses and sleazeballs who haven't gotten along with Bell River for decades. But no proof against anyone."

Dallas put his arm around Rowena. "The department has looked into it, and continues to do so. Is it okay if I send someone to the spa tomorrow to talk to you about anything you might have seen?"

Tess nodded. She thought about mentioning the dustup with Mrs. Fillmore, and especially the odd disappearance of Marley Baker, but she was too tired to go into it now. In fact, she felt more than a little woozy. She realized she hadn't ever stopped for a meal all day. She hadn't eaten a single bite since last night. No wonder she felt so bad.

"Tomorrow's fine," she said. "I don't think I have any clients around the lunch hour, if that would work for you."

"Tess," Rowena said, her voice suddenly urgent. "If you feel that…" She paused, as if searching for the right phrasing. "If it makes you so uncomfortable that you would rather not stay…I want you to know we wouldn't hold it against you. We would provide an excellent recommendation—"

"No." Tess appreciated the gesture, but no way was she leaving because of some snake like Marley Baker. "It doesn't make me uncomfortable at all. This is the work of a coward who doesn't even have the nerve to make his comments face-to-face."

With her last ounce of energy, she turned to Dallas, trying to project the certainty he'd shown his son. "I'll see someone from your office tomorrow, then?"

She thought she might have seen a glimmer of respect in his gaze. He nodded.

"Tess," Rowena said, "would you like to stay to—"

Again Tess interrupted Rowena. She was giving out. Her legs had begun to feel like wobbly strings, and her stomach churned acidly. She was afraid she might pass out, or even vomit, if she didn't get home.

Home. Well, the hotel that was passing for home right now, anyhow. The job included a cabin, but it wasn't ready yet, though Jude Calhoun was putting the finishing touches on it. Tonight, though, where she landed didn't matter. Anywhere with a bed and a cup of hot tea would suffice.

She mumbled something she hoped was civil and headed to the door. In an excess of courtesy, Rowena and Dallas escorted her, but if they made small talk, Tess didn't hear it. A dull roar had started in her ears, and she couldn't even hear herself think.

She must have said the right things, because finally the door closed behind her, and she was alone on the porch, with the lights and the scent of the garlands.

Oh, no. She put her hands against her stomach, feeling bile rise. She loved the smell of pine, and yet right now she found it the most repulsive odor in the world. Her stomach heaved, and she lost focus.

She had to get home. She pulled out her phone, but there was no one to call, was there? All she saw was the missed call log—two more from Craig, who simply would not give up. She hadn't even felt the vibration from incoming calls. She'd been running so hard all day.

She made an angry, whimpering sound under her breath, frustrated with him, with herself, with this ridiculous weakness....

She stumbled down the steps, fumbling in her pocket for her keys. Was she safe to drive? It had begun to snow again, and yet she was sweating inside her coat.

She heard her feet crunching across the snow. She saw the dizzying twist of white snowflakes spinning in the wind. A man was moving toward her, and she opened her mouth to say something, though she wasn't sure what.

"Tess?" Did he say that, or did she?

"Tess!" The man began to run. He cut through the snowflakes, rushing toward her, and the sight of his dark bulk against the driveway lights made her head spin. Her legs began to melt.

"I'm sorry," she said. And then, with an exhale of air that came out like a swirling white ghost, she collapsed into the outstretched arms of Jude Calhoun.

CHAPTER FOUR

JUDE HAD TO laugh at himself. Haley used to accuse him of having a pathological white-knight complex, never realizing how ironic it was for her to complain about that particular problem. If he hadn't had a thing for birds with broken wings, he wouldn't ever have been there for her to bitch at in the first place.

But right now, as he looked at Tess, sitting in the passenger seat of his truck, her head resting against the window and her pale lips biting into his leftover apple from lunch, he had to admit Haley might have had a point.

He might have taken the wounded-bird thing a little too far. Haley, waiting and hoping to hear he'd come back to her. His sister and the baby harboring at his house while Molly tried to gather the courage to ask Garth for a divorce. Now an exhausted, half-dead woman in his truck.

He ought to take her inside, of course. Bell River had a whole staff standing by to deal with emergencies like this. Hot soup, soft beds, warm blankets.

Rowena hovering and mothering, Bree organizing the troops, Penny sensing every unspoken need.

But Tess had become so agitated at the suggestion that he hadn't had the heart to force the issue. If she preferred a cold truck, hard seats and a badly bruised apple, he supposed they could try that first.

If she hadn't rallied, he would have insisted, of course. But as soon as she got halfway through the apple, some color began to seep into her lips and cheeks. Maybe she really had just been hungry.

He turned on the motor, so that he could get some heat in here. She'd been perspiring, obviously. Her shining brown hair was damp around her temples, and the notch of her throat glistened in the moonlight. If she sat here, wet, and got chilled, she could end up sick.

Once the heat was adjusted, he reached across her lap to recline her seat a couple of inches. She didn't seem to mind the invasion of her space. As the seat powered back, she wriggled, dropped her head against the headrest and shut her eyes.

"Thank you." She sighed. "I feel better." After a few seconds, she turned toward him and opened her eyes. "I'm sorry to be such a mess. I'll be fine in a minute, and I'll get out of your way. It's just that…I was so busy today I forgot to eat."

"All day? Then you need more than an apple." He wondered if he had any chips or maybe a package of crackers. He didn't cook much, and Molly obviously wasn't the Suzy Homemaker type. He mostly lived on Marianne Donovan's food these days.

He needed to get Tess something more substantial. She was staying in a hotel, so she probably wouldn't have anything there. Maybe he could drive her into town, and they could get some takeout from Donovan's.

But she didn't look as if she wanted to be on display right now. Even if, as she said, she wasn't sick, she looked whipped. For the past couple of days, he'd been focusing on completing her cabin, but he'd heard from Mitch that Tess was holding the spa together singlehandedly. The family was impressed, Mitch said.

So what she needed most of all was peace. But she also needed food.

"I know," he said, wondering why it had taken him so long to figure it out. "You wait here, okay? I'll be right back."

She nodded dreamily, as if she'd started to doze off. The apple core, with her tidy tooth marks scalloping the edges, was held loosely in her left hand. She looked far too tired to do a vanishing act on him in the next five minutes.

He engaged the emergency brake, grabbed his spare key, then climbed out and locked the doors. He dashed into the ranch, called hello to everyone, and headed for the kitchen. The cook had served roasted chicken, new potatoes, broccoli casserole and pumpkin pie to about forty people, so surely there would be enough left over to feed one hungry lady.

There was. One of the staff cleaning the kitchen dished up several to-go containers and didn't ask questions. Jude was in and out of the ranch often enough to be recognized as nearly family, and Rowena wasn't stingy with leftovers.

When he returned to the truck, Tess seemed not to have moved an inch. The windows were beginning to fog up, spreading the moonlight like a milky haze across his windshield. He turned on the defroster, and waited for the windows to clear.

While he waited, he couldn't help studying Tess. Her creamy cheeks bloomed pink again, and all the strain had left her face. She looked utterly at peace. And so exquisitely feminine that he felt his body respond in spite of himself.

He recalled Marianne's question—was Tess pretty? Of course the answer was yes, as Marianne had seen for herself. But right now, looking at Tess like this, unguarded, unmasked…he realized she was far more than that.

She was gorgeous. Not like Haley, who had been born with a movie star's face, a Greek goddess's body. Haley had heard all her life that she was destined for fame and fortune. She was terrified time would change any inch of her perfect face, her perfect body. At only twenty-five, she already spent a fortune on trainers and estheticians, on lasers and waxes and peels and shots. She knew age was coming, and was already stockpiling gold against the day she'd have to buy knives and toxins to freeze her beauty in place.

Tess couldn't compete with that. No one could.

Although no one would believe him, Jude wasn't looking for another glamour-goddess. Haley's beauty was meant to be seen but not touched. Worshipped from a distance. On a screen, on a billboard, where the surface was all that mattered.

No, if he'd been looking, he would have been trying to find something subtler. A quiet beauty with depths and textures. An empathetic woman whose beauty was as much in her spirit as in her bones. A spirit that listened and heard and felt... and changed with what it learned. A beauty that could age gracefully, finding meaning in real relationships, real work, real life.

If he'd been looking, he would have hoped to find someone a lot like Tess.

But he wasn't. Looking, that is. As he'd told Mitch, he had too many women in his life already.

In her light sleep, she touched her small pink tongue against her lips, sighed softly, then let her eyelids flutter open. She sniffed. "Something smells wonderful."

"I picked up some dinner from the ranch," he

said, gesturing to the backseat, where he'd stashed the laden bag. "I haven't eaten, either, so if you're up to it, why don't we take the food to your new cabin and eat there? They put the furniture in today, so we'd even have a table and chairs. I could show you around a little."

She stretched her arms, then her legs, as if she were testing her muscles. Then she smiled.

"That sounds fabulous," she said. "I'd love to see the cabin."

They didn't talk on the drive. The spa and its surrounding new cabins were only about a ten-minute walk from the main house, through the wooded paths and boardwalks. But by road it was a little longer. The landscape rolled past them like mounds of ice cream dusted with sugar. Yesterday, he'd been cursing this early snow for making his job harder, but tonight it seemed like the perfect backdrop.

The spa cabins—there would be five, in addition to the director's cabin—had a gingerbread quaintness. Even so, the spa was a bit remote, out here near Little Bell Falls. In rainy weather, or on moonless nights, it could seem kind of gloomy, especially with the cabins unoccupied.

But this sparkling moon-white night banished all that. The snowy trees and frozen waterfall, which could be seen from every cabin, would give it a magical charm.

He was glad. Maybe because she seemed so exhausted, so overworked and alone, he keenly wanted for her to like her new quarters. He wanted her first glimpse to make her feel at home.

He pulled the truck up close so she wouldn't have to walk far and so she could enter by the front door. The movers had been putting in the sofa, and Penny had been hanging pictures while he fiddled with the radiator today, and he knew that the front room was especially charming.

"The cabins are adorable, aren't they?" Tess had pressed her face to the window, as eager as a child.

"Yeah, they're cute. Rowena does things right." He chuckled. "For an outdoorsy, horsey, tomboy kind of gal, she's got quite the touch with design and decorating."

"I've seen them every day, from the spa windows, of course." Tess tucked her hair behind her ear. "It's very exciting to get to go inside, finally."

He felt ashamed that he hadn't thought to invite her over to take a look sooner. Why hadn't it occurred to him that she'd be curious? It would be her home, yet no one had consulted her on a single element.

As soon as the truck stopped, she jumped out. He grabbed the food and joined her on the porch. He hadn't left the outside light on, because he hadn't expected to return before daylight, but the moon was full and flooded the wide porch with its glow.

"You have a key?"

He nodded, wondering if she felt odd about that. She didn't know him well enough to trust, as Rowena did, that he wouldn't dream of misusing it.

"I won't, once you move in, but right now I come and go a lot. We had to redo the bathroom grout earlier this week. I'll be back first thing in the morning to check on it, but after that I'm just about done."

He'd opened the lock while he spoke, and he reached through to flip the light switch before stepping back to let her go in first. An overhead fixture, two table lamps and a strip of track lighting above the fireplace all shone a warm, amber glow.

A fire in the hearth would have been the ultimate touch, but obviously that hadn't been possible. If she felt the lack, she gave no sign. She entered slowly, her head turning, taking in everything she saw.

He noticed that she touched everything she passed.

"Oh," she said softly. It was just a syllable, but was uttered with such heartfelt joy that he had no doubt about her reaction.

Who could dislike this place? Rowena had chosen a color scheme of soft blues and browns, with spots of green here and there, in pictures, in pillow stitching and in the curtains. In a subtle way, it was like an interior reflection of Little Bell Falls in summer. Blue water, brown trees, green vegetation…and, though Tess couldn't know this, the yellow would echo the goldeneye wildflowers that carpeted the banks, all the way down to the edge of the deep, mysterious spill pool.

He led the way through the rest of the cabin, flicking on lights as he went, and pointing out various features, more to provide background noise than because he really thought she was listening. She moved solemnly, just behind him. He watched her graceful fingers glide over wooden tables, feather the fringe on drapery tiebacks and smooth the patchwork of the quilt at the foot of the bed.

She was an extremely tactile person, wasn't she? She learned with her hands, more than any other way. He remembered the feel of those knowing hands on his muscles, and realized she'd been learning him that day, as well.

"I know it's small," he said as they came to the end of the tour. The living space was only about nine hundred square feet—a bedroom, living room, kitchen and a bath. "But it's quality construction. The fixtures, the furniture, and all the guts of the house, plumbing, wiring, roofing, stuff like that—it's all first-rate. To Rowena, everything about Bell River is practically sacred. She doesn't do anything shoddy here."

Tess shook her head, a rote movement, as if she weren't even aware she did it. Lamplight slid across the brown waves of hair that cascaded over her shoulders.

She cupped the finial of the bed's footboard with her palm, moving her thumb rhythmically across the polished walnut globe as if it were alive. She turned her intense eyes toward Jude.

"It is almost as big as anywhere I've ever lived," she said somberly. "And ten times as nice. And a hundred times more beautiful."

The conviction in her voice made something move oddly inside him. She didn't say the words with any kind of pathos. She stated them as absolute, dry fact. But he heard so much more in that tone, and it made him hurt inside.

What had her life been like, if it had always been bounded by no more than nine hundred square feet of ugliness?

He wasn't sure how to respond. Every word he considered was rude or wrong. On some primitive level, all he really wanted was to take her into his arms. The muscles in his shoulders twitched, trying to send the signal that it should be done.

But touching her, even to soothe rather than to seduce, would be wrong on so many levels he couldn't even begin to list them. Where exactly was the line between comfort and seduction, anyhow? He'd started out wanting to comfort Haley, too, remember? And look where that got him.

So he told his muscles to shut up, settle down and

behave. They'd eat. He'd tell Tess how to operate the stove, open the flue on the fireplace, change the filter in the a/c. Then he'd take her to her car and say good-night.

"We should eat while it's still warm," he said, and he was surprised to hear the thread of tension in his voice.

"Yes." She sounded awkward and tight, as well, and he wondered whether he'd telegraphed his urge to embrace her, in spite of his determination not to act.

She headed toward the kitchen, and when she was safely on the other side of bar, she began pulling out containers from the bag and setting them on the counter. When she had them all arranged, she frowned.

"It just occurred to me. Should you call your wife? Is she home alone with the baby?"

"My wife?" For a minute he had no idea what she was talking about. But suddenly the comment made sense. He had told her, that first day, that he'd been up all night with the baby. He'd assumed that she knew his story, as everyone in Silverdell did.

But she didn't know. She thought he was a married man. No wonder she'd barricaded herself behind the counter, as if it could provide a shield against the sexual tension that was so obviously floating in the air between them.

"I'm not married," he said. When her frown

deepened, he hurried to explain. "The baby who keeps me up at night isn't my daughter. She's my niece. My sister's child. Molly and her husband have separated, so she and the baby are living with me for a while."

"Oh." Tess dropped her gaze and fiddled with the container of potatoes. "Oh, I see. I'm sorry to hear that."

But she wasn't. She wasn't sorry to hear he was single—any more than he was sorry to be so. He could tell because she held herself with an awareness that matched his in every degree.

She wanted him...wanted to walk into his arms and see where comfort took them.

Or if that were overstating it, at least she found him attractive, that the chemistry between them had reached across the space between flesh and flesh. The separate elements had touched, tested the compatibility and sparked a fire.

Maybe not tonight. Tonight was too soon. But someday. Someday, he knew, she might want to be his lover.

Someday...

A rush of sheer pleasure and anticipation moved through him, making his jeans feel too tight and his heart pound too fast.

Why was tonight too soon? They were both adults....

He moved toward the kitchen. She glanced up,

and her cheeks flushed to red. He actually reached out his hand, and touched her hair. To his surprise, she leaned her cheek into it—though he'd half expected her to pull away.

Her cheek was like rich velvet that had been sitting out in the sun. Warm, soft, smooth. Her hair fell forward to tickle his wrist. His jeans grew another size smaller.

He let his fingers drift gently over her lips. Those full, bowed lips with their own heat. They parted slightly, and he felt her breath against his fingertips. He had the insane idea that he'd like to let his fingers slip gently into that moist opening, to feel the soft inner edge of her lip, to touch the tiny, enchanting chip of her pearly tooth, and then to follow with his own lips....

He leaned toward her, mindlessly, like a growing thing turning toward sunlight. He wanted her. He didn't understand why he wanted her so intensely, when he hadn't wanted a woman since Haley....

He pulled his fingers away quickly. Haley. He hadn't even made a clean break with his last vulnerable, needy woman.

So, no. He wasn't doing this. He wasn't even going to *think about* doing this.

Sensing his withdrawal, she straightened and looked at him, her eyes large pools of liquid glimmer.

"We'd better eat," he said.

"All right." She blinked, clearly confused. As she had every right to be.

Damn it. He was a fool.

It probably would have been much smarter to let her go on believing he was a married man, a picked peach with a helpless infant depending on him. Because they wouldn't be lovers, tonight or ever.

He had sworn off wounded birds. Forever.

On the surface, there was nothing damaged about Tess. She was beautiful, talented, clearly independent enough to take on a new city, a new job and the Wright sisters without blinking. She was capable of saving the spa from the catastrophe Chelsea had left behind. That wasn't a job for sissies.

But he knew better than to judge by appearances, or even by a few days of superhuman effort. Tess might not realize it, but Jude learned with his hands, too. And tonight, when she'd collapsed in his arms, he'd felt the truth.

He'd felt the years of deprivation in her body, more skin-and-bones than slender. He'd felt the terrible, lifelong isolation that left her shocked that anyone was willing to catch her when she fell.

And he felt the hunger, far deeper than a lack of food. A chronic lack of love that made intimacy frighten her so much she fought it even when she was only half-conscious.

He had sworn off wounded birds. And this beautiful little sparrow was as broken as they come.

"HEY, RO." Mitch stuck his head through the door of Rowena's office.

She jumped slightly, and as if she had something to hide, she moved her computer mouse, clicked and quickly shifted the screen to a spreadsheet of salaries and withholding taxes. Then she put her hands over a letter she'd been writing, which lay, half-finished, on her desk.

All very odd. He wondered whether she was writing to her father—or at least the man who had been unearthed as her biological father. It was driving Bree nuts, he knew, waiting for Rowena to decide how to approach the man. He always thought it was kind of cute, how determined Bree and Penny were to bring Rowena and her true father together. No one ever seemed to mention the weirdness that resulted from the DNA bombshell—or the elephant in the room, which was that Rowena wasn't technically an heir, and this ranch she adored didn't technically belong to her.

But, hey, what would be the point of mentioning it? You couldn't separate Rowena from this land any more than you could move one of those mountains out there. She belonged here, and no one had ever, to his knowledge, questioned the situation even once.

So what was holding her back? He tried to conjure up a visual imprint of the split second he'd glimpsed before the screen blipped to the spreadsheet. He couldn't remember much except it looked like a hospital website.

Dr. Rowan Atherton worked at a hospital in Crested Butte, a real upright guy by all accounts, so it wasn't as if she were in danger of getting another lemon like Johnny Wright. Growing up believing that psycho was your father must have been hell—and so you'd think that discovering he *wasn't* would be heaven.

Oh, well. Rowena's secret internet browsing, and her DNA, were her problems. Mitch wasn't the type to interfere.

He pretended to have noticed nothing, plastered a smile on his face and adopted a lighthearted tone. "Mail come yet?"

Rowena raised her eyebrows, and inwardly Mitch winced, embarrassed by his bad acting. He had no idea why he tried to pretend he was nonchalant about the mail. Everyone—positively everyone—knew it was the most important time of day for him.

Though it stumped him why he continued to give a darn. Twenty-four out of twenty-five days ended in crushing disappointment. On those days, his only mail was bills or catalogues or junk from people who wanted to lend him money.

And on the twenty-fifth day, that rare day when Bonnie O'Mara actually deigned to send him a postcard, his misery was even greater. Because the only thing worse than not hearing from her was hearing from her.

She never said anything personal. And she darned sure never said what he wanted to hear—that she was coming home.

"Yeah, it came." Rowena smiled, but he could tell she saw through his act. She rummaged through the mess on her desk, then came up with a postcard. She raised it in the air. "Here you go."

Her bland tone told him everything he needed to know, but he took the postcard eagerly and read it anyway.

Damn it. It was exactly the same as last month's. And the month before.

"Having a wonderful time. Wish you were here."

He had tried, at first, to read something into the wish-you-were-here part. But this was the third month, the third postcard, and he had to accept the truth. She wasn't sending secret messages of love and longing. She was simply letting him know she was still alive. Nothing more.

And yet, just the sight of her handwriting did something to his heart. Partly he felt ragged and bleeding at the spot where she'd torn herself away. But partly he felt a primitive, flooding relief. She was still alive. Still safe. Still free enough to buy a postcard, write on it, stamp and address it. That was something.

In the end, it was everything, wasn't it?

"Card looks like New England," Rowena observed. "But I guess that means it's the one place we can be sure she isn't."

"Right." Mitch knew the routine well, and had confessed it to Dallas and Rowena when he returned in September. He and Bonnie had used it, the eight months they'd traveled together. They'd get the postcard ready, then approach some stranger with a license plate from that state and sell him a sob story about how they'd promised to write their parents from Nantucket, Florida, Chicago, wherever, but had forgotten to do so. Would the guy please mail it for them, when he got home?

Amazing how many nice people there were out there. Almost everyone had been happy to help the lovebirds out.

It had seemed like a lark, at first. He knew Bonnie was frightened, but in some post-adolescent, macho way he'd imagined she was blowing her problem out of proportion. He'd always assumed that someday she'd come clean with him, would hand her thorny problem over to him, and let big brave Mitch solve it.

But she never had and, like a fool, he'd been content to wait. He'd never been happier in his life. The eight months had passed like a dream, so full of fun and love, taking odd jobs in quirky towns. She'd wait tables and he'd sling hash. Or she'd answer phone banks, and he'd mix drinks at a neighborhood bar.

He'd signed up for a few business courses here and there. But mostly they didn't care what work they did, as long as they could come home at night, to whatever by-the-week apartment or extended-stay motel they'd chosen, and make love until their bodies gave out.

Then, one day, she was gone. Just like that. All she'd left was a note that said, "I'll be safe as long as you don't look for me."

He had to give her credit. As brick walls went, that one was about perfect. In one sentence, she'd made it absolutely impossible for him to do a damn thing. With eleven words, she'd shut the door on their love affair, locked it, thrown away the key and then dropped a bomb on the spot so that no one could ever find it again.

He'd gone home to Bell River, damn near broken. And now he lived for one postcard a month. One lousy postcard from a place she'd never been, saying words she didn't mean.

"I'm a fool, you know that?" He glanced at Rowena. He really liked her, and he knew she was too blunt and sensible to let him throw a pity party on her watch. "I ought to forget her, because she is obviously never coming back. In fact, I ought to start dating. Have you noticed how cute Marianne is looking these days?"

Rowena entered some numbers into her spreadsheet, her pencil in her mouth while she typed. She spoke around the shaft.

"Sorry, hadn't noticed." She squinted at the screen. "She's not my type."

Mitch grunted, tapping his foot against the desk leg. "You know what I mean. Marianne's a sweetie. I think she used to have the hots for Gray, but she's over that now. I should ask her out."

Rowena stopped typing, put down her pencil and skewered Mitch with her laser-green gaze.

"Yeah," she said, but he could tell from her tone, dripping with sarcasm, that she was about to let him have it. "Yeah, you should do that. Pick the nicest, sweetest, most vulnerable widow in town and see if she wants to have some romping rebound sex with you while you wait for Bonnie to get back. Awesome idea. I bet she'll jump at the chance."

He scowled at her. "Bonnie isn't coming back. That's my point."

"And that makes it better because…?"

Mitch opened his mouth. Then shut it.

"Exactly." Rowena flicked off her monitor. "I have to get out of here. I'm thinking of trying to squeeze in a ride before I have to take the kids tobogganing. Want to come? I'll let you ride Flash."

"Can't." Mitch would have loved that, but he was leading a trail ride right after lunch. Come to think of it, he didn't know exactly when he'd have time to date. Rowena had put the dude ranch on such a fast track that they all had to race around 24/7 just to keep up. "Is Dallas cool with your riding Flash this far along in the pregnancy?"

She wrinkled her nose saucily. "Dallas isn't the boss of me."

"Well, good for you." Mitch laughed. "That's more than I've ever been able to say."

Rowena stood. "Dallas knows I'm careful." She rested her hand against her stomach briefly. "I'm probably Hatchling's number-one fan. But she has to get used to horses, so I'm starting her lessons early."

"She? Her?"

Rowena shrugged. "Today it's she. Tomorrow, who knows? Either way, the future includes horses, so Hatchling had better get comfortable with them."

They started walking out together, when Mitch stopped short. "Darn it. I was supposed to tell you something. Fanny Bronson thinks she saw Farley Miller yesterday. Apparently he was in his dad's hardware store. She was going to call Dallas, but she wanted you to know right away."

He'd been a little worried about telling her. Last year, Farley had attacked her in the stables one night when he caught her there alone. She'd been ready to impale him with a tack hook, when Dallas saved his life by scooping him out of harm's way. You'd think the little jerk would have been grateful, but no. Farley was a scuzzbucket, and that's all there was to it.

To Mitch's surprise, Rowena didn't look distressed. In fact, she didn't even look surprised.

"I thought he had to leave town and stay gone," Mitch said. "I thought that was the deal, if you didn't press charges."

"No. I wasn't going to press charges anyhow. Dallas just suggested to Perry that it would be a good idea if Farley spent some time away from Silverdell. It's been more than a year. We can't expect him to stay away forever."

"But the guy isn't right in the head, not where the Wrights are concerned."

Mitch wasn't entirely clear on Farley's exact grudge, but word was that during the Wright murder trial Farley's father had testified. Apparently, somewhere along the way, crazy Johnny had accused Miller, a decent, ordinary Joe who owned the downtown hardware store, of sleeping with his wife. They'd even tested Miller to see if he might have been the father of the baby Moira was carrying when she died.

He wasn't, any more than Moira's husband, Johnny, was. They never had tracked down that little mystery, but given that both Moira and the unborn child were dead, it probably didn't get a lot of investigation.

Anyhow, Miller's mother had died not long

after the tragedy. Blaming the Wrights was nuts, of course, but Farley had been humiliated and infuriated. And he hadn't been playing with a full deck already.

"But Ro, are you sure Farley won't—"

"Not sure at all," she said soberly. "In fact, we're pretty sure he went into the spa yesterday and probably left one of those ugly notes we keep getting. Tess reports seeing a dirty little man who said his name was Marley Baker."

Mitch groaned. "Cute. Miller, Baker. Farley, Marley. That's his kind of sophomoric joke, all right."

"I thought so, too. Apparently he booked an appointment, showed up a little late and even let her show him to the massage room. But when she returned to get started, he'd disappeared."

"And you're sure it's Farley?"

"Yeah. When they interviewed Tess, she identified his picture. Dallas and Deputy Bartlett are going to pay him a visit this afternoon. We can't make him behave, but we can let him know we're watching."

She flashed him her trademark devilish smile, then turned to head for the door. "See you later," she said. "I seriously need some fresh air, and Flash is waiting."

"Hey, Ro!" He had a quiver of premonition.

"You sure you want to be out there alone, if Farley's hanging around?"

She raised her eyebrows, her eyes flashing. "You think I intend to hide under my bed because that little weasel is in town?"

He sized up his half-wild sister-in-law, from her black hair to her long, confident, athletic body. Pregnant or not, she was one impressive lady, and she was right. She ate "little weasels" like Farley for lunch, and washed them down with a punch made from the rest of the gossips and fools in Silverdell.

No wonder none of those fools had ever questioned whether she was Johnny's biological daughter. She was, in her way, even more fiery and powerful than he'd been. And she didn't need a gun to prove it.

"No," he said with a one-sided smile. "As a matter of fact, if you do run into the poor schmuck out there, I'm pretty sure he's the one who ought to be scared."

CHAPTER FIVE

TESS KNEW SHE was being a fool to let herself get so emotionally attached to her new cabin, but she couldn't help it. Everything was so charming, warm and fresh. Obviously every detail, from the sheets to the faucets, had been handpicked by someone with fabulous taste and a budget for beauty.

As she folded her last nightgown into the lovely walnut dresser—*real* walnut, not pasteboard, not balsa wood, not junk of any kind—she ran her hands over the shining, swirling grain one more time, trying to believe her luck. When she told Jude she had never lived anywhere this nice, she hadn't been kidding.

The spa was closed on Tuesdays, so she had the entire day to move in. Not that she needed it. Even though she didn't rush, by three o'clock she was done.

The rest of her free day stretched before her, luxuriously long and empty. She'd turned her phone off completely, so that she couldn't even see whether Craig was continuing to call. She wasn't going to answer, and sooner or later he'd have to accept that divorce meant forever.

So…freedom for a whole afternoon. What to do…?

A bath! A slow, hot, oil-scented bath. She stretched like a cat, thinking how delicious it would feel. All morning, she'd been eyeing the tiled bathroom, done in shades of creamed coffee, chestnut and white, with its whirlpool tub, its twelve settings on the showerhead and its towel warmers.

She'd turned on each one, just to see, like a kid in a candy store tasting something from every bin. These high-quality details wouldn't surprise her in the guest cabins. After all, the amenities lured in the customers, then brought them back for repeat business. In the guest cabins, frills would be looked on as investments.

But in a cabin that had always been earmarked for a member of the staff? Unheard of. Maybe she should pinch herself, but if she were dreaming she didn't want to wake up.

She picked out her favorite oils, discarded her jeans for a terry robe and turned on the water. She held her hand under the flow, waiting for it to get hot.

She waited. And waited. And waited.

The tub was halfway filled, but the water coming from the faucet was still stone-cold. She pulled her fingers away and dried them. Jude had given her the grand tour, but she couldn't remember him saying anything about the water heater. Had he mentioned some switch she should flip, some lever she should pull, but she'd forgotten to do so?

She went into the utility room, opened the closet and stared at the big gray drum stupidly. She didn't see anything that said *push me!* But, then, she wasn't particularly mechanical.

Her gaze moved to the window, which had a good view of the spa, and instinctively looked for Jude's truck. He was supposed to be there today, finishing the sauna walls.

To her surprise, instead of seeing the truck, she saw Jude himself. Dressed in a black leather bomber jacket, collar turned up against the cold, and a pair of jeans that rode his long legs softly, he was walking toward her cottage.

She hadn't expected to see him…maybe not for a long while. Last night, when he'd come very close to kissing her, but had pulled back, he'd seemed alarmed, as if the impulse surprised him—and not in a good way.

And yet here he was. It was almost as if she'd sent him a psychic SOS. Her heart sped up, if only because she knew she looked a wreck, half-dressed, with her hair untouched for hours and no lipstick.

She didn't have time to change into her jeans, but she tugged at her messy braid, hoping she didn't look absolutely crazed, and opened the back door as he lifted his hand to knock.

"Hey," she said. With one hand, she drew the sides of her robe together at the throat, not out of excessive modesty, but because it was freezing outside. "You must be able to read minds. I was thinking of calling you."

He smiled, clearly ready to put last night behind them and start over on friendly footing. "I don't know about the mind-reading part. I thought I'd see if you were settling in all right. Moving can be exhausting, and I know you were already pretty tired."

"Actually, I'm fine. The cabin was so fully stocked there wasn't much to do."

If he only knew how easy it had been. Talk about traveling light. Truth was, she owned very little. She'd sold or given away almost everything from her mother's house, and she'd walked out of the apartment she'd shared with Craig with one suitcase.

Once she'd hung her clothes in the closet, stocked the medicine cabinet with her soaps and oils, put her massage table and supplies here in the utility room and found a spot for her one plant, a cherished, half-dead Christmas cactus that she was nursing back to life, she was done.

"Good." Putting his hands in his pockets, he

raised one eyebrow. "So…you were thinking of calling me because…?"

"Oh. Right. It's the hot water." She gestured toward the heater. "There isn't any."

He frowned. "What? Joe—he's my assistant—said it was working when he installed it." He stepped forward. "Okay if I take a quick look?"

"Sure." She backed up, glad to be able to shut the door. It wasn't snowing today, but the bright, blue air was as sharp as a knife. "While you look at that, I'll just throw something warmer on, okay?"

But he didn't answer. He was already squatting, his elbows on his knees, studying the heater. She edged around him—not much room in the small space with all her massage supplies stored here—and went to the bedroom. Her jeans and sweater still lay across the beautiful blue-and-brown quilt at the foot of the bed, so she was able to pull them on in an instant.

By the time she returned to the utility room, he was dusting off his hands. "Good news. Joe left it unplugged, probably thinking he could conserve energy until you moved in. Guess he forgot to tell me. Sorry about that."

"No problem." She smiled. "I'm glad it was something so simple."

"Unfortunately, it'll be a while before you'll have any—" As he stood, he winced and, groaning, reached out to steady himself on the rim of

the water heater. "Damn it! Sorry. It's my leg…."
Glancing at her, he took a breath and smiled, clearly
trying to make light of it, though the strain on his
face told her how much it hurt. "No big deal. Just
acts up sometimes, if I stand on it wrong."

She waited for him to adjust. But after a few
seconds, she could see he still wasn't putting any
weight on it. Instead, he subtly rotated the foot, as if
trying to make something loosen, or fall into place.

The ankle, maybe? Or was the problem higher
up…the knee? She'd sensed there might be something wrong with his gait—but she hadn't realized
it was this bad.

She lifted his elbow and tucked herself under his
arm. "Come in and sit down. Let me see if there's
anything I can do."

He stiffened. "Really. It's nothing. It'll fix itself
in a minute."

But he couldn't pull completely away, because he
obviously still couldn't put weight on that foot. She
led him into the living room and helped him drop
carefully onto the sofa. She'd been running through
her mental files, and one thought kept coming up
highlighted. *High ankle sprain.*

"Thanks," he said as he sat. When he got situ-
ated, he leaned back and took a deep breath, shut-
ting his eyes.

"What happened?" Instinctively, she gently put
his leg across her lap. "Where does it hurt?"

He opened his eyes, but he didn't try to remove his leg. His dark hair, which he wore slightly long, spread out a little behind his head, very black against the blue fabric of the sofa. He really was shockingly handsome.

He stared at his leg as if it belonged to someone else. "I had an accident early this year. Twisted my ankle pretty bad, stretched the ligaments. I spent six weeks in a boot, but it still acts up sometimes."

She chewed thoughtfully on her lower lip. If he'd just "stretched" the ligaments, a grade one sprain, he would have healed by now. This must have at least been a grade two, with a partial tear...and maybe even a grade three, with a complete tear.

She put her fingers on either side of the leg and pressed very, very gently, nudging the tibia and the fibula toward each other. "Does that feel tender?"

He gave her a twisted smile. "Not like it used to. First time the ortho guy did that, I screamed like a baby."

She let go. "So...a high ankle sprain, then? Did they say whether it was a grade two or grade three?"

"Three. Torn like a piece of paper, apparently. It was doing fine, but I guess I went to work a little sooner than I should have, and that set me back. I'm mostly okay. Just now and then something gets tangled up in there, and I have to wait till it works itself out."

She began pressing along the lower leg. She'd had clients with high ankle sprains, and she knew the pain could be awful. Notoriously slow healer, too. He shouldn't have taken that boot off until the doctor cleared him. But it happened all the time—especially when people needed to earn a living, and the boot got in the way.

She probed gingerly, assuming he must have re-injured it. Had he been a carpenter in L.A.? But no... She had a sudden memory of Alec, stuck on the river-rock wall, waiting to be rescued, and saying he wished Jude were there, because a stuntman would know what to do.

Had he meant that literally? Surely Jude wouldn't have returned to stunt work before his ankle was fully healed.

Her fingers continued to explore, while her mind marched through the more concrete thoughts. She'd found several places that clearly were still sore, and she suspected some adhesions to the long tendons of the exterior ankle.

She looked at him, and saw that he was watching her, a half smile on his lips. She felt a flush creep over her cheeks as she realized how lost she'd been in her exploration of his calf. She'd even pushed up the jeans so that she could touch the skin directly, probing for knots, heat, flinching—all the signals of pain.

"Sorry," she said mildly. "I'm always working, I guess."

"No problem." His grin was easy, but she knew she should have asked permission first. She wondered what it was about him that made her forget herself so completely.

Maybe it was that he'd built this place, and clearly felt so comfortable here, on her sofa, with his leg across her knees.

Or maybe it was because his body had spoken to her so lucidly, so eloquently, during their massage that first day. All bodies communicated, but now and then, very rarely, a clearer channel opened, and true dialogue passed easily between her hands and the person on the table.

"What kind of accident was it?"

His silence was suddenly not comfortable at all. She bit her lip, wishing she could take back the words. She shouldn't have asked. He clearly didn't talk about it much, or he would have explained those scars on his back when she first saw them.

She started talking about something else quickly, to fill the awkward gap. "Have you tried regular lower leg massage? I've had a lot of success dealing with residual pain from high ankle sprains."

She pulled the denim over his ankle and rested her palm on the rounded curve of his knee, with an attempt at professional detachment. But her fingertips were still too sensitized to the shape of him, and the touch, which should have been natural, felt too personal. Too intimate.

She moved her hand awkwardly, letting it drop beside her hip.

"It was an explosion," he said, his voice casual, as if the silence hadn't happened.

"Oh?" She bit her lip again, to prevent pressing for more.

"Yes. I did stunt work in Hollywood for a few years. One day, someone miscalculated." He shrugged, as if it were no big deal. "Fake fire became a real fire, and I had to go from the second story to the ground without benefit of stairs. I landed on my ankle, rolled it out and something popped like a gunshot."

She winced. "I bet that hurt."

"Yeah. But I was lucky, all things considered. I did a Tarzan thing with a wire. It wasn't designed to hold so much weight, so it snapped halfway down. But it took about ten feet off the fall and probably saved my life."

With a chilled numbness, she saw the pictures, playing cruelly in her mind. She imagined him, as handsome, as dashing and tragic as any leading man could ever hope to be. Trapped but calm, of course. Reaching for the wire. Swinging. Falling.

The others must have been horrified, witnesses unable to help. How relieved they would have been, when he stood, limping but unbroken. Had they applauded? Had they rushed to his side with comfort and first aid?

Had they been his friends, as well as his co-workers? And what about Haley Hawthorne, the starlet who had called him that night at the diner? Had she been there? Haley had once been Jude's lover—perhaps still was. Tess had heard that in the whispers he'd left in his wake that night....

Haley Hawthorne. Of course Tess had heard of her. A true beauty, a rising star and apparently a Dellian by birth. What was she to Jude now that he was in Silverdell, and she was still on the silver screen? The whisperers had wanted to know that, too. Apparently he didn't speak of her and wouldn't provide any grist for the rumor mill.

Haley Hawthorne, with her black hair and red lips…and slim, graceful, red-tipped fingers. Tess realized that his film-set accident didn't account for the scars on his back. Perhaps they were love marks, after all. Perhaps Haley was a wild woman in bed…maybe Jude did that to a woman.

She squeezed her eyes shut and bowed her head, mortified at the direction her thoughts had taken.

She had to stop this. She certainly wasn't going to pry anymore. She'd already far overstepped the bounds of their fledgling friendship.

"Would you like some coffee?" She straightened her back, and he got the message. He lifted his leg and placed it on the floor, warily at first, then with more conviction.

"It's much better," he said happily. "That helped. Thanks."

"Great!" She stood, neatening the hem of her blue sweater and brushing her hair away from her face. "I do hope you'll look into getting some regular lower-leg massage. And you might want to tape your ankle whenever it feels unstable. It's so easy to reinjure this kind of sprain."

"I will," he said, standing, too. "I'll talk to Ashley tomorrow, see if she can work me in once a week or so."

Ashley. Tess had opened her mouth to say she'd be glad to do it when she realized that he'd put a delicate emphasis on the word *Ashley.* The other therapist. Not Tess. He didn't want Tess.

"Okay, then. Good," she said brightly, trying not to feel slighted. Just because she had felt a special connection when they worked together didn't mean he'd instantly prefer her to a therapist he'd probably known for years. "Now. How about that coffee, to thank you for the repairs?"

"No thanks needed," he said. He glanced toward the kitchen. "I should get back to work. Besides, your water should be hot by now, and a warm bath is probably what you need more than anything. You were pretty done in last I saw you."

"I'm fine, really. I'm honestly not ordinarily that

fragile. I've never fainted before in my life." He'd been so patient, feeding her, showing her around the cabin, then driving her to the hotel. And, even after the awkward moment when they'd almost kissed, he'd still been gallant, arranging for someone from Bell River to deliver her car to her. "I'm sorry to have been such a nuisance."

"No nuisance at all." He was already moving toward the utility room, as if he were impatient to get away.

She followed, surprised by the clingy sensation that had come over her. Why would she want him to stay, especially when he so clearly preferred to go? Before he came, she'd felt quite comfortable alone here, snug and cozy and fully at home.

But now...when she thought of the cabin without him, it felt oddly hollow and lifeless.

Absurd. She wouldn't allow herself to be so weak. Hadn't she learned anything over the past terrible year? Hadn't she learned anything from her mother's mistakes? And what about the example her mother had set for tough-minded self-reliance?

Obviously her mom had pushed Johnny out of their lives, and she'd brought up her daughter alone. It hadn't been easy, and Tess hadn't always appreciated it, but she was old enough now to realize how much courage it had taken.

Though sometimes she'd rebelled, and often she'd

been foolish—Craig was proof of that—still...she had her mother's blood and her mother's courage.

So no clinging. Depending on other people was a recipe for disaster. Tess didn't need anyone, least of all a near stranger who happened to be handy and kind. She would fix her own appliances. She would be her own friend, her own companionship, her own rock.

She, herself, Teresa Mary Spencer, was all she needed.

Which was a good thing. Because Teresa Mary Spencer was all she had.

Two days later, as the sunset began to dribble down the western sky like an overturned pot of watercolors, Tess stood at the edge of Silverbottom Pond, ice skates in hand, and tried to work up the nerve to join the crowd.

She hadn't thought she'd come at all. A native Californian, she'd been required to try Rollerblades, of course—though she'd never been very good. But she'd never ice-skated before in her life.

She wasn't in California anymore, though, and this world was very different. Just before the spa closed—they were closing early all week, because of holiday events—Rowena had poked her head into the Blue Room, holding out the skates.

"We're inaugurating a new holiday tradition tonight. We're calling it the New Year's Eve-Eve Ice

Derby." She jiggled the skates. "This is your official invitation."

Tess had raised her eyebrows. She'd finished her last massage, but she still had a lot of straightening up to do. "I'm not sure I'm familiar with that event."

Rowena chuckled mischievously. "Of course not! We invented it last night. It means a bunch of us, family and guests and staff, are going to skate on Silverbottom Pond and try not to kill ourselves. Most of us are rotten skaters. Especially me. It'll be nuts, and it'll be fun." She extended the skates a little farther. "I think these are your size. If you're not busy, why don't you come?"

Though she accepted the skates to be polite, Tess had demurred... Once she closed up, she was probably going to go to bed early, or work on the bookkeeping, or unpack a little more.

All lies, of course. She had nothing to do. Nothing but read, or take another long bath...

So she'd gone home to her cabin and pulled out the guide map to find out how far away Silverbottom Pond was. Not far at all—about halfway to the main house. She could easily walk there. Maybe it was a sign—maybe this would be a good time to learn more about her family.

Her family. She didn't remember ever having that phrase come so easily to the forefront, and it alarmed her slightly. They weren't her family. Liking them was one thing. She definitely respected Rowena, and they all seemed like good people.

But "her family"? Hardly.

Still…she stared out her window at the pinks and blues of the waning day. It was such a beautiful afternoon.

Before she knew it, she was digging out a muffler, gloves and cap, scooping up the skates, and heading off to find the party.

High hopes. But then, about a minute ago, she'd pulled up short at the edge of the pond, intimidated by the sheer scale of the event. *Wow.* If they'd "invented" this last night, they must have the organizational skills of a highly efficient army. The scene was bustling, cheerful and as pretty as a picture postcard.

At least fifty people were already skimming, stumbling and spinning across the pond, which was perfectly round, fully frozen and tinted a lovely shade of rosy pink by the sunset. Somewhere nearby, a sound system filled the air with "Jingle Bells." Stainless steel crowd-control stanchions gleamed at intervals around the perimeter, the ropes between them looped with fairy lights, so that the pond seemed to be the opal at the center of a circular diamond setting.

Off to the side, folding tables were piled high with refreshments, and someone was cooking over a small, open fire. Tess smelled coffee, hot chocolate, hot dogs and the unmistakable mouth-watering scent of marshmallows roasting.

Everywhere she looked, she saw couples holding hands, teens giggling and parents dangling their little ones by the arms, creating the happy illusion that the children could stay upright on their own. The banks were dotted with wooden benches filled with people tying and retying skates, or catching their breath after a turn on the ice.

She didn't see a single empty bench.

"You came!" A mittened hand pushed under her elbow and squeezed a warm welcome. Turning, Tess saw Rowena, who looked as round and apple-cheeked as Mrs. Claus. Her red coat with its white velvet trim struggled to cover her. "I'm so glad. Are you a good skater? I hope not. I don't want to be the only bumbling fool out here. Besides, I don't think you've met Penny, and you really should."

Rowena's confident stride swept Tess along, whether she was ready or not. They made their way to a crowded bench, a place where Tess wouldn't have dreamed of trying to intrude. But, as if it had been choreographed, the occupants of the bench parted to make room, smiling at them as if they'd been expected.

"Penny, come over here! I need you to meet Tess, and then I need you to help me tie these blasted skates." Rowena plopped down on the bench and held up her feet ruefully. "I haven't touched my toes in a month, and there's no way I'm getting down there now."

She patted the bench beside her, indicating that Tess should sit, too. But, though Tess set her skates in the spot to indicate that she would join Rowena soon, she wanted to remain standing to meet Penny. She craned her neck a little, trying to see who was obeying Rowena's imperious summons.

She saw one slight body separate itself from a larger crowd, and a young woman in pink came gliding toward them. When she reached the edge of the pond, she stepped carefully onto the snow, smiling at Tess as though she already knew who she was.

"Hi, Tess," the young woman said, offering her a smile that somehow managed to be both endearingly shy and warmly welcoming. "I'm Penny. It's so great to finally meet you. Rowena says you've absolutely saved our lives."

Penny held out both hands, and Tess held hers out, too, almost without thinking, as if Penny's sweetness were magnetic. For a minute she couldn't speak, couldn't really even think straight.

Because here, standing in front of her, was the recognition she'd been waiting for. Here, at last, was the kinship, the connection, the face that mirrored her own. This was the Wright daughter who was, somehow, truly Tess's flesh and blood.

Tess couldn't put her finger on what it was, exactly. Their coloring was similar...both of them were Bambi-brown-haired, with brown eyes and fair skin. Both of them were small women, not just short, but slight of build. They both wore their fine hair long and loose. It curled in much the same way around their collarbones, with wisps flying free, lifted by the wind, just as Tess had seen the wind tear off spirals of snow-dust from the mountaintops.

But those were details she probably shared with a hundred women. A thousand. The recognition she felt was deeper, and indefinable. It robbed her of her voice.

Luckily, the Wright sisters were easy hosts, chatter flowing from them like water tumbling down a bank to spill in a pool of hospitality. Penny held Tess's hands companionably as she drew her toward Rowena, continuing to compliment her on how well she'd handled the spa.

"—and we want you to know we're well aware how lucky we were," she concluded as they reached her sister. "Right, Ro?"

"Absolutely!" Rowena's eyes sparkled with impatience, and Tess knew full well she had no idea what she was agreeing to. "Now please, Pea. Put my skates on. I'm dying to get out there and fall on my face."

Penny knelt with a smile and began ministering to her sister. Still mute, Tess took the spot saved for her and started to unlace her skates.

"You're not going to fall, Ro," Penny said as she tugged off one of Rowena's glossy boots. "There's nothing athletic you can't do, and it'll take more than a baby belly to change that." She cast a smile toward Tess. "Now *me*…that's a different story. I haven't an athletic bone in my body. I'll be lucky if I don't break my neck out there tonight."

Tess smiled back. Another thing they had in common, maybe. Tess was a bit of a klutz herself, when it came to sports. Of course, Penny might be putting on a fake modesty. That was what royalty always did, wasn't it—part of the noblesse oblige? And there was no question that the Wright women were Bell River royalty.

The three of them stepped onto the pond together and, as predicted, Rowena found her feet first. She scissored a few tentative ovals into the ice, propelling herself forward slowly, and then began gliding with long strokes. As she left Penny and Tess behind, she grinned at them and wiggled a goodbye with her fingers.

Penny chuckled, but apparently even that distraction was too much for her skills. She faltered, her feet tangling. She grabbed onto Tess's sleeve for balance, but it was like one nonswimmer clutching another, trying not to drown. Tess's arms windmilled helplessly, and her eyes met Penny's with half alarm, half laughter.

And then they went down in a heap.

For a crazy moment, as other skaters veered to avoid them, Tess feared they might be like one of those fender benders on the Santa Monica Freeway that always dominoed into a thirty-car pileup.

But somehow, everyone stayed upright, curving around the two silly women who couldn't stop laughing long enough to untangle their coats and scarves and get back up on their skates.

"Penny, Penny." A dark-haired man appeared in front of them, extending a hand and chuckling. "Who let you on the ice without your helmet and kneepads?"

Tess pushed her hair out of her face and looked up. Oh, yes. Max. Penny's husband.

Penny made a rude sound as Max lifted her to her feet, but it quickly turned into a kiss. "My hero," she said, standing on tiptoe to rub her nose against his briefly. "You know I fall only so that you can save me."

"Right." Max smiled, then held his hand out for Tess. "Want a lift?"

Since she was in an undignified position, on her hands and knees, with her rump in the air, her skates refusing to hold steady long enough for her to raise herself, Tess accepted the hand gratefully.

"Thank you," she said sincerely, using his muscled stability to pull herself erect. She brushed snow from her pants, elbows and rear end. "Apparently Rollerblades and ice skates don't have much in common."

Max grinned. "You'll get the hang of it. Come around with us. We'll help."

Tess smiled, but she could tell by how contentedly Penny clung to Max's arm that the two of them were eager to skate together. As the sun began to drop farther in the west, the pond had taken on a decidedly romantic atmosphere. She would be in the way.

"Thanks, but…" She glanced around and wondered what she could use as a graceful out. "I think I see Jude over there. I wanted to thank him for fixing my water heater."

They believed her, of course. Why wouldn't they? They skated protectively behind her as she gingerly minced her way to solid ground. Someone had thoughtfully placed stanchions at the most convenient exit spots, and she reached out and balanced herself on the first one, breathing a sigh of relief.

Max and Penny waved and glided off. Tess noted ruefully that Penny became as graceful as a ballerina as soon as her husband's arm was around her waist, guiding her. Tess watched their silhouettes move away, their heads bent together, the gap forming an accidental heart-shaped piece of rose-red sunset.

Tess blinked, and the pond shimmered like crystal through a sudden sheen of tears.

She blinked irritably, clearing her vision. What was wrong with her these days? First that weird dizzy, half-fainting spell with Jude. Then that charged, high-hormone reaction to his presence in the cabin. And now this. Tears? Just because some other couple she barely knew briefly resembled a cliché from a Valentine's Day card?

Oh, well. She slipped the guards onto her blades and made her way to the bench where she thought she'd spotted Jude. It would look odd if she didn't actually speak to him, now that she'd said she wanted to.

When she got closer, she realized he was holding a baby. An absolutely adorable, chubby-cheeked infant—six or seven months old, perhaps—with a blue-and-pink-checked ski cap and a snowsuit that made her look like a miniature Michelin Man.

"Tess!" Jude waved, as if he were pleased to see her. Alert and eager to share in any excitement, the baby automatically arched her back and tried to launch herself toward Tess, imitating his wave with her tiny pink mittens.

So, of course, Tess had to greet the baby first. "Hey, there. You're a cutie, aren't you?"

The baby shouted, smiling toothlessly. Tess and Jude exchanged a grin.

"Tess, this is Beeba. Her real name's Barbara, but

obviously that doesn't suit her at all. Beeba, this is Tess." He jiggled the baby, who squawked with delight and continued to push against his thighs with her fat little legs, trying to keep the dance going. "Beeba has only one mode. Deliriously happy."

"I see that."

Jude scooted a couple of inches to one side, making room. Tess sat beside him, holding out her hand for Beeba to grasp. The baby's eyes widened, as if she couldn't believe her luck, and then, gurgling merrily, she guided Tess's finger to her lips and began gumming it. Her mouth was warm and wet and somehow ineffably sweet.

Oh, good grief. Tess took a steadying breath as a strangely poignant contentment spread through her. If she weren't careful, she'd find herself teary again.

"Is your sister here, too?"

Jude glanced toward the pond. "Yeah. She's skating. I'm hoping the fresh air and exercise might perk her up a little."

"Must be a really tough time for her." Tess saw how worried Jude's face was as he watched the skaters churn by. "I hope she and her husband work things out soon."

"God, *I* don't." Jude frowned hard. "Garth's a—"

He stopped himself with a wry smile. "Let's just say he was a rotten husband and would be an even worse father. Postpartum depression is nothing to joke about, but Molly's tough. She'll get through it."

He lightened his voice, and bent down to nibble playfully on the baby's ear. Beeba squealed and nuzzled her head against her uncle, tickling his mouth with the silly pompom at the top of her ski cap.

But she never let go of Tess's finger. That tiny hand had a heck of a grip.

Tess met Jude's eyes over the baby's head, and she tried to read the expression in his eyes. The reference to postpartum depression worried her. He didn't seem the type to toss around phrases like that carelessly, so probably his sister wasn't grappling with anything as simple as the everyday baby blues.

Tess smiled at the blue-eyed baby. Luckily, even if Molly were suffering from true postpartum depression, her little girl wasn't feeling any fallout yet.

Thanks to Jude, probably. Tess had a feeling he had made it his mission to keep the rainbows and sunshine in this little girl's life.

"Is there anything I could do to help?" She meant it, and she hoped he knew she wasn't merely being polite. "There are some aromatherapy ideas, and sometimes massage is—"

Before he could answer, a pretty brunette in a green coat came skidding up to them, making a noisy stop with the edge of her blades that scraped a small mound of snow from the ice.

"Thank you," the woman said, her fists clenched against her heart melodramatically. "Thank you, thank you! I haven't had this much fun in…" She glanced at the baby. "In forever!"

"Good." With a smile, Jude tilted his head toward the ice skater. "This, you may have guessed, is my sister, Molly. Molly, this is Tess. She's the new spa director."

The brunette turned her rosy-cheeked face toward Tess. "Great to meet you, Tess. I've heard a lot about you."

From where? Though she knew it was just a formal expression and probably meant very little, Tess couldn't help wondering. Had Jude talked about her?

"You were so right, Jude," Molly went on. "I'm having such a good time. And to celebrate, I'm going to get us the messiest hot dogs ever made. Sauerkraut, onions, ketchup, mustard, pickles… everything they've got. You want one, too, Tess?"

It seemed like popping a bubble to say no, so, though Tess wasn't very hungry, she nodded. "That sounds great." She tried to remember if she'd slipped any money into her pockets. "Let me give you some—"

Molly laughed and held up her hand. "No one

pays for anything at a Bell River party," she said. "You guys wait here. I'll be right back."

When she whisked off, Tess turned to Jude. "It's easy to see where the baby gets her personality."

But to her surprise, Jude's expression was somber, and his followed the disappearing figure of his sister.

"She's always been a cheerful person," he said, "but she seems a little manic, don't you think?"

Tess wasn't sure what to say, not knowing Molly well enough, naturally, to judge. As if lost in thought, Jude hoisted the baby higher on his shoulder, which dislodged Tessa's finger. Beeba didn't seem to mind, eagerly substituting the collar of Jude's jacket as a chew toy. Oddly, though, Tess felt a sense of loss as she lowered her hand and dried her quickly chilling finger against her thick leggings.

"Mood swings…that's one of the symptoms," Jude said, finally turning to Tess as if he'd remembered her presence. "She'll be hyper like this, and then some little detail will go wrong, and she'll end up in tears."

Actually, his description sounded too much like Tess's own mood swings these days. She shifted uncomfortably on the bench.

"I'm sorry," she said, knowing how ineffective it was but wanting somehow to lighten his burden. "It must be hard, watching someone you love be unhappy."

"Yeah. But not as hard as when she lived with Garth. He has a real temper. Back then, every time the phone rang at night I darn near had a heart attack. The guy's a psycho."

He pried his soggy collar out of the baby's mouth. For a second, Beeba glared at him, shocked, then balled her face up, ready to let loose a protesting wail. But before she could inhale fully, he distracted her by pretending to pop off her nose.

She paused, frowned at him, then jumped on his thighs and chortled, delighted. He did it again. And again. Apparently the sound he made as he pinched the tip of her tiny nose was endlessly hilarious, because she simply couldn't get enough.

For a few minutes, Tess and Jude sat without speaking, comfortably amused by the antics. Then, abruptly exhausted, Beeba dropped her head against Jude's chest, put her hand in her mouth, mitten and all, and sucked a bit before falling asleep.

Tess met Jude's gaze, and was touched by the baby's innate, absolute trust in him...and by the sudden urge she had to drop her own tired head against that capable chest.

Without warning, she found herself a little disoriented, her peripheral vision blurring, as if the world had narrowed, the skaters and the music and the laughter had disappeared, and they were the only two people at the pond.

Her breath came faster. His did, too. Then his eyes narrowed, and his gaze dropped to her lips.

Even though it had begun to snow, a starburst of heat exploded across her lips, and sparkled down, like firework tendrils, into her chest.

"Tess," he said quietly. "Tess, I want to, but I can't..."

Can't what? He didn't say, and her mind wouldn't think. All she knew was that she wanted him to kiss her...wanted it badly. And it horrified her to know that he knew.

She struggled for something innocent to say.

"So." She licked her lips, which didn't help, because then the cold air stung her wet mouth, and she had to lick again. "So, you don't skate? Is it your leg?"

He brought his gaze to her eyes slowly. He took a slow breath, as if it would steady him. The baby made a sound and adjusted her head into the hollow near his throat.

"No, the leg's been okay. And actually, the tight lacing of the skate feels pretty good. But I don't trust it enough to take Beeba out there. If I do a face-plant in the ice, that's one thing. If I do it holding an infant..."

"Here you go. Hot from the bonfire. Three jumbo

hot dogs with everything, including the kitchen sink!"

They looked over to see Molly moving toward them, a paper bag swinging from one hand. Tess straightened, and without knowing why she scooted over to put another inch between her hip and Jude's.

However, Molly wasn't paying any attention. She hadn't bothered with skate guards. She'd just stomped the few feet onto the bank, and plopped down on the other side of Jude. She'd already begun digging in her bag.

"Sorry, Beeba, but you can't have any. I got some crackers for you, because I don't think your little tummy can handle sauerkraut, or mustard, or any of this mess."

She held out a huge, cylindrical, foil-wrapped thing that probably was a hot dog—if a hot dog had been supersized by King Kong. "Here you go, Tess," she said, passing it across Jude's body without looking.

Tess reached out, oddly reluctant to touch the thing. How did you grow a hot dog this size? It was more like a watermelon. She peeled away the foil, and the pungent odor of sauerkraut hit her like a physical punch.

"Oh." She recoiled, folding the foil over the hot dog as quickly as she could. Her stomach heaved. "Oh…" She bent her head, shocked at the intensity of the wave of nausea that moved through her.

"What's the matter?" Jude bent toward her. He took the hot dog from her limp hand, but he'd already opened his, so the stench of the meat, the heat, the spices, was spiraling through the air toward her. Her stomach clenched again.

"I'm sorry...I just..."

But her stomach was like a machine, squeezing and then relaxing, tightening on itself, then going limp, over and over, as if it were a bellows. She tried to breathe, but a gagging sound came out instead. She stood, oddly panicked. Her throat spasmed, and she put her hands over her mouth like a child.

"Oh, no, it's the hot dog!" Molly's voice sounded stricken. "Oh, I should have thought. Some people just can't stand all these gooey things on top. I couldn't, either, remember, Jude? When I was pregnant with Beeba, I—"

Tess gasped. She looked at Jude's sister, her eyes so wide they actually stung, as if the air burned at the sensitive white parts usually protected by her lids.

What was the woman talking about? Pregnant? No. No.

No!

But even as Tess moved away, the palm of one hand over her stomach and the back of the other hand pressed hard against her lips, her mind was already doing the math.

Eight weeks. Two months. Two months since the night her mother died. Two months since, at the lowest, loneliest moment of her life, she'd made the fatal error of letting Craig spend the night.

Craig, her ex-husband. The divorce papers had already been filed by then, and she'd had no interest in changing her mind. But that night...she was weak. Just as weak as she'd been when she married him.

Thanks to her mother's eternal lecturing and iron-clad vigilance, Tess had grown up believing that giving in to physical attraction, indulging any physical needs, was weak—and, in fact, immoral. And so, even then, when she'd just turned twenty-seven, the only man who had ever kissed her was Craig.

His arms were the only ones that had ever held her. He was the only man who had ever been allowed in her bed. Craig, who had seemed, at that terrible moment, to be the closest thing to a life raft she could reach.

And so she'd let him stay. In her bed. In her arms. She'd let him make love to her. Just once, because once had been enough to learn that, even when your heart was breaking, even when you were drowning, the wrong man's arms couldn't save you.

You only ended up feeling more alone.

In the two months since then, had she...? She didn't think so. She'd been so busy, under so much stress. She hadn't really thought it was odd that her period didn't come on time.

She'd missed two periods now, though, hadn't she? Not just one. Two months. Two periods. And she'd been sick. Tired. Emotional.

Her hands felt limp at her sides. Her stomach had calmed a little, now that she was far enough away from the sick scent of the sauerkraut.

But her head still spun. The terrible word remained.

Pregnant.

No. No. No.

But yes. God help her. *Yes.*

CHAPTER SIX

TESS HADN'T EVER had to buy a pregnancy test before, and she found it surprisingly difficult to do. It was such a private thing to purchase, right out in public.

Silverdell's only drugstore was on Elk Avenue, on the town square next to Donovan's Dream, the café where Tess had eaten several nights ago…and where she'd seen just about everyone in town.

But so what? She wasn't going to drive to Crawford, or Montrose, just to avoid gossip. No one around here cared what she did, anyhow. She was a stranger, of little more interest than any of the tourists passing through for ski season.

If they'd known she was Johnny Wright's illegitimate daughter…

But they didn't. She could buy a hundred pregnancy tests without raising a single eyebrow, no doubt. Besides, if she really were pregnant, a gossipy drugstore clerk was the least of her problems.

So she got up early the next day, New Year's Eve, grateful that Ashley was well and could handle the appointments, and headed for Sterling Prescription

Shoppe. She parked at the east end of the square and decided to cut through the park. The clear, sunny sky was crisp and cheerful, the temperatures much milder than they'd been. The walk would relax her.

She wasn't the only Dellian with that idea. Though it was barely 9:00 a.m., the park was already dotted with a few joggers and dog-walkers celebrating the break in the weather. The overnight snowfall was already melting under busy feet, and one of the swings in the playground was carving arcs in the bright blue air.

So peaceful, so picturesque. Still decorated for the holidays, but without the Christmas-shopping chaos. On the cusp of a new year, a fresh start, but one you didn't have to begin until *tomorrow*. Today, everything stressful seemed suspended, all the hands of all the clocks frozen for the next twenty-four hours in this cradle of quiet.

Even for her, that calm-before-the-storm feeling was strong. All night long, she'd tried to tell herself she couldn't be pregnant. Surely she wasn't that unlucky—one dumb, lonely mistake couldn't really change her life this much, could it?

And yet, technically it was possible. Once she took the pregnancy test, her life might change forever. She felt her footsteps slowing, as if to drink in the pure charm of this innocent, unknowing moment.

The bells in the steeple of the church at the park's

west end pealed nine times, echoing like crystal into the clean air. Everyone she saw paused, their heads turning instinctively toward the sound.

But then, as the sweet notes rolled away over the mountaintops, Tess was surprised to hear the void filled by the piercing vibrations of a baby's scream.

She hesitated, looking around for the source of the noise. Halfway between where she stood and the playground, a woman in a green coat was bending over a stroller, trying to extricate her baby.

Tess recognized that green coat. It was Molly, Jude's sister.

Tess hurried over, alarmed by the escalating sounds of high-pitched distress.

"Beeba, stop. *Stop!*" Molly's voice was almost as frantic as the baby's. "What on earth is *wrong* with you?"

The latch of the harness seemed to be stuck, and Molly's tense fingers were yanking at it, as if she'd like to rip it free, destroying the whole stroller if necessary to get at her wailing child.

"Hey, Molly," Tess said, touching the other woman's tense back with calming fingertips. She spoke only loudly enough to be heard over the screaming. "Can I help?"

She hadn't been sure Molly would welcome her interference, but the young mother looked over her shoulder, her cheeks red and tear-stained, and her eyes swollen, as if she'd been crying for a while.

"Yes. No. I don't know. I don't know what's wrong with her. She won't stop crying. And now I can't get her out."

"Maybe a fresh pair of hands?"

Molly backed off, dropping the harness with a dramatic gesture. "Go for it," she said gracelessly, though Tess didn't take offense. The young woman was clearly at the end of her rope.

"I thought maybe I could get a run in this morning," Molly said, watching over Tess's shoulder as she felt the harness buckle, looking for any twisted spots that might be getting in the way. "Skating last night…it felt so good. I thought maybe if I could get out more, get some exercise…"

Her voice trailed off, as if she were tired of trying to justify herself. The baby had eased off a little when she saw Tess bending over her instead of her mother. Curiosity trumped whatever was upsetting her, but Tess knew the respite would probably be brief.

She found the twisted spot easily—as Molly would have done, if she hadn't been so upset. She unfolded the strap, squeezed the clasp and released the harness. She slipped her hands in, tucked one behind the baby's bottom and the other behind her head, and lifted Beeba out of the stroller.

"There you go," she said softly, giving the baby a smile. Beeba felt warm, but Tess didn't think it was fever. More likely the sweaty heat of too much crying and writhing in place.

She draped the baby across her shoulder and patted her back. The crying had eased off. After a few seconds, the baby lurched and let loose a comically loud burp.

"Oh, my gosh," Molly said. "Is that all it was?"

"That was probably part of it," Tess said, bouncing the baby gently to make sure all the air was gone. "But her gums might be bothering her. Is she getting her first teeth?"

"Yes. Sometimes she cries for hours."

Poor Molly. Tess put the palm of her hand over Beeba's little round head, snugging the ski cap tighter, to be sure it covered her ears. "She seems content for the moment. How about if I walk her around while you run?"

Molly's inner war played out clearly on her face. She probably felt she shouldn't take advantage— and, after all, she didn't know Tess all that well. But Jude had vouched for Tess…and besides, it was as plain as a neon sign that Molly desperately wanted to be free for a few minutes, to jog untethered and unafraid.

"I'd really enjoy it," Tess assured her. "She's a doll, and we made great friends last night."

Molly seemed to come out of her self-absorption. "Oh. That's right. You were sick. The hot dog."

She frowned. "Are you feeling better now? You look better."

"I'm feeling great," Tess said. She raised one corner of her mouth in a wry smile. "As long as you don't wave another hot dog in front of my face, I'm fine."

Molly grinned, finally reassured. "Okay, then, if you really don't mind…"

Tess made one last guarantee of her enthusiasm for babysitting, and then, with the quickest of good-bye kisses dropped on Beeba's head, Molly wiggled her earbuds into place, lowered her earmuffs and took off running.

Beeba watched her mother go, but didn't, as Tess had feared, break into new sobs at being abandoned. Instead, she turned toward Tess and grinned, as if the two of them had pulled off a successful coup.

"Fickle little rascal," Tess said, unable to resist running one fingertip over the downy velvet of Beeba's pink cheek. Amazing how a baby could transition from screaming horror to gurgling contentment in the blink of an eye. "What shall we do while Mommy runs?"

Beeba clearly didn't care. She was already distracted, her eyes widening, and her body leaning forward with intense focus. She made an excited noise, then reached for Tess's necklace. She closed her fist around the chain and started bending toward it, her mouth gaping like a fish.

"Oh, no, you don't." Tess unwound the gold from the chubby fingers and tucked the ruby-rose pendant deep into her shirt. Beeba stiffened indignantly, as if she'd been cheated. Tess felt her chest expanding as she inhaled, ready to inform the world of her disappointment.

"Hey!" Tess spoke so abruptly that Beeba froze in place, mid-inhale. "I've got an idea. Let's swing."

Beeba didn't seem to know that word, but she clearly knew the tone. She relaxed, the necklace forgotten.

"Okay, then. Playtime!"

Beeba rewarded her with a smile that was mostly gums, but right in the middle, at the bottom, a couple of tiny white caps gleamed. The first two teeth had successfully broken through, and more would follow quickly. Molly was probably in for a few more sleepless nights, poor kid.

As Tessa began to walk rapidly toward the playground area, the baby grabbed onto her lapels as if they were reins and happily twisted her face forward, curious to find out where they were going.

Small drifts of snow mounded on the grassy square like overturned scoops of ice cream. But mostly the playground had been packed down by the laughing, running children in padded snowsuits who ricocheted from one piece of equipment to the other, as random and silly as silver balls in a pinball machine.

Tess got lucky. One of the swings had just been abandoned, and was still rocking jerkily. She headed toward it and sat, with Beeba over her shoulder, her sturdy legs pushing hard against Tess's thighs.

Tess wrapped her left arm around the baby's back, tucking her snugly against her chest, and held the cold links of the swing's chain with the other. She brushed her feet lightly across the ground, creating a tiny wave of momentum.

The swing began to glide gently, cold air teasing across their cheeks.

Beeba chortled. She jumped in place with delight and squealed for more. Tess obliged, enchanted by the baby's laughter, and by the warmth of her sturdy body against her heart.

Whenever she allowed the swing to slow, Beeba shouted for more, and Tess couldn't resist her. But after only a few minutes, she felt dizzy, and ever so slightly nauseated.

She dragged her feet, stopping the swing. But her head still spun. Everything in the playground seemed to be in motion. A few yards in front of them, an indulgent daddy twirled the merry-go-round rapidly for his giggling children. Its silver handles flickered in the sun like strobe lights.

In her peripheral vision, a line of three or four seesaws churned relentlessly, each on a different tempo...up, down, down, up, both up and down...

"Wait just a minute, honey," Tess said, closing her eyes to make the winking, blinking, twirling, pumping chaos around her disappear. "Just a minute."

She realized how sensitive her breasts were where Beeba's body pressed her.

It was true, wasn't it? She hardly needed a test to confirm this. Her body had been telling her for days. This was morning sickness, and she was really pregnant.

She closed her lips over a small, agonized sound.

"Tess? Is everything okay?"

She opened her eyes, and found herself looking into Molly's worried face. "Sorry. Yes, I'm fine."

The baby turned at the sound of her mother's voice and thrust her body away from Tess, arms outstretched. Molly laughed, and plucked Beeba up happily.

"Have you been driving Tess crazy?" She buried her nose in the baby's belly and wriggled her face back and forth. Beeba erupted into giggles, grabbing Molly's hair and hanging on.

Tess stood. She clung to the swing's chain an extra moment, until she could be sure her legs were steady enough to walk. They were, just barely.

"I can't thank you enough, Tess," Molly said. "The run felt fantastic."

It seemed to have done her a world of good. Her cheeks were flushed, a little frost-burned, maybe, and her eyes sparkled. She looked about five years younger, and Tess realized suddenly that Molly probably was barely eighteen, if that.

"I enjoyed it," Tess said sincerely. "She's a sweetheart."

Molly laughed. "Sometimes." With her free hand, she swept her hair back from her damp face. "Wow, I'm so out of shape. I need to catch my breath. Do you have a minute to talk? I'd love to have an adult conversation for once."

Tess thought of the drugstore, and the test she'd hoped to take before she had to be at the spa for an 11:00 a.m. appointment. But how important was that, now? Didn't she already have her answer?

"Sure." The picnic table where Tess had parked the stroller was empty, so she settled on the bench, and Molly dropped down opposite her, sighing heavily.

Still holding Beeba over her shoulder, Molly used her foot to tug the stroller toward her. Then she rummaged in the diaper bag and came up with a bottle of juice. "This might buy us a few minutes of quiet."

Beeba reached for the bottle, settling contentedly in the crook of Molly's arm to drink it. Something pinched inside Tess at the sight of the two of them, and her arms felt strangely empty.

"So Jude tells me you gave him a massage."

Molly looked curious. "Part of your interview or something?"

Tess nodded. "Things were pretty crazy that day. I guess it's hard to hire anyone during the holidays, especially at a resort."

"Sounds as if they didn't have much choice." Molly wrinkled her nose disapprovingly. "I hear Chelsea took off with zero notice."

Tess wouldn't be enticed into gossiping about other members of the staff, even ones who were gone. She'd learned early on that office gossip was poison. People left, people came back, people knew people. Most of all, people talked.

"It's a lovely place to work," she said, avoiding any judgments. "It's a beautiful spa. Have you seen it?"

Molly nodded. "Of course it's beautiful—Jude doesn't build anything that isn't. He's a genius, and they are darned lucky he was available when they needed him. It won't last long, I'm sure. This is a waste of his talents. He'll be going back to L.A. in a few weeks."

"Really?" In spite of her determination to avoid gossip, Tess couldn't help registering her surprise. She hadn't gotten that impression.

"Of course." Molly frowned. "You know who Haley Hawthorne is, right?" When Tess nodded, Molly went on, gazing at Beeba, but with an odd tension in her posture. "Well, Haley has been the love of Jude's life since he was…like, in middle school. They went out to L.A. together, and if it hadn't been for Jude's accident, they'd probably be married by now."

Married? Had it been as serious as that? A wave of something cold moved through Tess's chest, as if the wind had picked up. Jude Calhoun's future shouldn't concern her—*didn't* concern her—and yet she couldn't picture him being happy as part of a Hollywood glamour couple.

Molly glanced up. "You know about his accident, right? If you gave him a massage…"

"He mentioned it," Tess said blandly. What he hadn't mentioned was Haley, marriage or going back to L.A. No reason he should, particularly, but…

She thought about the tight shoulders, white knuckles and fury-flat tone with which he'd answered that call from Haley in Donovan's café. He hadn't looked like a man in love.

"Anyhow," Molly said, "the whole thing was really messed up. It's no wonder it caused problems between them. I thought he should have sued. But Jude never listens to me. I'm just the little sister. You know? You have any sisters or brothers?"

Tess hesitated, then shook her head. It wasn't a lie. She didn't have sisters, not in the way Molly meant. She had no idea what the dynamics of siblings were like.

"He thinks I just care about the money. He even thinks that's why I want him to get back together with Haley. But that's not all of it. Sure, it would be nice if he'd be a movie star, too, and we could move to L.A., and we'd be so rich I'd have a live-in nanny for Beeba. I'll never understand why he didn't try for it. I bet Haley doesn't understand it, either. He's as handsome as any movie star, don't you think?"

Tess murmured something noncommittal. It was true, of course, but irrelevant. Only a child thought good looks were all it took to be a star. What about talent? What about training and desire, commitment and sacrifice? She'd met a lot of movie stars, in her years out there, and they had very little in common with Jude.

Suddenly she regretted agreeing to sit down for a chat. This wasn't an "adult" conversation. This was the kind of fantasy daydreaming high-school kids did. *Maybe my brother will strike it rich, and I won't be saddled with the baby when I want to go for a run....*

"Anyhow, I know he's going back, no matter what he says." Molly pulled the empty bottle away from Beeba, whose eyes were almost fully shut. She arranged the baby over her shoulder and began patting her back briskly, as if she were an expert at this sort of thing. "I know Jude. He can't hold a grudge forever, not with someone he loves. He'll forgive Haley, in the end."

BY ELEVEN THAT night, Jude was restless. Nothing against the Bell River New Year's Eve party. When the Wright women did a thing, they did it well.

But the truth was, he'd had his fill of partying during the Haley years. That might have been their biggest problem—bigger than money. Bigger, even, than sex. Haley hated being alone. She was like water, unformed, diffuse, disappearing unless she had something to pour herself into. If she did, she'd take the shape of whatever group she joined. But without a crowd, she began to fall apart again.

Jude was the opposite. Every time he had to make stupid small talk with fifty people he didn't know and didn't want to know, he felt his life slipping away. He wouldn't have minded if he could have picked one or two interesting people and spent the evening listening to them talk about their work, but no. *Circulate,* Haley hissed. Find the *important* guests, and make nice.

He found Molly by the fireplace, where the teenagers were roasting marshmallows. He knew all of them—good kids, either in high school or not long out of it. He was glad to see Molly so comfortably ensconced among them.

He was even happier to see she had sticky fingers and a rim of white around her mouth. She'd been obsessive about losing the "baby weight," and he had started to worry about an eating disorder.

"Hey," he said, smiling. "I think I'm heading home. You okay?"

"I'm fine. I'm having a ball. I can't believe you're leaving before midnight. You'll miss the fireworks!"

"I'll probably be able to see them from the house," he said. They lived in the hilly subdivision north of town, not along the ranchlands, but as the crow flew they were less than three miles from Bell River Ranch. The fireworks Bree had planned were professional grade. Bell River's first annual New Year's Eve party was the social event of the year.

"You haven't seen Tess tonight, have you?" He gave the fireplace group a quick scan. "I thought she might come, but I haven't seen her."

"Me, either. But I haven't really been looking. It's pretty crowded."

Jude noticed that Molly's expression lost a little of its marshmallow glee. He wondered why. Had she decided she didn't like Tess? The two women hardly knew each other…and surely she hadn't taken offense at the hot-dog incident.

"Well, she was in fairly bad shape last night," he reminded her. "I hate to think of her in a new place on New Year's Eve, alone and sick."

"Oh, she's not sick. Didn't I tell you I saw her today? She was fine."

"No. You didn't tell me. Where?"

"Downtown. I was hoping to go jogging this morning, but when we got to the park Beeba just would not stop crying. We ran into Tess, and she offered to distract the baby for me while I ran. She seemed perfectly normal, not sick at all."

He winced at Molly's careless tone. Maybe he indulged her too much. She was developing an un- attractive habit of taking other people's help for granted. Especially when it came to babysitting. Tonight Beeba was being tended by a crew of Bell River staffers in the nursery, and Molly was among a lucky group of guests who had been offered free rooms at the ranch, so that they wouldn't have to drive home.

Jude had, of course, declined, but Molly had jumped at the offer, like someone stranded in the desert leaping toward an oasis. He'd been annoyed at first, but he got over it. He forgot sometimes how very young she was. Just barely eighteen. And a coddled, sheltered eighteen, at that.

She might have a child of her own, but in many ways she would have fit in better at the children's party, being held right now in the old stables.

"That was thoughtful of Tess," he said slowly. "I hope you thanked her for it."

"Of course I did. God, Jude, you're so judgmen- tal. I do have manners, you know. I was *very* nice to her. I'm simply saying you don't need to leave an awesome party early to check on her, in case that's what you had in mind."

Ah. *That* was why her mood had soured. Molly was determined to see him reunited with Haley, and she wouldn't be a fan of any other woman in his life.

"It's just that…truly, she's not sick." She shrugged. "Maybe she hates parties."

He smiled at the not-so-subtle dig at his own antisocial ways. Molly and Haley were so alike. He wondered sometimes whether that was why he'd been drawn to Haley in the first place. He'd felt an instinctive, big-brother longing to take that wistful look out of her eyes, to give her the glamour and excitement she hungered for.

Too bad Molly and Haley couldn't pair up and live together. They could party till they passed out, and he could have his nice, quiet life back.

"What are you laughing at?" Molly's frown was suspicious, and he realized he must have been enjoying his inner joke. "I'm just saying—"

"I know what you're saying, Moll." He bent over and kissed her on the top of the head. "Happy New Year, kiddo. Next year's going to be fantastic, I promise."

She reached up and hugged him hard, her fussiness dropping away.

"I know it is," she said softly, resting her head against his shoulder. "Thank you for taking us in,

Jude. I know you wanted me to go stay with Flora in Chicago, but—"

"Just because it would have been farther away from Montrose. From Garth." He would have sent his sister to Jupiter, if he'd thought it would help her forget Garth. The man hadn't shown any signs of wanting his family back, but you never knew. Some night when he was lonely, when he got tired of being a big shot on the rodeo circuit, he might return and sweet-talk his way into Molly's bed.

Life was so ironic sometimes. He'd had to threaten jail to get Garth to marry Molly, who was underage when she wound up pregnant. Brilliant move, huh? Now he had to threaten jail to make sure the violent bastard never came back.

"You know I love having you and Beeba. But I still think Flora is a good option. She's got a big house in a big city, and a housekeeper, too. Lots of chances for you to go back to school. And she'd be a real help. You know how focused she is."

"I know how strict she is."

He frowned, but this wasn't the time to rehash the past. And she had a point. Flora, the family rocket scientist, truly was a martinet. But that was why Jude liked the idea. Her disciplined life would be good for Molly. Or, if Molly were too resistant, at least for Beeba. Just knowing there was a housekeeper around to help out would make Jude feel safer.

"Jude, don't be mad." Molly pouted. "I know I've been a pill sometimes, but I do love you so much."

Relenting, he tugged teasingly on her hair and kissed her head one more time. "Ditto, dork," he said, using their childhood slogan to lighten the mood.

He gave her one last smile, then headed out into the darkness.

The night sky was having a party, too. The snow clouds that had arrived that afternoon and felt so low and oppressive had blown away, leaving a vast, arching blackness silvered by a thousand stars.

He had to trek quite a way to his truck—parking was crazy at a party this big. By the time he climbed into it, he knew he wasn't going home.

Maybe he'd known it all along.

It took only about fifteen minutes to reach Little Bell Falls, and as soon as he rumbled over the small bridge over Cupcake Creek, he could see the glow from Tess's cabin windows. The spa building was dark, and the other four cabins were still unfinished and uninhabited, so her little squares of lights looked poignant against the trees and frozen waterfall. Brave, but alone, like an illustration from a book about a child lost in the woods.

He pulled in the drive, parked behind her car and headed to the front porch. Once he got there, he felt awkward, as if he ought to have something in his hands. He should have brought a bottle of champagne, maybe. Yes, that would have been a good excuse to come knocking at her door at eleven thirty on New Year's Eve.

He was actually considering zipping back to get one when, out of the corner of his eye, he sensed movement of the curtain. He glanced at the window, and saw Tess's face there, a small, pale oval that didn't do much to dispel the Hansel-and-Gretel mood he'd imagined earlier.

He smiled and waved, adding an extra dose of friendliness so that she wouldn't be alarmed. She must have recognized him, because she wiggled her fingers in greeting then let the curtain fall into place.

Two seconds later, he heard the locks snapping open. The door moved noiselessly on its hinges.

"Hey," she said, looking surprised but not displeased. Not really pleased, either, of course. He studied her face, trying to read it. She looked wan and tired, oddly somber for a holiday night. Maybe Molly had it wrong. Maybe Tess was sick, after all. "Everything okay?"

"Everything's fine," he said. "I was heading home from the party, and I thought I'd make sure you were all right. I wanted to be sure you weren't catching anything. You seemed pretty sick...."

He stopped himself, aware that he was making too many excuses. He felt as young and gauche as

Molly, trying to be subtle, but aware that he was probably as obvious as a sledgehammer.

"Actually, I just wanted to see you," he said, giving up the facade. "I had hoped you'd be at the party."

"I wasn't really in the mood." She smiled, a one-sided thing that was almost apologetic. "I'm not a big party person."

"Yeah," he said. "Me, either."

There was one heartbeat of silence, just enough for him to get a sinking feeling that he'd made a mistake, and she was going to send him away. He was about to fill the awkwardness with some dumb excuse to retreat—*well, better go, gotta get some sleep, just wanted to be sure*—when she stepped back and peeled the door open another six inches.

"Want to come in? I don't have anything fizzy to celebrate with. But Bree brought over some of the party food earlier, so I wouldn't miss out. And I've made some hot chocolate, if— "

"Hot chocolate sounds great." Relieved, he moved through the open door before she could change her mind. The room was blessedly warm after the cold night. She'd set a brisk fire in the hearth, and the lamplight pooled like spills of sweet syrup around the room.

She must have been sitting on the sofa, because the pillows were tumbled and the quilt was piled messily in one corner. But what had she been doing? Just staring at the fire? Napping, maybe? There was no TV in the room, and he didn't see any books or magazines.

"Were you sleeping?" He should have checked her clothes, but he'd been too distracted, too eager to come in. Luckily, she wasn't in a robe, or anything else that said bedtime. She wore jeans and a sweater, the only concession to the late hour being that she'd kicked off her boots beside the sofa, exposing a pair of fuzzy pink socks. "I know it's late. If I'm interrupting—"

"No, I'm glad you came. I was getting tired of my own thoughts." She moved into the kitchen. "Were you serious about wanting some chocolate?"

"Deadly," he said, with a grin. He stood on the other side of the bar while she prepared a mug for him, and when it was ready, took it between his palms gratefully.

She led the way toward the sofa. As she sat, pulling her feet up under her to make room for him, she checked her watch. "You left the party before midnight?"

He nodded as he settled himself at the other end of the sofa. "I've always been weird like that. Even when I was a kid, I liked to be alone when the ball dropped. It's almost superstitious, in a way. I believed I had to be alone, or my New Year's wish wouldn't come true." He took a sip of chocolate.

"Sure sign of a kid from a big family. Quiet time was always hard to come by."

"Molly's not your only sibling, then?"

"Lord, no. There were six of us. You couldn't move at our house without stepping on a Calhoun. It was like living at the dog pound. Somebody was always fighting, or whining, or nosing around in your stuff."

To his surprise, she looked wistful. "That sounds lovely," she said.

"No, ma'am, it was definitely not." He laughed. "Not even a little. And if you really think so, I'm going to make a guess here...you're an only child?"

She nodded. "It was just my mother and me. She was an administrative assistant, often for high-level executives who required her to work about sixty hours a week. I had all the quiet time a kid could want. And then some."

"What about your dad?"

She shrugged. "Never met him."

He started to ask more, but her shoulders had lifted subtly, and her grip on her mug had tightened. She didn't want to talk about it.

He should back off. He didn't have a right to pry into her personal life, even if they were alone, cozy in front of the crackling fire, waiting for the clock to tick its way to a new year. Still, seeing her withdraw into herself, he felt a sharp disappointment.

Sharper than it should have been. Why? Truth was, he'd known her less than two weeks.

"Does your mother still live in L.A.?"

"No." She lifted her gaze, and something lurched in his chest when he looked into her round, brown eyes. Her body might not be sick…but her heart was. "My mother died two months ago."

"I'm sorry," he said, inadequately. She was completely alone, then. No father, no siblings, no wedding ring, and even if there had been a serious relationship she'd obviously left it behind when she moved to Silverdell.

No wonder he felt that strangely wounded vibe whenever he was close to her. He set his mug on the end table, freeing his hands…though for what he couldn't say. It wasn't as if he could reach over and put his arms around her.

It wasn't as if she would want him to.

Would she?

But she'd rearranged her face, and the sadness was gone.

"How about your parents?" Her gaze was politely curious, and her tone matched. "And all your sisters and brothers? Where are they now?"

"My parents are gone, too," he said. "My father died when I was fifteen, and my mother died about a year ago. My sisters are all younger than I am. In the past few years, they've scattered, the way people do. They got married, got jobs, got restless."

He smiled, so that she wouldn't misunderstand. He wasn't sorry they had moved on. After his father's death, he'd essentially been the surrogate father in the house until he left for L.A. at twenty-two. One of his reasons for going—other than Haley's constant nagging— was that the pay was so good. Stunt work allowed him to provide college money, grad-school money, house-deposit money, baby money.

Still, he'd been relieved when they found happy, fulfilling homes and careers. It had felt like putting down a heavy load he'd been carrying for far too long.

Only Molly, the youngest, had stumbled. Jude had sensed from the start that Garth was trouble. But Molly had been indulged all her life—and had never learned much about patience or self-denial. She'd been only twelve when Jude went out to Hollywood…not that he probably would have been any stricter than their mother had been, even if he'd been in town. He'd always been a pushover for Molly.

He'd done his best, long-distance, to make her see the truth about Garth—that he was a bully and a liar. But she'd been pregnant before she could come to her senses. And before Jude could come home to stop her.

He'd always felt guilty about that. But now that

they had Beeba in their lives, Jude couldn't really regret it.

"They come back often enough, with their husbands and boyfriends and babies and dogs, to remind me how much I *don't* miss living with them."

Tess was smiling now, too. "All five of them are sisters?"

"Yep." He tapped off on his fingers. "Flora, Diane, Renee, Tricia—they're practically stairsteppers, with Flora only two years younger than I am. And Molly, the surprise, five years younger than Tricia."

"Wow," Tess said, obviously impressed.

"Right. My poor parents. Two tomboys, two princesses and one rocket scientist. Literally. The princesses—Molly would be one of those—are royal only in their own minds."

Tess laughed. He liked her laugh. It started softly, then flowered, like music. But most of all he liked that her laughter banished the sadness from her eyes.

Like a teenaged show-off, he realized that he wanted to make her laugh again. He wanted it a lot. He would have stood on his head, if she'd think it was funny.

Out of nowhere, he heard the scattered pops of the fireworks, like gunfire in the distance. She frowned, glancing toward the window. "What was that?"

"Come see." He stood and held out his hand.

She looked dubious, but the sound repeated. She put her mug down and, accepting his hand, let him tug her up. He didn't let go as he led her to the window.

"It's midnight," he said. With his free hand, he nudged aside the curtain. Just above the falls, shimmering green tendrils were spreading through the sky, disappearing as they fell.

"Oh." She breathed the word softly, and he felt an answering shimmer move through her body, as if the fireworks had come straight through and touched her.

The next explosion was gold and white, like an eruption of stars. Then red, like fire. She let go of his hand and moved in front of him, their bodies so close her shoulder grazed his chest, and the rounded swell of her hip came warm against his thigh.

He shut his eyes, feeling her. He had to fight to keep his hands at his side, and not to put them on her shoulders. He didn't want to scare her into moving away.

But she showed no signs of fear. She either didn't notice the intimacy, or didn't mind. Though the motion pressed her hip harder against him, she leaned forward, putting her palms against the glass, as if she could touch the sparkling sky.

"It's so beautiful," she whispered. She watched in silence, until finally the last twinkling streaks of color were gone, leaving behind only a sky full of white smoke and stars. Then she turned toward him, impulsively, her face alight.

"Thank you," she said, as if he'd somehow created the magic show himself. "Thank you for coming…and for staying. I thought I'd be sad tonight. I thought I'd be confused, and afraid. But I'm not."

"I'm glad," he said. Belatedly, he made his New Year's wish. For the first time, he didn't wish health and contentment for his sisters. He didn't wish for Molly to feel better, or for world peace, or for the whole mess with Haley to be resolved.

Instead, with a wish that was as selfish and irrational as it was fervent, he wished that Tess Spencer would always be as happy as she was right now.

Without letting himself question the wisdom of such a move, he put his hands against her cheeks, which were chilled slightly from the outside air that seeped in through the glass. That cool, smooth skin made his palms feel very hot.

"I'm glad," he said again. And then, mesmerized by the tiny white, wet gleam of her teeth between her parted lips, he lowered his head. He had to kiss her. He felt suddenly that he'd explode like one of Bell River's fireworks if he couldn't kiss that wide, beautiful mouth.…

He was close. So close he could smell the chocolate on her warm breath. So close his lips tingled from the static electricity that arced between them. So close he didn't see how anything could stop him now.

Nothing did.

Ignoring all warnings from his brain or his conscience, he closed the distance between them, as smoothly as if the air were liquid and he was caught in its current. His mouth found hers, warmth meeting warmth, creating passion.

She made a sound, a cross between confusion and pleasure. But she didn't pull away. His lips moved over hers, driving harder, finding the wet sweetness between. Without conscious choice, compelled by pure instinct, his hands slid from her cheeks to her shoulders, and then to her hips. He pulled her closer. Their bodies melded, breast to chest, hand to hip.

He pressed her against the wall, and she wound her fingers into his hair, panting behind his mouth. He let his hand drift behind her thigh and lifted it, bringing her closer. The burn that had begun on his lips sank slowly, muscle by muscle, bone by bone, into the depths of him, as if he'd swallowed fire.

"Tess," he said. It struck him again...the power of this chemistry between them. Once again, the startled realization came. He hadn't wanted a woman like this in...

He hadn't *ever* wanted a woman like this.

He bent his head, dragging his mouth down her

neck, across her collarbone, and finally, desperately, sweeping over the swell of her breast.

Her breathing hitched. And then her body, which had been as fluid and shimmery as fireworks in his hands, stiffened.

"No," she said.

And, with that fatal syllable, time stood still. Like a frozen frame on one of the Hollywood movies he hated so much, his whole body stopped in this impossible moment.

"I can't," she said.

He raised his head and looked at her, though he knew his eyes were burning and bewildered. Hers were made of liquid that gleamed in the shadow cast by his impossibly balanced head.

"Why?" And then again. *Why, why, why?* Did he say the words, or did he merely will the question into her mind?

Either way, she heard him. She blinked, and she moved away, an inch, two inches. A mile.

"I'm pregnant."

CHAPTER SEVEN

"TESS?" THE POUNDING on the door was insistent, and the woman's voice was loud. "Tess, are you awake?"

Tess stumbled toward the noise, tugging the sash of her robe closed. She hadn't slept much last night, not after Jude left.

And, of course, he *had* left. Even after that kiss, which had been beyond description. He'd walked away without anger, but also without hesitation.

The ache of watching him leave had taken her by surprise. She hadn't wanted to stop with one kiss. She'd wanted to go on kissing him. She'd wanted to take him to her bedroom and make love to him.

Realizing how ready she'd been to abandon all inhibition was more than a surprise—it was a true, unsettling shock. She didn't do things like that. She'd known him only a couple of weeks. She didn't have casual sex.

That was what had kept her tossing and turning all night.

She pulled open the door to find Penny.

"Oh, I did wake you! I'm sorry. But we're in a

bad way, and I was hoping that maybe you could come help."

"Of course I can," Tess said, without even asking what the problem was. And that surprised her, too. She'd been at Bell River such a short time, and already she found herself doing, saying and feeling things that didn't seem like her. "I'll need a minute to get dressed."

"Great." Penny was more diffident than Rowena, so she didn't bustle into the cabin without permission. She just hugged herself against the cold and smiled.

"Come in," Tess said. "I won't be long."

She pulled on work clothes and gathered her outerwear as Penny filled her in.

"Not sure if you heard, but right before Christmas the snow collapsed one section of the roof on the new activities building. I feel guilty about that, of course, because I picked the contractor."

Tess had to smile. So Penny was the sweet one—the one who internalized all the guilt, took all the blame, in order to keep the peace. Tess couldn't imagine Ro or Bree accepting responsibility for something that wasn't their fault. In fact, with their powerful but conflicting personalities of fire and ice, Tess imagined they would be at loggerheads much of the time.

"Anyhow, we've had it repaired, but it took longer than anticipated. We've got a huge shindig set to christen the building tonight, a New Year's thing for the guests. Ro's about to strangle somebody, and everyone is pitching in to keep her calm and get things finished. There's painting, reinstalling baseboards and molding, rehanging the lights…" She sighed heavily. "Not to mention decorating for the event."

Tess presented herself, coat on and gloves in hand, and a smile on her lips. "I'm not touching the electricity. But I probably can wield a paint-brush without killing anyone."

Penny gave Tess a quick hug. "That's exactly what I said!" She took Tess's hand and led her out. "We're supposed to make a coffee stop by the house on our way."

Not long afterward, they arrived at the large rect-angular building that had been erected to house the ranch-wide activities. The car was rich with the perfumes of blueberry muffins and coffee, which hadn't made Tess's stomach turn yet.

Apparently morning sickness responded well to yummy scents.

As they entered, they were welcomed with loud cheers and scattered applause. Tess scanned the group, realizing she recognized only about half of them. Ro, of course, who was totally indifferent to the arrival of muffins, Dallas, Mitch, Barton James…and Jude.

Jude. Tess's stomach pinched, a tweak of desire,

just from seeing him across the room, standing at a table saw, disheveled and utterly gorgeous.

She had to look away, a little overwhelmed by these emotions, which were at the same time awkward and exhilarating. Regret at the way they'd parted last night hit hard. Why, when she'd finally found a man she admired and respected, did she have to be pregnant by, and forever tied to, her ex-husband? It seemed grossly unfair.

"Thank you, my friends," Penny said, with a curtsy. "It's so nice to feel loved." She turned to Tess. "They don't give a hoot about us. It's the muffins they're cheering."

"Not true." With a deft move Max snagged a muffin in one hand while scooping Penny in with the other. "Thanks for being willing to help, Tess. Really, we're not clapping just for the muffins. We'd cheer for any extra workers who walked through that door."

Penny nodded sagely. "Told you. We're cogs in the wheel that's Bell River Ranch."

"How about you put the faceplates on while I keep Rowena from beating the electrical inspector over the head with his clipboard?" Then Max glanced at Tess. "You willing to feed molding to Jude, and take dimensions? That molding profile is tricky, and if he's going to get it right on the first pass he's got to stay focused."

Work with Jude? *Now?* "That's fine," she said,

trying to sound indifferent to her assignment. But something about the way Max looked at her made her wonder if she'd succeeded.

"Jude." Max raised his voice. "Tess is going to work with you, okay?"

If Jude felt any of the awkwardness roiling through Tess, he didn't show it. "Sure." He smiled at Tess. "Thanks."

Either he was a better actor than she was, or he really hadn't been impacted much by last night—either the kiss or her announcement.

Attempting to match his nonchalance, she grabbed a muffin and coffee and made her way through the melee. When she reached Jude and his table saw, she held both out to him.

"Sustenance." She avoided his gaze, instead taking in the wood shavings that covered the floor like curly ivory grass. "And an assistant—though I have to warn you I don't know a single thing about miter saws and molding profiles."

"No problem," he said, taking the cup and knocking back a long swig before setting it on the windowsill beside him. "I've got that part covered. If you have two hands and know how to read a measuring tape, I'm glad to have you."

His words brought her gaze to his and she flushed. Funny how, with this man, a certain tone, a certain light in his smile, could pull a blush out of her like water from a tap. She glanced away, and saw Penny and Bree standing a few feet away. They seemed to be watching Jude and Tess curiously. She wondered what drew their attention.

Her absurd blushing, perhaps?

He tilted his head and gave her a smile that wasn't quite as indifferent as she'd thought. "In fact, even if you can't read a measuring tape, I'm still glad to have you."

No blushing. "Tell me that again, after I've given you a few bad measurements." It was an absurd joke, since she was good with numbers.

"Okay, I will."

There was nothing flirtatious about his smile. It was simply the smile of one friend to another. So why did it make her heart race like this?

She didn't know where to look, then. Not at him, and she didn't want to meet the curious gazes of Penny and Bree. So she picked up the molding he'd been working on, as if she needed to understand it better.

He took a bite of muffin, groaned appreciatively. "Lord, that woman can cook." He looked around for Tess's muffin. "You not eating? Are you feeling okay?"

"I'm fine," she assured him. "I don't want to push my luck. If I get sick or pass out here, I'll have to explain. And I'm not quite ready to do that. Not before…"

She didn't finish, knowing he'd understand. Last

night she'd told him she planned to call Craig—she would have phoned him as soon as she woke, in fact, if Penny hadn't arrived first.

Though obviously Jude was attracted to her, and might even have taken that attraction further than a kiss, he'd backed off instantly when he heard she was pregnant. In his mind, clearly, a baby was the trump card. Craig had won the hand. The woman. The future. The letdown she felt at that realization seemed too big for the short time she and Jude had known each other, for the fledgling status of their relationship.

"I get it," he said. "I'm glad you're feeling well enough to be here. I know you hadn't felt up to the party, and—"

"Not a party person, remember?" His concern warmed her. Really, would it be so bad to call Jude a friend? "But I *am* a work person. I was glad they asked me. It's nice to be a part of it all. They're very welcoming, aren't they? They make everyone feel like family."

"Well, yeah. But I think most people are welcoming to the idea of extending their family if it gets them free labor."

Suddenly Tess noticed Bree and the inspector dancing to the music coming from the boom box. Mitch and Marianne were unpacking a chandelier, and Mitch had crystals dangling from his ears, which made people giggle.

"Oh, you'd be surprised," Tess said softly. "I think maybe you've lived around Bell River so long you forget how cold and self-serving the rest of the world can be."

He was silent a minute, watching her carefully. "I might know more than you realize. Remember, I've had my years in the big, bad city, too."

In spite of the crowd, the moment felt intensely intimate, as if they were reading each others' minds. In his, she felt a mysterious sadness, maybe even an unhappy ambivalence. Was it Haley? Was he wrestling with the decision of whether to return to L.A.?

She wondered what he sensed as he probed her mind. She tried to steer clear of all thoughts of sexual attraction and thwarted passion. She wanted to keep those to herself. If she could.

"Tess, about last night—"

His cell phone, which lay on the window sill, buzzed angrily, like a trapped fly.

She couldn't help wondering whether he'd answer. Was it Haley, as it had been that night in Donovan's café? Did she call him all the time? Where did his relationship with the starlet really stand?

He eyed the caller ID with a frown. "It's Molly. I'll let it go to voice mail. She just wants to continue the argument we started this morning."

"Oh. I'm sorry. Is everything okay?"

He ran his hand through his hair. "Not really.

I suggested she think about going to live with Flora—our sister in Chicago. She's got to get back to school, make new friends, get her life on track."

His words confirmed what she'd wondered about Molly, that getting married and having Beeba had disrupted the life Molly had been enjoying. Losing everything was a shock, but if you let the shock paralyze you, then your life was over. It was the choice Tess had faced two months ago. It was what had brought her here.

"It's unlikely she'll do any of that while she's brooding away in Silverdell," Jude went on. "I'm wondering if, instead of helping her, I might be enabling her."

Tess felt sad, glimpsing the frustration and deep concern in his face. "I'm sure you'll know when it's time to let go."

He laughed. "Don't bet on it. I'm not known for my clearheaded tough love."

She wondered what that meant.

"The truth is, it's time for me to give up the idea that I can save everyone. If she gets too dependent on me, what will she do if the day comes that I'm not there?"

Not there? Why wouldn't he be? He was young, healthy…

But then she realized he meant that he might be involved in something that took him to another city, another state. Something that wouldn't allow for a little sister and niece clinging to his coattails.

Something like a love affair—a marriage—with Haley Hawthorne.

IN THEORY, Mitch understood that this first year of Bell River's operation was all about working out the kinks in the resort.

They needed to see how much it cost to heat the cabins, versus how much they could charge to keep them filled. They'd learn how many people wanted to travel over the holidays, how many liked snowshoeing, whether anyone came for the amateur archaeology lectures, whether they had too many deadheads in the stable, or not enough trail guides on the staff.

And he also knew that the debt they'd taken on was so steep that they had to move full steam ahead to generate enough income to make the installment payments.

But darn it. He was desperate to have a day off. Just one lousy day. Was that too much to ask?

He'd spent all morning finishing out the activities hall. But was that the end of it? Of course not. Now he was in the supply warehouse with the other guys, unloading crates of saddles and snowshoes.

Midafternoon on New Year's Day, a day when normal people were sitting by the fire, writing a list of resolutions they wouldn't keep, and he was drowning in packing material. He needed to get out of here. He had no intention of making a list, but he needed some clean, cold air in his face and an energetic horse between his legs.

Or maybe even an energetic woman…

What he did *not* need was to be holed up inside. Mitch wasn't an inside kind of guy.

"What the devil is this?" He held up a disgusting floppy sack that looked like the bladder of a gigantic sheep. He'd been whipping through cartons, unwrapping supplies to be catalogued and stored by the others, but his mind had been a million miles away. He kicked at the empty boxes, trying to see what the label was on the one this horror had come from.

Barton James, their ranch manager, let loose a whoop of delight. "My bagpipes!"

Mitch glared at the nasty thing. "Bagpipes?"

Barton was a darned good manager, but he also fancied himself quite the cowboy poet and musician. He held sing-alongs every week, which Mitch tended to skip, because they always included a bunch of tearjerker, lonesome-trail songs that made him think about Bonnie.

Of course, everything made him think about Bonnie.

Barton's guitar was fine, but…bagpipes? Mitch imagined the low drone, the high screech, all those tragic, dying-rhino sounds… "No. *No. Hell* no."

Barton barged forward, fairly rhino-like himself. "Give me those, boy."

Mitch was too grouchy to comply. He held the bag over his head, which infuriated the old man. Barton was tall, but Mitch was at least an inch taller.

"Those bagpipes cost more than two thousand dollars, you young barbarian, and the bag was hand-sewn by—"

"Stop it, you morons." Dallas's authoritative tone cut through the skirmish. Barton and Mitch both looked toward the far side of the small warehouse, where Dallas had been organizing the supplies. He held up a small piece of paper.

"What?" Mitch knew it had to be something important, but his rotten mood just wouldn't let go. "What's the matter?"

"It's another note."

No one asked what kind of note. They all knew. They'd received five in all—this made six—since the ranch opened early this year. With a start, Mitch realized it was more accurate to say "early *last* year."

New number on the dateline, but same old problems.

"Nasty little coward." Gray stared at the paper. His normally affable voice was low and steely. "What does this one say?"

Dallas didn't even look at the note. He obviously

knew it by heart after only one reading. They all knew all the notes by heart. The note-writer was always succinct, and always repeated essentially the same message of hate.

"This one says, 'No one wants you here.'"

"Bastard," Mitch said, oddly glad to have somewhere to direct his frustration and anger. Dallas shot him a glance, as if to say that ugliness wasn't the answer to ugliness, but Mitch didn't care. He couldn't think of any other word that fit this jerk.

The tension in the warehouse grew so thick it made the air hum. Max stepped forward. "Where did you find it?"

"Tucked into one of the snowshoe boxes. If I hadn't opened it to check the shoes, a guest probably would have been found it."

"Diabolical," Max said. "This guy isn't just trying to insult them. He's trying to destroy them."

Max might be the newest member of the family, but he was obviously as furious as any of them. All three of the husbands were protective—they felt it their missions to make the futures of the Wright sisters as beautiful as their past had been hideous.

For a minute, Mitch envied them. At least they had their women by their sides, and *could* protect them. At least they knew what the demons in their past looked like and could fight them, head-on. Whereas Mitch had no idea what Bonnie was running from, or how he could help her. Even if he could find her.

Immediately he felt ashamed. Surely he hadn't sunk so low that he saw every event only in terms of his own emotions. So far, the note-writer showed no signs of violence, and the worst crimes he could have been charged with were harassment, and maybe trespassing, but they all knew where it could lead.

"Damn it," Mitch breathed. "Who *is* it?"

"Gotta be Farley Miller," Barton said. "He's the biggest little hyena in Silverdell. I mean, the worst. I mean…" He ran his hand through his salt-and-pepper Gregory-Peck hair. "Oh, you know what I mean."

"Actually, I'm not so sure it is Farley." Dallas glanced at the note. "He was still in North Carolina when the first three were found. We checked. Ironclad."

"Could have had someone deliver those three for him," Barton said. "Even hyenas have friends. And family."

"You think *Perry* might have done this?" Mitch liked Farley's father, who owned the hardware store, and the implication that he could be tied to the note-writer made Mitch feel warm under the collar. "Or Farley's uncle Bill? Bill's done some local history lectures for us here. The guests love him."

"See? Access!" Barton sounded smug. "Has anyone compared those lecture dates with the dates of the notes?"

"No one needs to." Mitch felt his fists ball up. "I've known Perry and Bill Miller all my life. They donated time and materials to build my kindergarten playground. Heck, Bill's taught every Silverdell kid how to use a hammer for the past thirty years"

"That doesn't mean anything," Barton began, but stopped when Dallas held up his hand.

"Come on, guys. We need to stick together. Barton, we've been looking at everyone, but nothing points anywhere in particular yet. The creep will make a mistake eventually, though. They always do."

Gray took the note from Dallas's hand and went to the door, where he could look at it in bright light. "Whoever he is, he's pretty smart about keeping it generic. Block letters, standard printer paper, no fingerprints, no idiosyncratic vocabulary or phrasing. You'll take this in, I guess, but you know it'll come out the same. He's no fool, even if he is a hyena."

"Are you so sure it's a he?" Max lifted one shoulder. "Just wondering why it would have to be male. No sexual overtones in any of the notes, right? I mean, the notes call them *dirty,* but that could as easily be a jealous woman as a rejected male."

Dallas nodded. "We've looked at several women. Esther Fillmore, of course. I'm sure a few of her emotional wires are crossed. And Gray's got a couple of ex-girlfriends who aren't exactly models of mental health."

"Old girlfriends from when I was about fifteen, but hey." Gray chuckled. "As the song says, there's no getting over me."

Dallas rolled his eyes. "For a small town, Silverdell has proved to be surprisingly rich with suspects. Of course, you're talking about at least three beautiful, strong-willed females, five if you count Bonnie and Moira. Women like that always have long lists of people who've wanted them, who've been rejected by them, or who just dislike gutsy females."

"What about Fanny Bronson?" All the men stared at Mitch, surprised but curious. "I'm just saying, speaking of people who dislike feisty females. At the party last night, she got pretty plastered, and she was shooting daggers at Rowena. My guess is she has a voodoo doll of Ro under her pillow, and a lipstick-covered picture of Dallas in her locket."

"Oh, yeah." Gray grinned. "Remember how drunk she was at the costume party? I can see Fanny, for sure. Functional most of the time, but now and then her jealousy takes over, and she climbs into bed with a bottle of gin and her little red pencil."

"Good grief." Dallas shook his head, as if to shake off the mental picture. "But you're right, in principle. The notes seem to focus on the gals, but who knows? Max is too new, probably, but there's Gray and Mitch and me, and everyone we dated or didn't date, and in my case everyone I've arrested or questioned."

Gray nodded. "And of course Johnny was never short of enemies. You see? Gets complicated fast."

Max whistled softly, obviously recognizing the problem. "Okay. I hear you. So we just wait for a mistake? Should we hire more security? Are you going to tell Rowena you found this new note?"

"Of course," Dallas said. "You know they hate that kind of coddling. They may look fragile, but all three of them are more dragon-slayer than princess."

Max smiled stupidly, and Mitch knew he had gone into a momentary bliss-fog, thinking about his wife. The jealousy monster growled in the pit of his chest one last time. *Damn it*. Where the devil was Bonnie? He knew she was the dragon-slayer type, too—and he wouldn't change that for the world.

But was there some rule that said the prince couldn't tag along for the fight?

He stepped outside, leaving the others discussing how much security they could afford to hire. As he went, he pulled his cell phone out of his pocket, then fumbled for his sunglasses, blinded by the unclouded glare of the sun.

He dialed the number he'd sworn to himself—and to Bonnie—he'd never dial again. It was the throw-away phone they'd bought that was never, ever to be used unless there was an emergency that couldn't be solved any other way. They'd never spelled it out, but he had assumed she meant he could call if he were on his deathbed, but nothing less dire than that.

He practically held his breath while he punched in the number. He had no idea why he thought he had the right to do this. He had no idea why, today of all days, he had to violate their agreement.

He couldn't justify it to himself, and he didn't even try. All he knew was that he had to hear her voice, even if she were telling him to go to hell.

But it didn't ring. It went straight to a recorded message, telling him that the number was out of service. His heart began to pound like a drum, but he didn't let himself think about it. He just punched in the numbers again, more slowly this time, to be sure he didn't misdial. He pressed the little black rectangle against his ear so roughly it hurt, as if listening harder would make him hear something he liked more.

But he was a fool. A fool. The number was out of service, the perky, impersonal voice assured him. Translation: *Hang up, idiot. She's thrown away the phone.*

She doesn't want to talk to you. Even if you're dying.

He shoved his cell into his pocket, and started toward the warehouse. He needed not to think about this yet. He needed time to chill out, calm down. He needed to lift boxes and lug and haul and sweat until his muscles ached so bad he couldn't feel what was happening to his heart.

He'd just reached the doorway when a little body slammed past him, racing inside like a cartoon tornado.

"Dad!" Alec staggered forward, hands extended, rendered helpless by coming so suddenly into the intense shadows of the warehouse after playing for hours in the sun. "Dad! Where are you?"

"I'm over here." Dallas moved toward his son quickly, alerted by that high-pitched tone. "What's wrong?"

As Mitch's own eyes adjusted, he saw that the boy was streaked with dirt, and he sported a whopping black eye. In spite of himself, Mitch smiled. *That crazy kid.*

"Rowena said I had to come see you." Alec sounded more aggrieved than hurt. He wore his trademark scowl. "She's mad at me, but it wasn't my fault, Dad, honest. He was making fun of Ellen, so what was I supposed to do?"

"Slow down, buddy," Dallas said patiently. "Who was making fun of Ellen?"

"Benny McAvee. You know what a turd he can be."

Over in the corner, someone, probably Gray,

smothered a chuckle. Rowena had warned every male on the ranch, on fear of death, not to encourage Alec's vulgarity. But they also knew Benny....

"What did Benny say?"

"He said she was uglier than a monkey's armpit."

Dallas glanced at Max, who didn't seem perturbed to hear his daughter denigrated. Why should he be? Any fool could see that Ellen would be a looker when she got older, even a hopeless fool like Benny.

"Well, you know that's not true, right?" Dallas was studying the black eye, though they hadn't mentioned it yet. "And Ellen knows it's not true, so what's the big deal?"

"It wasn't a big deal. Ellen told him to shut up, and he should have seen that she was about to blow her top, but he didn't. He said he'd shut up when he felt like it, and there was no stupid girl who could make him, especially not one like Ellen, who couldn't ride for sh—"

Alec seemed to realize he couldn't repeat that. "Couldn't ride for nothing," he said. "So I had to defend her, didn't I, Dad?"

"Well, if by *defend her,* you mean—"

"I had to! I looked him square in the eye, and I said that wasn't fair. I said she couldn't help being a crummy rider, coming from the city like she did."

Dallas tilted his head. "Let me get this straight... Benny gave you a shiner just for saying that?"

"*No.* Of course not. Benny's too big a wuss to hit anybody." Alec glowered, huffing as if Dallas were being deliberately dense. "*Ellen* did."

It was nearly five o'clock. Still in her paint-splattered clothes, Tess stood at her window, her cell phone in her hand, trying to force herself to make the call.

She'd vowed not to let New Year's pass without finishing the odious chore. But every time she touched the phone, her fingers recoiled, as if it were a hot burner.

The bare tree limbs against the orange sky looked like the black veins on a monarch butterfly's wings. The snow caught some of the reflected sunset color, making the world look as if it were a big, sparkling gumdrop, glazed with marzipan.

The beautiful New Year. Her hopeful new life.

And she had to bring Craig into it.

Why? The renegade question kept rearing its head. Did she *have* to tell him? He wouldn't want the baby…he wouldn't care about it at all, unless he imagined there might be profit in it for him.

She remembered his reaction when he heard she'd learned who her real father was. Her mother had died three days before. They'd come to her mother's apartment after the funeral. Tess had been in tears. Her whole life, the foundation of her entire self-definition, had been altered forever. And what did Craig say?

Does he have money?

She was glad, now, that she hadn't shared any details. She'd merely laughed harshly. "Hardly," she'd said. "He died in prison." Then she'd told him to leave, that, even though she'd slept with him the night her mother died, she still wanted a divorce.

He didn't believe her. He'd been so sure that, alone now, she'd have to turn to him for comfort. When whining, tears, anger, commands—even a disgusting attempt at seduction—hadn't dented her resolution, he'd turned vicious. He'd knocked over a lamp, upended a table. Finally, with one furious arm, he'd swept her mother's Christmas cactus from the windowsill.

The minute it crashed, he seemed to realize what a terrible, fatal mistake it was. That plant had sat there, on the same sill, for more than ten years. It had given her mother so much joy during those last terrible months. She'd prayed to live long enough to see it bloom one more winter…and she hadn't made it.

In some weird way, Tess thought, it might have been easier to forgive Craig if he'd hit Tess herself. Instead, it was as if he'd hit her mother's ghost… and she would never, ever forgive him for that.

And now, just when she had felt free of him, when she might have met a man who made her feel all the things she'd never felt for Craig…she was having Craig's baby.

Why did she feel so sure he had the right to know? What idealized, romanticized Hollywood movie had she seen, what dewy-eyed book had she read, in which the heroine's Victorian morality forced her to give her faithless lover a second chance? How did those stories end? With the baby's father on his knees, repenting and begging to be allowed to love them both forever?

Her story would not end like that, with roses, violins and tears. She felt the tussle to come, the awkward attempt to share custody, at best, and hated the prospect, hated it in the deep core of her heart.

And yet, she'd grown up without a father, and the hole in her life had been so big it had almost eclipsed her. It had nearly swallowed up any identity for little Tess Spencer, no matter how hard her mother tried to fill the void. When her mother told her about Johnny, Tess had faced the almost unimaginable truth: she would rather have had a terrible father, a *murderer* father, than no father at all.

And so, she had to tell Craig. Not for his sake, but for the baby's.

She dialed his number.

"Tess?" No normal hello. He'd seen her number on the caller ID. His voice sounded boyishly eager, and she thought of the dozens of calls she'd ignored in the past couple of months.

"Yes," she said. She tried to continue, but her throat felt as dry as sand.

"Are you all right? I've tried to reach you so many times. Where are you?"

"I'm in Colorado."

"Colorado?" He couldn't have sounded more shocked if she'd said the moon. He obviously hadn't really believed she would move away. Across town, maybe, as a statement of temporary independence. But not far, far away, where he couldn't find her. "Why?"

"I got a job," she said. "A good job."

"But why Colorado? Why so far?" He paused. "Are you following information about your father?"

"No." She spoke fast, then wondered if she'd rushed the denial. She didn't want to trigger his curiosity. She was grateful anew for whatever instincts had prevented her from telling him any details. He didn't even know she had sisters. "No. It was a good opportunity, and I wanted a change."

He let that hang in the air a minute. Then, in a coaxing voice, he said, "I miss you, Tess."

She breathed several times, looking for an answer. This conversation was like a kite in no wind. She simply couldn't think of anything to say. She wouldn't lie, but the truth was unkind. She didn't miss him. She would give almost anything not to be making this call.

"Don't you miss me? You must miss me, honey, or you wouldn't have called."

"No," she said, again too fast. "I don't want to

send mixed signals here. I don't miss you. Our marriage was a mistake from the start—and the last time we were together…really together…that was the biggest mistake of all."

"It wasn't a mistake," he said, denying her reality easily, as he always had. "You were emotional because of your mother, and that made everything seem strange. You weren't yourself that night—you can't expect the sex to be particularly satisfying when—"

"For God's sake, Craig. I don't give a damn about the sex. The sex was always terrible, every single time."

His silence conveyed he was shocked and offended. What was wrong with her these days? Were her hormones so out of whack that she'd say anything, even things she'd sworn never to say? Or was it that, after Jude's kiss, she no longer felt guilty and ashamed, as if the unsatisfactory sex were her fault alone?

She put her palm against her temple, where her pulse beat too fast, and a light perspiration had broken out. She tried to drink in peace and calm from the vista. She felt the queasiness rising, and that made her feel strangely helpless.

"I'm sorry. I mean that there's no reason to discuss all that anymore. It's over, Craig, just as I told you that night. It's over forever, and I don't want you to think that's why I'm calling."

"Okay." The syllables were colder than the snow. "So why *are* you calling?"

"I thought…I thought you had the right to know." She leaned forward, resting her forehead against the glass, and letting its sting seep into her. "I'm pregnant."

CHAPTER EIGHT

ONLY JANUARY SECOND, and already another party.

Jude couldn't believe he'd been roped into attending this one—the second in three days. Who would have thought that a dude ranch and a trio of scandalous Wright women would turn sleepy little Silverdell into the social hub of western Colorado?

He should be at home. In his workshop. He'd been looking forward to it all day. His ankle ached from climbing a ladder, and his psyche ached from the cacophony of the group finishing work on the ranch building.

Jude pictured his solitary, well-organized little space, and felt a yearning to be sitting there, with a heavy piece of wood in his hands, letting the silence wash the tension of the day away. He was like his father that way, and he'd realized it even as a child. His dad didn't talk his troubles away or convert them to rage, the way Haley's father had—or Garth, Molly's ex. Even at ten, though, Jude had recognized a certain inward-focused intensity on his father's face that had meant he should be left alone while he worked.

His dad had always built the most beautiful pieces under stress, like the headboard he'd carved for his wife the month his mother, Jude's grandmother, died. Similarly, Jude knew that the playpen he was making for Beeba had reached a tricky point, and concentrating on that would make all his other worries go away.

He probably wouldn't even think about Tess Spencer.

Pregnant Tess Spencer. Thank goodness he'd found *that* out before things got out of control. It was easier to see today. That night, it had nearly killed him to pull back, to act as if he hadn't turned to ashes on the inside. He'd been in fairly foul humor yesterday. Molly wasn't speaking to him, and had spent all her time crying on the phone to Flora about what a beast he was.

Good, because the more Molly trusted Flora, the sooner she'd agree to move to Chicago. She needed a life.

And so did he.

When he thought those words, two women flashed before his mental eye. Haley. And Tess.

"Jude?" Fanny Bronson touched his elbow, jolting him out of his reverie. "Have you met Acton Adams?"

Reluctantly, Jude brought his mind to Fanny Bronson's bookstore, where Adams, the golfer behind Silverdell Hills, was signing copies of his biography. His new golf resort, designed by Max, wouldn't be finished for at least another six months, but Adams apparently couldn't wait that long to surround himself with adoring fans.

Jude had sized up the man in an instant. Early fifties. Too many beers, too much money. One shade too white on the veneers, one shade too dark on the tanning machine. The guy probably had been a big deal some years ago. Apparently, he hadn't noticed that the parade of time and fame had kept on marching, while his rose-covered float was standing still.

"No, I haven't." Jude held out his hand. "Nice to meet you," he lied.

Acton's grip was mighty, and the ensuing shake was like someone trying to get water out of an old hand-pump.

"So *you're* Haley Hawthorne's boyfriend." Acton's white grin was knowing, and he swept his free hand in the air, as if shaking off a burn. "Gawd, you're a lucky mother. What a woman!"

Jude felt his smile harden in place, like plaster. He could have corrected Acton, but that would have invited more Haley discussion, and he had no intention of letting this jerk salivate while he probed for juicy tidbits.

"Excuse me, emergency, gotta steal Jude a minute." Bree appeared like a magician. Gently, with an apologetic smile aimed toward Acton and Fanny, she tugged Jude free. "So sorry, hate to be selfish, but we need him over here to settle a rather silly little…"

The nonsensical sentence died off as soon as they were out of earshot. Good thing, too, because obviously Bree had no emergency, and nothing to settle. She slipped her hand through Jude's elbow.

"There. I saved you. Now let's find something to eat."

Jude tightened his grip on her hand. Bree was such a good egg. There weren't many people who could have persuaded him to attend another party so soon after New Year's Eve, but she was one of them.

He'd been recruited as her date, a last-minute substitution for Gray, who had to guide a new foal into the world tonight but hoped that his breeding stables would have a good relationship with Acton's resort.

"Food sounds great," he agreed, making a left turn by the new releases. "I hear the desserts are over in the self-help section."

He realized he was starving. He'd skipped lunch, as he'd been trying to frame the windows in the new dining hall. Winter wasn't the best building season, but Bell River couldn't afford to wait.

He picked out an éclairlike thing that looked fantastic, and Bree took a lemon-colored tart. Then she took another one.

Apparently the rest of the guests were more health-conscious, either not eating or grazing at the fruit-and-vegetable table. Jude and Bree seemed to have this little nook to themselves, and neither of them seemed inclined to wander out. Bree was an extrovert, so probably she was trying to provide an oasis for him.

Like he said, a good egg.

"So, if Wright was convicted of killing her, who got the land?" Just over the tall shelves of self-help books, a man's deep voice could be heard, low but clear. Jude didn't recognize it. "That property's gotta be worth a fortune, right?"

"It could be, if it were handled properly." This sniffing, disapproving voice, Jude did recognize. It was sour, old Esther Fillmore.

"Esther, don't be like that." The soft-spoken reproach sounded like Alton. He was forever trying to get his wife to be kinder. Good luck with that.

"It isn't being run properly?" The stranger sounded deferential, as if Esther were the world's leading authority on moneymaking.

"Of course it is," Alton said mildly.

"Of course it is *not*." Esther's overbearing tone said volumes. "Those trashy girls don't know the first thing about running a business."

Jude jerked forward instinctively, as if he could barge straight through the copies of *Think Yourself Smart* and *Make Love, Not Divorce,* and tackle

Esther to the ground. But once again he felt Bree's cool hand, and he glanced at her. Her blue eyes were calm, and she shook her head slowly.

"Not worth it," she whispered almost without sound.

She was right, of course. The old witch didn't like anyone or anything.

Still, he hated Esther for gossiping, and he hated this faceless stranger for encouraging it.

Eventually the Fillmores and friend moved away. Their voices drifted off as the man was saying something about "just the three of them?" Esther's response was lost.

"Jude, my friend, I should have known I'd find you in the happy place."

Jude looked up, his mouth still full of chocolate and custard, irritated that someone had invaded their hiding spot. But then he smiled. It was Mitch. The rusty-haired goofball leaned against the self-help stacks, grinning.

And then, slipping in behind him came Marianne Donovan. Also smiling.

"Hey, buddy," Jude said. "Hey, Mari." As the women exchanged greetings, Jude offered Mitch a subtle nod, the less-obvious version of a thumbs-up for the guys.

Mitch smiled, accepting Jude's approval happily. And he did look happy. Jude was so darned glad to see it. It had been painful to watch Mitch mooning over Bonnie O'Mara these past few months.

Mitch Garwood wasn't made for pining. He was a born hellion, Jude's childhood partner in crime. The whole world had seemed tilted slightly, while a muted Mitch nursed a heartbreak.

Jude glanced at Bree, and was surprised to see that, though she was being perfectly polite to Mari, she didn't look quite as pleased. Of course, the Bell River ladies had adopted Bonnie, in all her mysterious vulnerability. Probably they were still hoping for a happy ending to the Bonnie/Mitch tearjerker.

Just like everyone was still hoping for one in the Jude/Haley fairy tale. *Juley.* That was the combined nickname Haley had hoped they would get someday, when she had finally talked Jude into becoming a big, hunky movie star. Like Bennifer and Brangelina. It had made her furious, reduced her to tears, when he refused to look for acting jobs and "settled" for stunt work instead.

He swallowed the last bite of éclair, which tasted as if it had turned. *Women.* Did they really think you should adopt their dreams? Wait forever while they disappeared, or put off having a family until they were ready for stretch marks, or bedded their directors to get a juicy role?

Did they think you should forgive them anything, just because you had loved them, once upon a time? Didn't they know that love wasn't a marble statue you erected in your heart that would always stand there, unflinching, unfeeling, through wind and rain and pigeon poop?

It wasn't, damn it. Love was a vital, breathing entity that needed tending.

And, like any other living thing, with enough cruelty, enough neglect, you could kill it.

"You okay, Jude?" Mitch looked at him oddly, and he realized he must have been letting his emotions play out on his face.

"Yeah. I'm great." He shrugged it off with a grin, but deep inside he was alarmed at this eruption of bitterness. He had thought he'd come to terms with it all.

Still... Sorry, Bree. If Mitch is ready to let go of that dead dream and be happy, I'm all for it. I think I'll join him, as soon as I get the chance.

A chance at happiness. God, that sounded good.

But then, to prove he'd probably always be a sucker and a fool when it came to love and women, the first face that popped into his brain belonged to Tess Spencer.

Pregnant Tess Spencer.

TESS WOKE LATER than usual that Sunday morning, surprised to see that the sun was already golden on the snow. For once, she didn't feel queasy. To celebrate, she went outside to enjoy the fresh air and silence.

On Sundays, the spa opened at noon instead of nine. So, even though she'd slept late, she had three whole hours before she had to go into work. It felt like such a luxury to have both a warm, lovely, private cabin she could putter around in and a gorgeous landscape to explore.

She went to the falls first, because the icy sculpture looked so magnificent. As she stood watching the snow diamonds sparkle, and the frozen water throw rainbows, she realized how rare it was not to hear a saw, or bulldozer, or drill groaning and wheezing in the distance. Bell River was inventing and improving itself every day.

But Sunday mornings were for quiet things—church services, family bonding, communing with nature. It felt good to begin to understand the ranch's rhythms. She'd been here a couple of weeks now, and at least she could find places and people...most of the time.

And she needed quiet time, rather desperately. She needed to sort her thoughts. She'd told Craig last night that she would fly to L.A. soon, so that they could talk things over. She had resisted promising even that, but he had put on such a show of love, of excitement over the baby...

How could she deny him even a chance to talk about it, face-to-face?

She heard a rhythmic crunching sound, as if someone, or something, was coming toward her.

A deer, perhaps? She'd heard someone mention that the wildlife moved in closer when it got colder—drawn by the promise of warmth or the hope of food.

When the puffy-coated, hooded figure broke through the trees, Tess recognized Rowena.

"Hey, Tess!" Rowena's gorgeous face was wind-scalded, her long hair whipping around her green plaid hood like black flames. But her smile was full of welcoming warmth. "We both had the same idea. I was… Well, I was trying to write a letter that I'm finding it ridiculously difficult to finish. Whenever I'm edgy, I come here. Aren't the falls gorgeous when they're frozen? It's one of my favorite spots in all of Bell River—at any season."

"They are beautiful," Tess said.

"This part of the property had been let go for so long," Rowena said, glancing around. "We used to call this 'the wrong side of the river,' because all the inhabited buildings and nice gardens were over by the house. But I loved how wild it was. When we decided to put the spa here, I asked the landscapers to keep at least some of that feeling. Bree says I drove them half insane, with all my interfering."

Tess could easily imagine Rowena micromanaging the workers. Tess had come to understand the family a bit, and she could sense the division of duties, and the balance of power.

Gray and Bree, who had been married in September, lived the farthest away from the nucleus of the main house. Their horse-breeding business, Gray Stables, was under construction on the far reaches of the ranch, somewhere they called the Western Slope.

Max and Penny, who had married only a few weeks ago, lived in the main house right now, with Max's daughter from his first marriage. But they planned to move out as soon as expansions on their cabin, River Song, were completed.

Dallas and Rowena were indisputably the king and queen of the place. They'd been married a year, and they lived with Alec in a private wing of the main house.

Though technically all three sisters were equal partners in the dude ranch, Tess had intuited instantly that Rowena's vote weighed more. And with good reason. She seemed to feel personally responsible for everything that happened at Bell River, from the laundry to the bank loans. She knew every inch of every building, and her eye spotted a drooping soffit or peeling paint long before anyone else noticed.

And the land... Rowena singlehandedly answered the old riddle about whether a tree falling in the forest made any sound. If it was a Bell River tree, its falling made a sound in Rowena's heart.

Rowena Wright Garwood didn't just *own* Bell River. She *was* Bell River.

Watching her now, and feeling the love for the land radiating out as she surveyed the spot, Tess realized she envied that more than anything else. Far more than the material trappings of wealth.

Maybe it was because she had always been like a bird on a wire, perched but precarious. Completely ungrounded. That was partly why she clung to her dream of owning her own spa someday, if she could ever save enough money, and move to a city big enough to support the kind of business she imagined.

"What is the waterfall like in the summer? I imagine it's lovely."

Rowena moved closer, as if she could direct Tess's mental vision. "Oh, yes. It's not showy, but it's very special. It's a little like…well, you know how you'd rather have a small, fiery diamond than a big cloudy one?"

Tess laughed slightly. "I do." The one Craig had given her when they got engaged was huge and horribly flawed, which should have told her something about the relationship.

"Well, that's what Little Bell Falls is like. It's what's called a horsetail fall, which means it stays pretty close to the bedrock as it comes down. It's a lot of water, but in a narrow passage, like a chute. See the frozen circle at the bottom—looks like a tiny frozen pond?"

Tess nodded.

"That's the plunge pool. It doesn't always freeze completely, especially not this early in the season because it's very deep. In the spring and summer, it's the most magical shade of blue—almost neon, in some light. And all around here, on every bank, wildflowers grow so dense you can hardly walk through them."

Tess's lips parted slightly as her focus blurred and she imagined the landscape morphing. In her mind's eye, she saw it greening, blooming, the water rushing down to sparkle in the blue basin beneath.

Rowena stared mistily for a few seconds, too, and then she squeezed Tess's forearm happily. "You can see it, can't you?"

Tess blinked and smiled, slightly embarrassed. "You describe it well." She cleared her throat to remove the excessive emotion from her voice. "It'll be gorgeous, for the spa's clients."

"Absolutely." Rowena's dreamy gaze sharpened into her businesswoman's eye. "I keep thinking there has to be some way we can do massages outside in the summer. Our location is so much prettier than Silverdell Hills—and we'll need to distinguish ourselves once they open up."

Tess knew exactly what she meant. "Once, I worked for a spa that offered wonderful nighttime treatments, where couples would soak in deep copper tubs overlooking a creek. Stars, moonlight, candlelight, champagne and strawberries—people loved it. It was like something out of a fairy tale."

Rowena whipped around to face Tess. "That's brilliant," she said fervently. "We must do that! Can you work up a proposal? Be sure to include liability considerations, and everything that would be needed to meet the health codes. I don't know exactly how you'd sanitize an outdoor tub, but..."

Tess was taken aback by how quickly Rowena had adopted her casual idea.

"I know it'll be time-consuming for you," Rowena said. "We'll give Ashley some extra hours, to free you to work on it." She laughed. "We're already up to our eyeballs in debt, so what's a little more?"

"I'm sure I can do it without adding any hours," Tess said, to her own surprise.

Why should she care if Bell River took on more debt? She'd never intended to stay long-term. And if, when she talked to Craig, he found a way to convince her that they needed to be in the same city—somewhere else, not here where he might ferret out the truth of her paternity—for the sake of this baby, she might not even be staying short-term. She would be gone long before the first wildflower bloomed on the banks of Little Bell Falls.

Even if she decided to exclude Craig from her baby's life, who knew what the Wrights would say when they learned of her pregnancy? Would they want an unmarried pregnant woman running their spa? They didn't seem like the type to quail before the gossips, but they might not think she was up to the task, especially once she had an infant to care for.

She realized that, whether she were here to see it or not, she wanted Rowena's venture to thrive. She wanted these courageous, vibrant women to hold their own against Silverdell Hills, and against a bad economy, and, most of all, against whoever was sending those hideous, anonymous notes.

Dirty bitches, indeed. Well, whoever Mr. Notewriter might be, he wasn't dealing with just three dirty, bitchy Wright sisters anymore.

At least for a little while, he was dealing with *four.*

JUDE DIDN'T REALLY *need* to check on the exercise room at the spa that Sunday night. The space was basically finished—at least his part was. Someone else would paint it, and nail on the baseboards.

Okay, fine. Honesty check. He didn't *need* to stop by the spa. He *wanted* to. It was eight o'clock—technically at least an hour later than Tess normally worked, but the lights were on. So the way he figured it, if she were the one who happened to be staying late, and he happened to stop by...well, that was Fate's decision, not his.

Maybe, if she were there, she'd *happen* to tell

him what her ex-husband had said when she gave him the news about the baby. If she had done it, that is. She clearly hadn't wanted to. She might have changed her mind....

Either way, Jude wanted to know. Maybe then he could stop obsessing about it.

So he used his master key on the back door and let himself in.

"Hi, Jude," Tess called from the dimly lit storage room, where she kneeled over a large cardboard box piled high with green-and-white-and-gold garland. She looked over her shoulder toward the door, her face honey-gold, reflecting the metallic loops. "You're working late, aren't you?"

He walked toward her, not even glancing at the exercise room, as if he were a moth, and her golden face was the flame. "Nope. Not working. I just wanted to stop by and make sure everything's good with you."

Well, great. So much for playing it cool, pretending they *happened* to find themselves in the same place at the same time.

"I'm feeling much better," she said, nesting a box of green glass Christmas ornaments into the cushion of garland. "I haven't been sick in two days."

She knocked the surface of a wooden shelf in playful superstition. As she did, one of the garlands in her stack slid off, and she had to bend to retrieve it. He tried to get there first, but he was too far away.

When she straightened, though, he was in the room, only inches from where she knelt. Her eyes widened, as if his sudden proximity surprised her.

"I was going to pick that up for you," he said awkwardly, wondering if he'd regressed to the point that he came across as a creeper. "I just—I was all the way over there, and—"

"That's okay. Thanks." She gestured to a folding chair. "Want to sit down? I was so slammed, I could only stuff the decorations in here when I first took them down, so I thought I'd get them organized. I'll be a while. I mean, if you wanted to talk, or…"

She hesitated, and the overhead lighting was weak enough that he wondered if he imagined her flush. "I guess you probably don't have time to chat."

He smiled. He liked her slightly reticent manner. It matched his own. Neither one of them was slick or glib or overly social. More importantly, neither one of them was fake. She was so natural, so unaffected and comfortable to be with—at least when he wasn't too close, too flooded with desire to think straight.

That sexual tension was over, anyhow. It had to be. She wasn't merely an attractive single woman he could kiss whenever the whim moved him. She was a complicated, vulnerable, confused, recently divorced woman carrying another man's baby.

He liked her, and he cared what happened to her, but that was as far as it went. As far as any honorable man could allow it to go.

So there wasn't any reason he couldn't come out and ask her about the developments, the way he'd ask Bree, or Rowena, or any female friend.

"I've got time," he said. He sat, crossing his leg over one knee, then draping his jacket over his lap. "The truth is I want to say I'm sorry about the other night. New Year's Eve." He avoided saying the word *kiss,* for fear it might make him want to do it all over again.

She waited.

"We haven't had a chance to talk about it—not alone, anyhow," he said, remembering when they'd been forced to act normal as they participated in the repair of the activities hall. "I shouldn't have put you in that situation."

Her cheeks grew pinker. "It was my fault, more than yours. I'm the one who knew…knew how things really stood."

He tried to smile, though talking about it made him feel fiery inside. But it was done, the mutual apologies had been made and they could return to a simpler kind of friendship.

Right?

"How did your phone call go? Did you talk to your husband?"

"Ex-husband," she said. The correction was abrupt, like a reflex. After that, she seemed tongue-tied, looking at the box.

Darn it. He hadn't meant to make her uncomfortable. "Look, Tess. If you don't want to talk about it, just say so. We haven't known each other very long, and maybe you—"

"I did tell him." She raised her gaze to his, and he was pierced by the confusion and sorrow he saw there. "I'd like to talk about it, if you really don't mind. I don't have—" She swallowed, absently wound a green garland around her hand. "I don't have a lot of people I can share with, and for some reason it's easy to talk to you."

"Me, too," he said. He met her sad eyes straight. "Anything you want to tell me, I really want to know."

She was silent a moment. Her hair was loose tonight, falling around her shoulders and down her back, which made her look young and vulnerable. Seeing her this way, it was difficult to believe she was going to be someone's mother.

"Craig was shocked, of course. Neither of us imagined...neither of us dreamed..." She grimaced. "You see, we'd already filed for divorce, when my mother died. We hadn't lived together for three months. I'd been living with my mother ever since her cancer came back."

He could imagine how difficult that had been. A marriage falling apart, a mother dying. No siblings, no father. For once, he saw that his crowded childhood had been a safety net against that kind of loneliness.

"I think I told you," she went on, putting the story together piece by painful piece, "that my mother died two months ago."

He nodded.

"Well, the night she died was… It was very bad. She'd wanted to be at home for the end, so it was just the two of us. After…" Another pause. "After they took her away, someone…I don't know who, one of my friends, I guess, called Craig."

"Why? If you'd been separated for months, why him?"

She shrugged. "They meant well, I'm sure. Most of our friends thought we shouldn't be divorcing. They thought I was overly emotional about my mother. They probably thought it would break the ice, give us a chance to mend the relationship. It was foolish, but they don't know Craig like I do."

He could almost see her shudder of distaste. What were Craig's sins?

"Anyhow…" She straightened. "He came over, and I…was so lost, and so…"

"So alone."

She looked at him somberly. "Yes. I don't mind that, usually. I'm used to it. But that night was different. That night I needed…"

"You needed comfort. So you slept with him." He didn't have to filter out any judgmental tones. He didn't feel judgmental. He knew why people turned to sex for anesthesia. It did, in the short term, block out the pain.

"Yes." She lifted her chin. "And now, because I was weak, I'm pregnant."

"And how does he feel about that?"

Her eyebrows drew together slightly. "He says he's happy about the baby. He says he hopes we can start over. He says he wants to be a father. A husband."

He says… He says…

Jude could hear Tess's doubt, the disbelief in every statement. Was that why tears shimmered against her lower lids, threatening to spill at any moment? Did she fear that her husband's protestations of delight weren't sincere? Was she hopeful, but simultaneously afraid that her hopes would be dashed?

"Well…" He shifted on the uncomfortable metal chair, suddenly furious with this Craig bastard, who had shamelessly exploited Tess's deepest vulnerability—and whose lack of conscience had enabled him to catch the golden ring. He would get her back, after all.

"That's good, then, right? That he's happy?" He found a smile and tacked it on his face. "That's good, isn't it?"

"No."

He had been about to spout some other stupid platitudes, but her heartsick syllable stopped the words in his throat.

"What?"

"No." She squeezed the tinseled garland so tightly it snapped in her hand. She unwound it, tossed it into the box with the others, then lifted her agonized face to his again. "No, it isn't good. I didn't even want to tell him, though I knew I had to. But even then I was hoping…praying…that he'd be furious, that he'd deny responsibility. I was hoping he'd say he wanted nothing to do with me or the baby."

Jude didn't respond right away. He wasn't sure what the right answer could be.

"What does that say about me?" She slid her hands into her hair and pressed against her temples. "What kind of terrible person would wish that? What kind of person am I, if I would deny my baby a father just because I don't love him, and I don't want to be tangled up with him again?"

His chest tightened. He'd had no idea.…

She'd probably been beating herself up for a long time—for having resorted to sex as comfort in the first place, and now for wishing the consequences didn't have to be so permanent.

"It doesn't make you a terrible person, Tess. If you don't love him, it's perfectly natural that you wouldn't want to be tied to him."

"But the baby…" She let her hands fall to the flat plane of her stomach, which didn't yet reveal her pregnancy by even the smallest swelling. "The baby deserves a father. I know that better than anyone. Every child needs…"

She didn't seem to be able to finish the sentence. As if her muscles had gone limp, she lowered her head, her chin almost touching her breastbone.

He couldn't stand it. Without thinking, he stood, and dropped quickly to his knees behind her. He put his arms around her and clasped her hands.

"Bottom line, some men shouldn't be fathers," he said. He was thinking of Molly and Garth mostly, but here on Johnny Wright's land it was hard to ignore his gold standard of bad paternity. "If Craig is abusive, or—"

"He's not." She shook her head hard. "He doesn't drink, or hit me. He hasn't committed any terrible sins. That's the problem. If he did anything like that, I would have the right to shut him out of our lives."

Suddenly, she was breathing so fast it was as if she were running in place. He kept his hands over hers, pressing against her stomach, and her heart was beating so hard he could feel it even from there.

He hated that she was in so much bewildered pain, and trying so valiantly to be tough on herself, and fair to this jerk of an ex-husband. He wanted to reassure her, to convince her that she didn't need to sacrifice herself. She had every right to reject a husband she didn't trust—whether there was a baby on the way or not.

But the cold, hard facts of the case didn't matter. What she was feeling was what was important.

And, in his heart of hearts, he knew that if he were the father he'd want to know, too. He didn't really have to guess at this. He knew. He knew, one-hundred-percent absolutely, that he wouldn't tolerate being shut out. He would want a place in his child's life. He would demand one.

Still…this rapid breathing wasn't like her. She was calm, and this seemed almost like an impending panic attack. More like Molly, than what he knew of Tess. Molly had had the attacks ever since she was a child. Tess, he sensed, would be a stranger to this loss of control.

"It's okay, Tess. You'll find a way to work it out." He inhaled and exhaled slowly, his chin near her cheek, to try to calm her breathing. He moved his thumbs soothingly against her hands.

It seemed to work. After a minute or two, the

drumbeat of her pulse grew less frenetic, and he felt her shoulders relax.

"You'll make it work," he repeated. And because he believed it, his words carried a note of conviction.

"Thanks for having faith in me." She angled her face slightly, a fraction of an inch toward him. Her voice sounded calmer. "But honestly, I don't see how, when all I have is a feeling about Craig. No. It's more like a—a *knowing*."

A shimmer of the earlier emotion passed through her. "He's not a good person."

"Then that's enough."

"Yeah?" She took a deep breath, but when she spoke again her voice had a certain wry amusement that he found reassuring. "I wonder if a judge would think so, if I tried using it in a custody hearing."

"He would if he knew you. I suspect you've got pretty good instincts about people."

Finally, he felt her cheek move, the curve of a small smile changing the contours of her face. "Apparently not good enough to save me from marrying him in the first place."

They both laughed softly, both of them all too aware what a mess people could make of their love lives.

Then, as if realizing how intimate this embrace in the darkness really was, she shifted subtly. She twitched, as if she'd like to ease her hands free, and he took the hint. He let go and rocked back on his heels, to give her space.

"But thank you," she said politely. She faced him, her cheekbones still damp, but the shine of her eyes was less liquid, more normal. "Thank you so much for being so patient. I'd say I'm not always this emotional, but that doesn't seem to be true anymore, does it? Practically every time we meet, I'm causing some kind of scene."

Grinning, he stood and held out his hand to help her to her feet. "Well, hey, at least you have a great excuse. Everyone knows about pregnant women, right?"

He should leave. He was well aware of the danger of this moment, the power of the feelings she brought out in him.

And yet, he didn't move. Neither did she. They stood, inches apart, in the small, shadowy space. Her heart-shaped face, round penny-brown eyes and baby-fine hair were so close, so tantalizingly close. He could smell the soft lavender of her skin. And her lips, half-parted, the subtle glistening of pink shadows between...

He grabbed himself by the scruff of the neck and yanked up hard. Was he crazy?

For a second, he thought he'd do it anyway. Maybe it made him crazy, but he was going to kiss her, damn it, because he wanted to, because *she* wanted to. Because she did not love the creep who was coming here and was going to try to take her away.

The creep who had created this baby the way you might put a tracking chip in a kitten, or a hook in an angelfish—so that Tess could never run too far away, and he could always reel her back in at will. Like Garth thought he'd done with Molly.

Jude's shoulders tightened. Okay, that was true about Garth, but it was a crappy thing to say about Craig, a man he'd never met. Jude had no proof of the man's motives. It was just, as Tess had put it, a *knowing*.

"Tess…" he began with a strange urgency. "Don't—"

But apparently the creep had a *knowing* of his own, because before Jude could finish the sentence, a glow of light appeared on the shelf behind them, and Tess's cell phone chirped.

She stepped back, put her hand out and picked up the small rectangle of blue radiance. She glanced at the screen, then looked at Jude. Her face was pale, her eyes wide and dazed.

"It's Craig," she said. "He's here."

CHAPTER NINE

THE FOOD AT Donovan's was delicious, but as Tess
sat across from Craig, watching him devour pasta,
she found that she couldn't eat a bite. It wasn't the
pregnancy. She'd had trouble eating since she was
a child. Her stomach always rejected food when
she was nervous.

And Craig definitely made her nervous.

He was strung tightly, underneath his concerned
facade. She knew she'd annoyed him by insisting
they meet here, instead of at her cabin. "God, Tess,"
he'd complained on the phone. "You want witnesses
to protect you? What do you think I'm going to
do?"

Frankly, she had no idea what he was going to
do. That, in a nutshell, was the problem. He wasn't
predictable. He wasn't genuine. There was no "real"
Craig you could count on. His moods were mer-
curial, and half of his attitudes were just masks he
wore to suit his needs.

For the moment, he was wearing the "caring"
mask, his handsome face smiling, his eyes soft and
protective. He was trying to convince her that he

wanted to take care of her—and their baby. But something didn't ring true.

"I think it's understandable that I'm uncomfortable with your showing up like this. I mean…I called you only two days ago. How did you find me?"

He shrugged. "You said Colorado. After that, not really a problem. You aren't exactly James Bond."

She tried to think where she'd left a weak link. Mail forwarding? Her credit-card companies? It made her feel strangely dizzy to think that he'd been nosing around, like a bloodhound after a scent.

"Aren't you hungry?" He waved his sauce-coated fork toward her plate. "Remember you're eating for two now."

She tightened at the paternalistic tone. She kept her gaze on the table, and turned her fork over and over, tines up, tines down, on her napkin. She felt several pairs of curious eyes on them.

Most of these people were strangers to her, which was a piece of luck. She'd wanted witnesses, yes. But witnesses who were associated with the ranch, no. Fortunately the only customer here connected to Bell River was Mitch. And though he'd waved as Tess came in, he was too busy flirting with Marianne Donovan to show much curiosity about Craig.

"We need to talk about how to handle our situation." She spoke as calmly as she could. "I told you about the baby because I recognize that you have rights. But the fact is that we're divorced, and you can't keep acting as though that isn't true."

"I know it's true," he said. "But I also know it can be changed. We can get remarried, and we should, so that our child has both a father and a mother."

He put down his fork and reached for her hand. Instinctively, she withdrew it, and dropped it onto her lap. His fingers closed over nothing but her fork, and his expression hardened for a second. He had never liked looking foolish.

He rearranged his features, returning to his long-suffering patience. "Okay, you're angry with me, I get that. You feel I betrayed you, even though nothing actually happened. I wouldn't ever even have looked at another woman, if you—" He shook his head. "You were so distant, Tess. So caught up with your mother…"

She almost rolled her eyes. Even in a full-throated apology he couldn't resist trying to justify himself. *Of course* it was her fault that he'd come within an inch of having an affair with his secretary. *Of course* a man like him couldn't stand being second in line behind her dying mother.

The part he'd never understood was that she didn't really care about the flirtation with Glenda. She felt sorry for Glenda, who had fallen in love with Craig, but when she found the woman's love letters in Craig's glove compartment, her main emotion had been relief.

She'd actually hugged the letters to her chest, as if they were a long-awaited gift. *Finally,* after six years of marriage, she had an excuse—a reason to leave the husband she could hardly stand to touch.

"I don't want to go through all that again, Craig," she said now. "It doesn't matter. Our marriage was a mistake, and we can't make that mistake again just because there's going to be a baby. We need to think about some kind of joint custody."

Even as she said the words, a pain passed through her. She didn't see how she could ever relinquish her child, even temporarily, to anyone—but especially to a man she didn't trust.

But, as her mother would have said, she should have thought of that before she had sex with him, shouldn't she?

"Joint custody?" He inched his plate away with a small twitch of repressed violence. "Don't be ridiculous. Look, are you afraid I won't want to move here? I don't have a problem with that. The real estate business never rebounded like I'd hoped in L.A., so obviously we'd do better at Bell River, and—"

"What are you talking about?" Vaguely alarmed, she leaned forward, determined to read the truth behind that strangely smug expression. That was the face he wore when he was closing a very lucrative deal.

"Why would you assume I wanted to live in Silverdell? I told you this ranch is a temporary job."

He looked at her, his eyes narrowing the way they did when he was doing internal calculations. Then he wadded up his napkin, tossed it onto the table and took a deep breath.

"I *know,* Tess," he said. He waited a beat for that to sink in. "I know Johnny Wright was your father."

As horrified heat boiled to the surface of her cheeks, she shot a glance around the café, hoping his voice hadn't been loud enough to be heard. She was relieved to see that Mitch was still deeply engaged in conversation with Marianne.

Finally, she looked at Craig. She'd never been good at lying. But she tried. "I don't know what you're talking about."

"Oh, come on, Tess." His tone was indulgent, as if she were a child fibbing about tracking mud on the floor. "Two months ago, you learn that your father murdered someone and died in prison. Then you go haring off to Nowhere, Colorado, to work on a ranch owned by a man who murdered his wife and died in prison. That's a coincidence?"

Her throat felt paralyzed. "Where did you hear that?"

He was still smiling. "See that woman over

there? The one with the book, who is pretending she likes eating alone?"

Tess refused to turn around. She'd seen the woman earlier.

"Well, anyhow, *she* told me. She owns the bookstore. When I checked into the hotel last night, someone mentioned she was having a party, so I went. Everyone there confirmed what I'd already figured out. Apparently Johnny Wright is like the Loch Ness monster of this town. Practically a tourist attraction."

"You crashed that woman's party?" But that wasn't the point, was it? Tess was so blindsided by the whole thing she couldn't think straight. "I mean…you've been in Silverdell since *yesterday?*"

"I didn't crash. It was open to the public. I even bought a book. But yeah. I came right away. I got here last night. I wanted to—" he smiled "—scope things out."

Before Tess could respond, the notes of "Danny Boy" rang out as the door opened, and the customers all stopped talking to sing their part.

Tess didn't turn around, but out of the corner of her eye she saw Esther Fillmore making her way toward the take-out counter, a diffident, stooped man two subservient paces behind her. Her husband, probably. It still surprised Tess to know that the awful Esther actually had a husband.

"Cute," Craig observed sarcastically as the singing died down.

Tess felt hot all over, as if her nerves were catching fire. She *liked* the Danny Boy tradition.

"Damn it, Craig," she said. "What made you think you had the right to snoop? What made you think you had the right to *scope out* my town, my job, my *life?*"

He dropped the saccharine smile. His eyebrows came together in a counterattack. "I think the better question is…what makes *you* think you have the right to hide an inheritance of this size from me?"

She swallowed hard, squeezing the hem of her sweater in her palm.

"There is no inheritance," she said in a low, fierce tone. "No one knows for sure who my father is, least of all you."

"Bullshit."

Tess felt as if she'd been struck by the unvarnished profanity. She stared at her ex-husband, momentarily speechless.

"Everything okay over here?" Marianne appeared, as if out of nowhere. The café's owner smiled placidly. "We have a killer pumpkin pie, if you're not too full."

Craig waved an annoyed hand. Tess managed a smile, though. Marianne seemed like an observant restaurateur, and she might well have been stopping by to defuse the bomb of Craig's temper.

"Honestly, all I need is a to-go box," she said, gesturing apologetically to her untouched pasta. "It's wonderful, but I couldn't finish it."

"Will do." Marianne cast a quick look at Craig, smiled at Tess and disappeared. But Tess noticed that Mitch's gaze was on them, as if Marianne's attention had attracted his. How long before it got back to Rowena and Bree?

Craig didn't speak, even when they were alone. His hazel eyes were as hard as marbles, and he stared her down with an unblinking gaze.

"I haven't mentioned my...what my mother said...to anyone here," she said quietly. "I doubt that I ever will. I wanted to see them, yes. And get to know them a little. But they're good people, Craig, and they've been through a lot. It's been difficult for this family to rise above the scandal. Another coal on the fire of local gossip might burn the whole place down."

"That's absurd." He folded his arms over his chest. "You have to tell them."

"No. I don't."

"Well, if you don't, I will."

Her heart skipped two beats, then raced, as if to make up for the lost time. Her chest felt so tight it was difficult to take full breaths. She wanted desperately to slap that arrogance from his face.

Arrogance and avarice. Finally she understood

his endgame. It wasn't the baby. It wasn't even Tess herself. It was money. It was Bell River.

Or at least a quarter of it.

She should have known. With Craig, the bottom line was always money. The minute she'd finished her training, he'd pushed her to set up her own spa, and had been furious that she wanted to delay, first to get experience in the business, and later so that she could care for her mother.

She leaned forward, so that she could speak quietly. "You will not. Do you hear me, Craig? You're no longer my husband. This has nothing to do with you."

"The hell it doesn't. This place is a gold mine. Do you know how many acres those girls inherited? It might be tricky, and we'll have to get a look at the will…."

His eyes were unfocused, seemingly unaware of Tess as he followed his thoughts. "I say we start by telling them. Who knows? If they're as afraid of bad publicity as you say, they might do the right thing voluntarily."

She balled her fists on the table. "Are you crazy? I'm not going to extort—"

"Who said anything about extortion?" He laughed, as if he found her attitude an amusing overreaction. "Don't be such a prude. No way we're letting this slip through our fingers because you don't want to get your hands dirty."

"*Our* fingers?"

He lifted his glass of iced tea and knocked it back in one toss, as if it had been liquor. He stood, flicked a hundred-dollar bill on the table and then slowly rotated his neck, as if to work out a kink.

"Yes, ours. I may not be your husband, but I'm that baby's father. It's our child's inheritance, too, and if you won't look out for it, I'll have to do it for you."

What a liar! He didn't give a snap about the baby, and suddenly she knew it as absolutely as she knew her own face in the mirror. She pressed her palms against her stomach, thinking, illogically, of how gentle and protective Jude's hands had felt there just an hour ago.

"Don't do this, Craig," she said. But that sounded like begging, and no way she'd beg this wretched excuse for a man. "I won't *let* you do this."

He laughed, loudly enough to turn several heads toward them.

"How are you going to stop me? You've got twenty-four hours, Tess. Either you tell them, or I do."

MITCH TOLD HIMSELF, as he had every hour, on the hour, since he had dinner at Donovan's last night, that he was an idiot. A moron. He'd promised himself he'd take this slowly—if he took it at all. Now look at him. One flirtation at a book signing party, one chitchat at Donovan's...and the very next day he was going to have sex with the woman?

"Giddy up!" He dug his heels into Flashdancer's side, and whipped through the night, letting the wind smack his face, since obviously no one else was going to, and he clearly needed it.

"Moron," he said again, loud enough to echo off the nearest rock wall.

Two minutes later, Flashdancer stumbled over a loose rock on the western trail, and he knew he'd pushed the horse too hard. Flash never lost his footing, not unless he was beyond tired.

Not cool, moron. Definitely not cool to treat any horse this way, especially one as gifted and giving as this beautiful young paint, which he co-owned with Rowena.

You're out here in the darkness, galloping aimlessly in the snow, because you hate yourself, not Flash.

"Sorry, boy." Mitch pulled the reins to slow to a canter. Flash responded instantly, clearly relieved to sense that the rider on his back was good old Mitch again, and not some guilt-driven demon.

When they reached the edge of Little Bell Falls, Mitch eased from canter to trot, and finally to a walk. The horse's exhausted breath rushed out of his flared nostrils in loud puffs of cold, misty air and Mitch felt guiltier than ever.

By the frozen moonlight, he checked his watch.

Almost eight. He was already twenty minutes late, no surprise since he'd begun by saying he'd take the long way into town. Just to make sure Flash got some exercise. And then, with the devil driving him, he'd ended up galloping down the darkest, most heavily forested trails of Bell River's western wilderness.

He'd turned around ten minutes ago, but he'd kept riding east, passing up the shortcut to town, and now he was almost at the main ranch buildings. The spa was only yards away.

Clearly he wasn't at all sure he *ever* wanted to reach his destination.

His destination. Marianne's sweet little house, complete with stables, on the far side of town. The house where she was undoubtedly waiting for him, trying to keep her home-cooked dinner from drying out, and her candles from guttering, and her thoughts from turning to the fresh sheets she'd put on the bed, and the condoms she'd bought at Sterling Prescription Shoppe, just in case.

She'd made it clear, when she invited him, what she had in mind. She wasn't the coy type. It was one of the things he loved about her.

"We might be good for each other," she'd said. "For a while, anyhow. We're both still carrying a memory around, but we both know it's hopeless. It might be a relief to put that burden down for a while. I'm tired of being alone. Aren't you?"

Darn right, he had told himself. He *was* tired of being alone, of sinking like a stone emotionally because he wouldn't let go of these heavy, hopeless dreams.

Why shouldn't they have a pleasant, short-term affair? They were adults. They weren't breaking vows to anyone. Marianne's husband was dead, which was different, of course...but not *terribly* different. Bonnie had cut off all communication, even that last-ditch, emergency-only phone line. So the relationship was dead, even if she lived.

And hell...she might even really be dead, for all he knew. He seriously doubted she carried his name around as next of kin. If the worst happened, he probably wouldn't ever know, unless someday Isamar reported seeing Bonnie's ghost beside the familiar Moira Wright.

He shivered, realizing how damp and cold it was. Plus, out here, with the fantastical shapes of the frozen falls beside him, with the snow winking and glimmering, and the trees like spellbound shapes, caught at the cruelest moment of their twisted, outstretched begging...

Well, for the first time Mitch could remember, this spot didn't feel beautiful or blessed. It felt...a little strange. The idea of ghosts didn't seem quite so crazy here.

"Shut up, you fool." His angry voice echoed in

the darkness, and Flash flicked his ears nervously, not recognizing the command.

"Sorry, boy," Mitch said again. "I'm being bitter and dumb. I don't mean it. God knows, I don't mean a word of it."

The horse nickered sympathetically, as if he understood that the apology wasn't really directed at him. Which, of course, it wasn't. Mitch wanted to tell Bonnie how sorry he was. He wanted to tell her that she mustn't die, not now, not ever.

But as soon as Mitch allowed himself to feel that searing longing, he got angry all over again. Anger didn't hurt half as much as missing her did. He had to move on.

He just had to. Or he'd drown in his own self-pity.

"Come on, boy." He gave the reins a subtle flick. "We're keeping a lady waiting."

He cut across the path between the spa and the cabins, noting that Tess's lights were on, though all four other cabins, still unoccupied, remained black. He kept Flash at a walk, because they weren't sticking strictly to the trail.

It should have been a simple cut-through. So Mitch was surprised when Flash balked, then sidestepped, tossing his head and neighing, as if he didn't like what lay in front of them.

The trees were thick here, and the shadows

dense, so at first Mitch couldn't see what the problem could possibly be.

"What's wrong, buddy?" He tried to urge the horse forward, but Flash had no intention of taking another step. There must be something in the way. Reins loose in his hands, Mitch bent forward and peered at the lumpy, shadowy ground.

"Aw, crud." Something did lie there, something rather large and crumpled. He hoped it wasn't an animal. He'd have to take care of that. It was always heart-wrenching to see a deer, or an elk, or even a fox, lying dead like a stain on the snow. But it happened on a ranch. A lot.

The worst was when the animal wasn't quite gone. That was the absolute pits. He was a native Coloradan, but as a preacher's son he hadn't been brought up with ranching, and he was still getting used to this part.

"Okay, let me take a look." He patted Flash's neck, then slid from the saddle. "You wait here." Unnecessary, since Rowena had trained the horse to be smarter and more cooperative than most humans.

He crunched across the snow, pulling out his cell phone to use the built-in light. As he drew closer to the bulky mess, his heart sank. It was too big to be anything but a deer or an elk. If some criminal fool had shot one, he'd use this phone to get Dallas out here and arrest his sorry ass....

As he squatted, he clenched his gut hard and took a deep breath, preparing himself for whatever he'd see.

Good thing he did. Because what lay there wasn't an animal at all.

It was a man.

Biting back an exclamation of shock, he shone the light on the man's bruised face. What he saw rocked him on his heels, and almost sent him rump-first into the snow.

Tearing off one glove, he thumbed his phone and hit the auto-dial for Dallas—not the sheriff's department, though Dallas was on duty tonight, but his private cell.

Thank God, his brother answered on the first ring.

"Dallas," Mitch said, a little breathlessly. "Remember that man I told you I saw arguing with Tess at Donovan's last night?"

"Hi, there, Mitch," Dallas said wryly. "That's how phone conversations begin, little brother. Someone says hello, and—"

"Not this conversation. Do you remember that man, or not? Because he's lying out here on the snow behind the spa cabins. And he's dead."

TESS HAD TOSSED and turned most of last night, trying to find a way out of this mess with Craig. As soon as she had closed up the spa tonight, though, everything had suddenly become blessedly clear.

She knew what she had to do.

She had to go up to the main house and ask for a meeting with Rowena, Bree and Penny, and she had to tell them the truth. Then, even if they were forgiving enough not to fire her on the spot—a long shot, at best—she'd have to leave Bell River.

Leaving—a total break—was the only way to avoid a scandal. It was the only way to prove she had no designs on their inheritance.

She could have left the minute she got home from dinner last night. But that would have been cowardly, fleeing into the night with no explanation.

She wanted to tell her sisters the truth. And she'd wanted another day at the job she had grown to love. Another night in her cozy little cabin.

Craig had given her twenty-four hours, and she wanted every minute. All day, she'd worked hard—Mondays were practically back-to-back clients—and the work, as always, had soothed her. By the time the spa closed, she felt quite calm. Almost strong. She had returned to the cabin, packed her clothes, loaded her equipment and things into the car and mentally readied her speech.

There's something I should have told you....

You may be contacted by my ex-husband, and I wanted to warn you that he isn't to be trusted....

All I really wanted was to meet you, and to know a little of where I came from....

They'd be shocked—and suspicious, of course. Anyone would be. They might even think she'd made it all up. She didn't have any DNA tests to prove her parentage. All she had was her mother's confession. All they had was her word that her mother had confessed. The word of a liar, passing on the accusations of their father's supposed mistress....

She'd known from the minute she set eyes on Bell River that she'd have to leave eventually. The only shock was that she had to leave so soon. But if it hurt she had no one to blame but herself, did she? If she'd told the truth when she arrived... Or if she'd never married such a money-grubbing scumbag as Craig Marsh in the first place...

But she *had* made those stupid mistakes. So what else could she have expected the outcome to be? This was the pill she had to swallow, and she would do it without complaint.

It was only when she thought of Jude that her resolution wavered. Jude...

There had been something almost magical there. The way he made her feel—

Stop that.

She grabbed her coat, shoving her arms into it roughly. Jude was a pipe dream. He was a lovely man, kind and gentle and indescribably sensual. He was the kind of man she should have held out for, instead of settling for Craig. But she hadn't. And Jude wasn't free for the taking, anyhow. According to Molly, his heart already belonged to his childhood sweetheart, no matter how complicated their situation might be at the moment.

She buttoned her coat slowly. If she could have stayed... If she weren't pregnant... If she hadn't come to Bell River under false pretenses...

She had to laugh at herself. Even if all those things were true, then what? Did she really think that, if she had a little longer, she could have banished thoughts of Haley Hawthorne from his heart? She glanced in the mirror at her small, pale, sad face under its cascade of messy curls. Few women could compete with a glamorous starlet, and she wasn't one of the lucky few.

So he'd kissed her once on New Year's Eve? He might even have slept with her. But she would probably have been no more than a placeholder, until he worked it out with Haley. Whatever "it" was. Though she'd listened guiltily to the gossip whenever anyone mentioned Jude, no one seemed to know exactly what had gone wrong with the fairytale romance.

So enough dithering. Enough self-pity. She had to hurry. It was almost eight, and Craig's twenty-four-hour deadline expired at ten. He'd come by, or maybe he'd call. But he wouldn't let it pass.

She hadn't entertained any false hopes on that point, not even during the darkest hours of her restless night. She'd seen Craig get hold of a promising deal before. He was worse than a dog with a bone. He maneuvered and danced, exploited and cajoled. He wined and dined, even muscled and schemed and misrepresented, if he had to. The one thing he never did was give up.

She took one last moment to stand at the window and stare into the night, as if, magically, she could imprint the scene on her brain. Maybe, like a hawk flying overhead, she could map the layout of the ranch, with the sparkling silver bell of Bell River bisecting it, and her square window of light burning beside the frozen falls.

But she wasn't a hawk or a magician. Though the landscape was luminescent with moonlight, she couldn't see any farther than the trees that stood between her cabin and the spa.

She wrapped her scarf around her neck, stuffed her gloves into her pockets, picked up her last suitcase and opened the door.

To her surprise, Mitch stood there, his hands in his pockets, his jacket collar turned up against the cold. He was breathing heavily, in white clouds of condensation. His face was gray, and his auburn hair windblown.

"Tess." He looked startled to see her, which was

strange, given that he stood on her porch. "Where are you going?"

She froze, too surprised to move past his bulk. Too surprised, even, to ask him why he would be here in the first place, blocking her door.

"I'm going up to the ranch," she said. "Were you going to— Did you need me?"

"Yes." He shook his head, though the motion was a curious mismatch with his answer. He glanced at her suitcase. "I mean…I think you'd better go inside."

"Why?" She was starting to find this unnerving. He looked upset. He kept glancing into the night, as if something out there bothered him. "Is something wrong?"

"I think you should go inside," he said again. He didn't quite meet her eyes.

And suddenly, with one of those hormonal swings she was starting to realize came with pregnancy, she was angry.

He was trying to stop her now, without even the courtesy of an explanation? After everything it had taken for her to find the courage to do this in the first place? No, by heaven. She wasn't going to be shuffled into her cabin like a naughty little girl, without even the simplest explanation.

She stood as tall as she could, then raised her chin for an extra inch. "As you can see, I was about to leave," she said with an unaccustomed ferocity.

"And I'm getting in my car right now, unless you've got a darned good reason why I shouldn't."

"I do," he said, and his voice had an oddly gentle sound.

Before she could insist on more, the trees around the cabins began to flash with alternating blue and white lights. The crunch of cars coming up the snowy drive, fast and unwavering, filled the quiet air.

"What is it?" Dropping her suitcase, she turned to him. She dropped her artificial antagonism, too. "Mitch, please. What is it?"

He seemed to struggle with himself for a minute. He glanced at the arriving vehicles. Then he took a deep breath.

"That man I saw you with last night," he said, his voice low and urgent. "Who was he?"

"He…his name is Craig Marsh," she said numbly.

"And what is he to you?"

"My ex-husband. Why?" She watched the cars with a sense of fatalism, knowing something terrible had happened, but having no idea what it was. Dallas stepped out of his truck first. Then a marked car parked behind him, from which a uniformed sheriff's deputy emerged.

Behind them, a third vehicle crunched to a stop. It was an ambulance.

Her stomach churned, and her legs began to feel warmly liquid.

"*Tell me*. What's wrong? Is this about Craig? What has he done?"

Mitch laid his hand on her wrist. His fingers felt cold against the sick heat of her skin. She knew before he spoke. She knew because touch always spoke to her louder than words.

"He hasn't done anything," he said. "He's dead."

CHAPTER TEN

AN HOUR LATER, Tess still didn't know much more than that.

Mitch had left, to alert the others at the ranch. Members of the sheriff's department, including Dallas, continued to comb the area around the spa, black shadows pacing back and forth in the moonlight, like methodical wolves. For a while, the interior of her cabin had sporadically flashed with a blue-white light, and Tess knew that meant the photographer was documenting the scene. She tried not to imagine how Craig's body would look in the merciless glare, whether he looked broken, or whether the snow around him was stained with blood.

A young deputy with a terrible head cold had been sent to sit with her while they waited for Dallas to be free for an official interview. The deputy's name was Linz. If he'd broken into his twenties, he'd done so very recently. His chin still had spots, and his manner was diffident, even sensitive, as if he'd been sent to make sure she was all right. But she suspected his role was more warden than nursemaid. He was probably tasked with making sure she didn't try to flush a weapon down the toilet.

Not that she even knew whether there had been a weapon. She assumed, from the number of police vehicles outside, that Craig hadn't died of anything as simple as a heart attack. But she had no idea whether to imagine knives, or guns, or...

She shuddered, then wrapped her arms around her chest, hugging her elbows. Deputy Linz shot her a nervous glance, clearly praying she didn't do anything bizarre on his watch.

"Can I get you something? Hot milk?" He glanced toward the kitchen, looking worried that he'd offered something he couldn't deliver. He had no idea, of course, whether she had milk in the refrigerator.

She felt sorry for him. Poor guy, having to sit here while he was clearly so miserable, blowing his nose every few minutes, trying to be courteous while privately preparing to handle either the emotional breakdown of a grieving widow, or the vicious attack of a murderer.

"Thank you, but I'm all right," she said reassuringly. "Though I'd be happy to get you something, if you'd like. Coffee?"

He shook his head stalwartly, and then turned with obvious relief as her door opened, and Dallas entered, stamping his feet at the threshold to avoid bringing in the slush. To Tess's surprise, Rowena

KATHLEEN O'BRIEN 263

stood behind him, unwinding a green scarf from around her hair. When Dallas began unzipping his jacket, she moved past him, coming forward with outstretched arms.

"Tess, I'm so sorry," she said. Without waiting for Tess to respond, she enfolded her in an uninhibited hug. Her baby bump hit first, but she didn't seem self-conscious about it. "Are you okay?"

"I'm fine," Tess said, awkwardly. It seemed wrong to accept a hug from Rowena, knowing that, before the night was over, she'd undoubtedly have to reveal her true motives for coming to Bell River.

And that was the least of it. Her relationship with Craig was so complicated. Their divorce had been ugly. Their argument had been public. She wasn't so naive that she didn't realize the implications of those facts. If foul play were suspected in Craig's death, Tess might be the prime suspect.

Would Rowena still want to hug her then?

"Craig and I were divorced," she added, so that Rowena wouldn't feel doubly deceived. Tess didn't deserve the comfort and solicitude awarded to heartbroken widows. She hadn't lost her soul mate. Far from it. "It's dreadful something has happened to him, but it's not as if we—as if I—"

"I know." Rowena pulled back and looked Tess in the eyes, her own brimming with sympathy. "But an ex-husband was once a husband. And losing someone you loved, even if things got complicated…"

"Ro." Dallas put his hand on his wife's shoulder. He'd hung his jacket on the coat tree by the door. "You promised that, if I let you come, you'd let me do my job."

"I'm not stopping you. I just wanted Tess to know she has a friend in the room." She kissed Tess's numb cheek, then, peeling off her jacket, plopped herself in one of the armchairs by the fire. "I'll be absolutely silent from here on."

Dallas's answering smile was wry. "Ri-i-ight," he said, the elongated syllable dripping with sarcasm. He turned to Tess, his face handsome, pleasant and carefully neutral. "I need to ask you some questions. But first, I imagine you probably have a few questions for me."

A minute ago, she'd been burning with the need for answers. Now that he was here, radiating authority from some innate place, her thoughts felt scrambled and incoherent. She wasn't sure where to begin.

"I don't really know anything except that Craig is dead," she said. "What happened? How did he die?"

"He seems to have hit his head," he said. "On one of the large rocks beside the sidewalk, we think. But we'll have to wait for the medical examiner's report."

Tess swallowed. "It was an accident?"

Dallas hesitated a fraction of a second. "That's unclear at this point."

Without really planning it, Tess felt herself drop onto the sofa. "I see." And she did. She could hear in his voice that he did not, for a single second, believe it had been an accident.

Dallas waited, as if to give her plenty of time to keep asking questions. But she couldn't think of a single thing that mattered. Craig was dead. Someone had killed him. And they were going to think that she had done it, to prevent him from revealing her secret.

Someone had killed Craig. She thought it over again, to see if it sounded any less insane. While she had packed her clothes exactly the way a guilty woman planning to flee would do, someone had killed her ex-husband.

"I'm sorry to have kept you waiting so long. We had a lot of paperwork and details to take care of." Dallas looked as solicitous as the deputy had for the past hour. It must be an expression they taught in sheriff school. "Are you up to answering a few questions?"

She nodded.

"Okay if I sit?"

She nodded again.

"Thanks." Dallas took the other armchair, opposite Rowena. He nodded subtly to Deputy Linz, who opened a notebook, and then turned to Tess with an emotionless expression. "When did you last see your ex-husband?"

"Last night. Around nine o'clock. We had dinner at Donovan's café." She had no idea whether it made her sound guiltier to volunteer so much so fast, but she couldn't bear to sit here and let him pull the shrapnel out of her, detail by detail. "We argued, as I'm sure you've heard from some of the other customers. I think your brother was there."

Dallas didn't openly react to the cascade of information. He simply nodded. He was a good listener, which probably came in handy for an investigator.

She wondered, though, how many investigations he'd had to conduct, in a sweet little burg like Silverdell. She wondered how many suspicious deaths there were. Maybe Moira Wright's murder had been the only other one, and he was obviously too young to have been involved with that.

She wanted to glance at Rowena, to see how she felt about what she was hearing, but she didn't. Dallas was clearly waiting to see whether Tess had more to volunteer before he had to prod her with another question.

She saved him the trouble. "Craig and I agreed to meet again tonight, to talk things over some more. I was expecting him to come here, to the cabin, at ten. So he may have been on his way when he... when he...hit his head."

She frowned, realizing that didn't quite make sense. She'd felt quite confident that she had another couple of hours. If she'd believed for a moment he might ignore the deadline, she wouldn't have been dawdling, saying goodbye to every room in her little cabin like an idiot.

"But I wouldn't have expected him to come early," she admitted, rubbing her hand anxiously along the sofa's fabric. Something about Craig being out there, hours before their appointment, watching her cabin, made her feel slightly ill. "That wasn't like him. He was very precise, very literal. If he said ten, he meant ten."

Dallas glanced at her fidgeting hand, then returned his bland gaze to her face. "Sounds as if your husband might not have been an easy man to deal with."

"Ex-husband," she corrected automatically, though the minute she said it her cheeks burned. It made her sound exactly like what she was—a woman who deeply regretted her marriage and was very glad it was over.

"Of course. Ex-husband." He didn't quibble, though he could easily have done some correcting himself. *Your* late *ex-husband,* he might have said.

"Craig had a temper," she said, keeping her back straight and her chin level. Why deny it? Everyone in Donovan's Dream had seen that temper in action. "I didn't kill him, Sheriff. I know what you're thinking, and I know how it looks. But I didn't kill him."

"Dallas," Ro said, twitching slightly, as if it were making her crazy to have to remain silent and still.

He ignored her. His focus was impressive. "We don't know that anyone killed him," he said mildly. "We don't know much of anything yet. But I would like to know what you were arguing about, and why he was coming here tonight."

She wondered whether she should ask for a lawyer. Deputy Linz hadn't looked up from his notebook since the questioning began, and Dallas was so poker-faced she knew she could easily be in serious trouble. Rowena's warm offer of friendship wouldn't mean much if it turned out that Craig's death hadn't been an accident.

The one thing she didn't consider was lying. She was in too deep for that. Her only hope now was the truth…the whole truth and nothing but the truth. She didn't kill Craig, and if she muddied the water with a bunch of lies she would only make it more difficult for them to find out who did.

"I'll tell you anything you want to know," she said. She gave up the ramrod pose and let her back rest against the sofa. She felt the need of a bolster. "In fact, I was coming by the ranch tonight to tell you, anyhow. To tell Rowena, Penny and Bree, that is."

Everyone glanced at her suitcase, which still stood by the door, where her numb, shocked hands had dropped it when Mitch told her Craig was dead.

It was small and plain and brown, but it seemed to glow with radioactivity—as if it pulsed with the telltale message, *Liar. Liar…*

"When I explain, you'll understand," she said. "It's true. I *was* planning to leave. I assumed you would want me to, when you heard what I had to say."

The silence hung like a physical thing in the air.

Rowena watched Tess's face, as if she sensed a bombshell approaching. "What were you coming to tell us?" Her voice was tight, but not unfriendly, even now.

"It's what Craig and I were fighting about. He'd discovered something I didn't want him to know. Something I didn't want *anyone* to know." She turned to Rowena, who sat with her hands protectively clasped over her stomach. "Especially you and your sisters. I didn't want to upset you, or to make things any harder for Bell River than they already are."

Rowena's dramatic raven's-wing eyebrows knitted together. "I don't understand," she said.

"I was coming to admit…to admit who I am. When I took the job, I didn't tell you the truth about myself." As she spoke the words that marked the point of no return, Tess felt a little odd, untethered, as if she floated a few inches above the sofa instead of sitting on it. As if she were dematerializing, losing substance.

She would like that, she thought with a weird, dreamy sense of being outside her body—to be looking at the scene from somewhere above the room. But it wasn't that easy. She couldn't vaporize and reform somewhere else, somewhere less complicated and cruel.

"What do you mean?" Paradoxically, as the situation grew more complex, Rowena seemed to become more real, more solid, more forceful and fiery. That was her gift, Tess recognized with a vague sense of envy. Rowena was a fighter, and when anything unsettled her she grew strong to face it.

"What didn't you tell us about who you are?"

"Ro." Dallas leaned toward his wife, as if trying to warn her to ease up. He probably saw what Rowena didn't—that Tess was on emotional overload, and very close to fainting.

Rowena didn't seem to hear him. Her gaze was locked on Tess. "Who are you?"

"I'm pregnant," Tess said, but she knew that wasn't a direct response. That was merely to explain why she wasn't tough like Rowena, why she might pass out, why she might look pale, why she might disappear before their eyes. She was sick, and pregnant, and her baby's father was lying dead in the snow behind her house. And she was frightened, though she knew she was innocent, because no one else knew that, and she had no way to prove it.

"But *who are you?*"

Tess used Rowena's green gaze as a lifeline, as a prop. The force of the other woman's concentration felt like the only thing holding Tess in one piece.

"I'm Johnny Wright's illegitimate daughter," she said.

"What?" Rowena breathed out the word, her lips falling open.

"Yes." The room seemed to go black and white, and then to vanish entirely. But, from that distant place, Tess heard herself say softly, "I think I am your sister."

"WELL, IF SHE'S willing to take on a quarter of Bell River's debts, then I'm happy to give her a quarter of its profits," Rowena said, sounding tired and more cantankerous than Mitch had ever heard her in all the years he'd known her. And that was saying something.

She shrugged. "Profits that, at the moment, amount to, about a buck fifty?"

"Don't be an idiot, Ro," Bree said, and she sounded crabby, too. Gray gave her a worried look. Everyone was treading lightly, because no one could quite believe all the bombshells that had been dropped into their world tonight.

"What's idiotic about it?" For the past half hour, Rowena had been sitting on the floor in front of Dallas, leaning her cheek against his knee as he rubbed her shoulders. "If Tess is really the old lunatic's daughter, then she's got as much right to the ranch as we do."

An awkward silence hummed.

"Okay, somebody might as well say it." Rowena scowled, which Mitch recognized as her habitual expression when she was trying to hide some insecurity or emotion. "If she's really his daughter, then she's got more right to the ranch than I do."

Mitch cringed. Jude was the only person in the room who wasn't family, by blood or by marriage. Mitch had run into him tonight, as he was leaving Tess's cabin. Jude had been driving up.

Mitch wasn't a fool. He knew what that meant. Heck, he'd known it since practically the first few days the woman was here. Jude was hooked. Fine with Mitch—Tess seemed sweet, and, best of all, she wasn't Haley. But until they found out whether Tess was a murderer, he wasn't going to mention his suspicions about Jude's feelings to anyone. Not even Jude.

On the other hand, when he'd learned they were having a meeting to decide what to do about Tess tonight, Jude had insisted on coming. It would have taken every man on Bell River Ranch to prevent it.

No one tried. Jude had earned a place at the family confab by virtue of long association and loyalty. Besides, maybe more of them had guessed at his feelings than Mitch realized.

Still, Rowena's DNA wasn't something the family talked about openly very much. Or ever.

Rowena had discovered she wasn't Johnny's biological daughter before they launched the dude-ranch project. She'd been relieved, of course—who wouldn't prefer to be as *unrelated* to that murdering psychopath as possible?

But the news had rocked the Wright world for a while, because it meant that, technically, she wasn't one of the people Johnny had in mind when he wrote, in his will, that if his wife predeceased him his estate should be divided equally "per stirpes." Apparently that was lawyer-talk for "equally among his bloodline," and Rowena had proved she didn't have a drop of his blood in her veins.

That had been crazy enough.

Now they were discovering Tess Spencer might carry his bloodline instead.

The implications, if paternity could be proved, stretched out so far, and around so many twisted corners, that none of them could really predict where it might lead.

The doctor had given Tess a sedative, though he'd pronounced her basically sound, and the baby safe. So they had a few hours to decide what to do.

But when she woke up…what then?

For a few minutes, no one spoke. What was left to say? They'd been going around and around, with no resolution in sight.

Mitch, who sat on the piano stool in the Garwood family quarters, had reached the end of his patience. He plunked a few notes that sounded suspiciously like Chopin's funeral march. *Dum, dum, da dum...*

Then he swiveled, putting his hands on his thighs, and sighed irritably. "Look...there's a bigger issue than who her daddy is. What about her dead husband? What if she actually killed him?"

Jude frowned. "She didn't."

Everyone turned toward Jude, their faces wearing similar looks of surprise.

"What?" He clearly hadn't meant to blurt it out like that, but he seemed to find the idea too ridiculous to consider. "Come on. You know that woman's not a murderer."

"I don't think she is, either," Penny said quietly. Jude tossed her a grateful glance.

"Oh, Pea." Bree's voice was more weary than waspish. "You never think anything bad about anyone. Ever."

"Of course I do," Penny retorted with a smile. "For instance, right now I think you're being unfair and cranky, and you should probably go to bed."

"Maybe we all should," Dallas said, refereeing instinctively. "We might reason more clearly after a good night's sleep. I've got to be up early so I can brief the Bureau guy first thing."

Mitch exchanged glances with him, aware that

it had been a difficult, but inevitable call to bring in the Colorado Bureau of Investigation. Dallas couldn't be the one to look into this death. No matter how ethical Dallas was—and everyone around here knew their sheriff was beyond reproach—the conflicts of interest were too glaring to ignore.

The body had been found on Bell River land. The deceased was related to one of their employees, who might be his wife's half sister. The man had died after threatening to expose a secret that could jeopardize the ranch's future.

So when Dallas had phoned the Bureau and requested that he be allowed to recuse himself, they'd agreed, without hesitation. They would take over in the morning.

"Is Linz staying at the cabin all night?" Gray glanced at Dallas. None of them wanted to admit they needed to keep an eye on Tess, but...

Well, she had been packed and ready to leave town, hadn't she? If that didn't scream "flight risk," nothing did.

"Yes." Dallas rubbed his temple. "Poor Linz. He's sick as a dog, but he's hanging in there."

"Maybe we should send someone else, too," Jude said. "I mean, if Linz is sick, he shouldn't get too close to her. She's clearly fragile, and with the baby—"

"He's not planning to crawl in bed with her,

Jude," Mitch said, chuckling. "He's just going to make sure she doesn't climb out the window."

Jude tapped his fingers on the end table, somehow keeping a lid on his temper. Ordinarily Mitch's irreverent jokes made him laugh, but apparently not tonight.

"Mitch, you're a moron," he said. He turned toward Dallas. "I think it might be nice if, when she wakes up, she could see a friendly face. She's going to be confused, maybe a little shell-shocked. I don't want her to feel as if she's under house arrest. You know?"

Mitch rolled his eyes. "I take it you're volunteering?"

Jude glared at him. "I'm not planning to crawl in bed with her," he said. "But yeah. I'm volunteering."

Dallas was shaking his head. "Bad idea."

"Look. No one guarantees Tess will sleep till morning. You want her lying there, dreaming of her dead husband, lying in the snow behind her cabin, then waking up in the darkness, disoriented and alone? Because if you do, then I'm not sure I give a rat's—"

"Jude." Rowena's voice was uncharacteristically gentle. "Dallas is trying to protect Tess. Don't you see? If someone killed her ex-husband, they are going to be looking at her first. And if it seems that she's already got another lover…"

Jude continued to breathe hard for another minute, but he couldn't pretend he didn't see. Finally he leaned against his chair, checkmated, clearly unwilling to do anything to make it worse for her.

"I'll go," Rowena said, suddenly.

"Whoa." Dallas jerked and laid his hands firmly on her shoulders. "What are you talking about?"

"I'll go. I'll sleep on the couch. I'll be there if she wakes up, so that she won't feel alone."

A rumble of protests sounded, but protesting against Rowena, once she'd made up her mind, was an exercise in folly.

"Ro, do you think it's really wise?" Bree looked genuinely worried. "I mean…what if she did kill her husband? Even if it wasn't intentional…even if they were fighting, what if she—"

"She didn't." Rowena used Dallas's knees to help herself to a standing position. She sent her fierce glance around the room, pinning them, one by one. "Come on, guys. Listen to your gut, for once, instead of your head. *Bree.* Dallas. We've been there. We know the difference between bad people and good people. And the truth is, you *know* she didn't kill anybody."

Finally, Dallas shook his head, wise enough to know he was outnumbered. "Okay. I'll drive you over. But I'm staying, too."

"Excellent." Rowena leaned down and kissed him hard.

And then a small "wup-wup" of exultation sounded from the doorway.

Alec stood there, his thatch of blond hair sticking out in all directions. His favorite pajamas, which he refused to throw away or replace, were about three inches too short, and exposed his skinny shins and bare feet.

"I'm going, too, right, Dad? You wouldn't leave me here alone, right? I mean, I would be so scared." He tried to look scared, and failed horribly. It was a sensation with which he clearly had no experience.

"Alec…" Dallas began, working hard to hold back a smile.

"Come on, Dad, I *have* to go," Alec interrupted eagerly, his blue eyes gleaming, "Ellen will be so jealous! I bet she's never spent the night with a killer before!"

CHAPTER ELEVEN

THE SUN WAS shining when Tess woke, filling her room with so much warmth and color that, for about a split second, she didn't even remember what had happened last night.

Then it all came crashing back over her.

Craig was dead. And everyone was going to think she killed him.

She'd ended up bringing more darkness and scandal to Bell River than she had ever imagined.

"Hey. You awake?"

She turned her head toward the voice that had appeared out of nowhere. Alec stood in her doorway, dressed in jeans and a flannel shirt, looking like a miniature version of his father...except with a giant load of devil mixed in.

"Yes." She sat up. She glanced down and was glad to see that she wore her most boring flannel nightgown. She vaguely remembered changing into it last night, after the doctor had checked her over. "I'm awake."

"Awesome. Can I come in?"

This was just one more surreal moment in a chain of weirdness, so she waved a hand. "Sure."

He clearly had no idea what shyness was. He entered and circled the room quickly, looking at everything, touching everything. Then he sat on the foot of her bed and smiled. "So. Did you really kill a guy?"

He said it so matter-of-factly that somehow she wasn't particularly insulted.

"No," she said. "I didn't." She let her tone express the absolute, unequivocal certainty.

And he believed her. His face fell, his mouth twisting in disappointment, and his eyebrows scrunching up comically.

"Dang it," he said, sighing heavily. "That would have been so cool. I've never met anyone who killed someone before."

She bunched the pillows up behind her so that she could lean back. "Why would you want to?"

He looked at her with new respect, as if she'd asked a very interesting question, one he hadn't considered before.

"Well, now, I don't really know. I guess it's just because I've never done it. You know how it's fun to do new things? Like I'd never seen a dog ice-skate, so I made these skates for Trouble, he's my dog, out of Cookie's butter knives...."

He chewed on the inside of his lower lip. "Well, that may not be a good example, 'cause it didn't

work out so well, but take my word for it. Sometimes it's cool."

"I believe you," she said.

He seemed satisfied with that. He dug in his shirt
pocket, then brought out a couple of Tootsie Roll
candies. "Want one?"

And, though she hadn't expected to smile for quite
a while, she felt her lips curving up. "Yeah." She
took the little chocolate, warm and soft from being
tucked away against his skinny chest. "Thanks."

He opened his solemnly, then munched in silence, with a kind of determined pleasure, as if he
didn't want to let a moment's enjoyment go uncel-
ebrated. She decided to eat hers the same way, and
sure enough it tasted twice as good as any candy
she could remember.

She thought of him as she'd seen him last, clinging to the wall of Bell River's great room, like a
doomed but determined superhero. His outlook on
life wasn't exactly practical, but it was refreshing,
and his courage was indisputable.

Plus, he was right. It could be exciting to do
things you'd never done before.

For instance, she'd never had a baby....

"Tess? Are you awake?" Rowena appeared at
the door, and her face instantly grew stormy when
she spotted Alec.

"Oh, buster, you are in *so* much trouble. Didn't
I tell you to leave Tess alone?"

"It's not my fault," he protested vehemently. "She invited me in. It would have been rude to say no."

Rowena shook her head, clearly unimpressed with that logic. "Well, I'm inviting you to get out. Go gather your schoolbooks, and wait for me in the car. I want to talk to Tess alone for a minute."

Harrumphing sullenly, Alec jumped off the bed. He stopped briefly on the threshold to grin at Tess. "Later?"

She nodded, though she wasn't sure what she was agreeing to, exactly. "Later."

When he was gone, Rowena took his place on the edge of the bed. Tess knew Alec was her stepson, but they shared a lot of traits in common, nonetheless.

"Sorry about that," Rowena said. "Technically, he's mine, but in reality he's a force of nature. There isn't any controlling him. Mostly we try to keep him from destroying civilization as we know it."

"He's fabulous," Tess said, and she meant it. She felt as if she'd had a visit from the courage pixies, and he'd left her stronger than he'd found her. But now it was time to face the day, and all the horrors it might include. "How long did I sleep?"

"It's about eight-thirty," Rowena said.

"Oh, no." Tess glanced around anxiously. "I probably should have— I know Dallas said he'd want to talk to me again in the morning." She squeezed her eyes shut for a minute, trying not to imagine

Craig, the way she'd done over and over last night. "Has there been any news?"

"Yes, some." Rowena's face sobered. "But I'm afraid it's not good. Dallas called in the state investigators, and they're pretty sure it wasn't an accident. They want to see you downtown, when you feel up to it."

"I'm fine," Tess said, willing it to be true. She swung her legs over the edge and was relieved to find that they were quite steady, and that standing didn't activate any nausea. "I'll go right away."

"No rush," Rowena said. She'd put out her hand, as if she feared Tess might keel over again. "Have some breakfast first. Take a shower. I hate the new state guy, anyhow. He thinks he's God's gift. It'll do him good to cool his heels a while."

Tess picked up her robe, and glanced ruefully at Rowena. "Easy for you to say. But I'm not exactly in a power position here. I don't want to give him any reason to dislike me right from the start. You know?"

Rowena gave a sheepish smile. "Yeah, I know. You're right. Don't ever take advice from me. According to Dallas, I'm always being uppity. He says it's a miracle no one's slapped me in jail already."

Then she seemed to realize her faux pas and sighed. "See? I always say the wrong thing."

"It's okay." Tess wondered, though, whether she'd ever think the word *jail* was funny again.

Everything seemed different when you feared that at any moment you might be arrested for murder.

Rowena put her hands gently on Tess's shoulders. "Seriously, Tess. There's no reason to be touchy about it, because nobody's putting you in jail."

Tess tried to smile, but she knew she didn't look convinced.

"I mean it." Rowena's voice was firm. "You're one of us now, and we're going to make sure that doesn't happen."

Tess stood, momentarily frozen as if Rowena's slim hands were as powerful as shackles. She happened to be in a shaft of sunlight, and it was a little like standing in a spotlight. She shook her head, unsure she could have heard Rowena properly.

"What do you mean…*one of us?*"

"I mean we're a team. I mean we're *sisters*. I mean anyone who wants to give you a hard time has to take us all on now." Rowena grinned. "And there are a lot of us. Four kick-ass men, three gorgeous, uppity women, a cowboy poet and a stable full of fast horses. And hey, Alec alone is the equivalent of a small army."

In spite of her determination to stand on her own two feet, to fight her own battles, Tess felt the magnetic appeal of such camaraderie. It would be such a luxury to be a member of a motley team like that.

Sisters. The very word sounded magical, too

good to be true. Sisters were blood, not choice. Immutable, not subject to the whims of mood and fate.

And yet, was it even true? Rowena obviously was passionate, and operated more on instinct than on evidence. Tess couldn't let her sweep them all away on a current of emotion—especially if it swept them into disaster.

Especially if it would sweep Tess into a tidal wave of disappointment. Better never to hope than to have such a glowing possibility evaporate in front of your eyes.

"Rowena," she said cautiously, "I want to be honest with you. Things were so crazy last night I didn't get the chance to explain very well. The truth is, I have no proof your father really was my father. I've got only my mother's word for it. And even though I believe her, there's no reason for you to—"

"Sure there is." Rowena's smile was placid and unwavering.

"There is? What?"

With her slim, capable fingers, Rowena touched Tess's rosebud necklace. "This is my reason. And frankly, it's all the reason I need."

"My necklace? What does that have to do with—"

Rowena slowly lifted her hair away from her face. The gesture exposed her ears for the first time this morning, and Tess realized she wore a pair of dangling earrings.

Lovely, rosebud earrings, with twining gold

stems and leaves, and tiny, glowing rubies for the flower. Impossibly, and yet undeniably, the earrings were the exact match to Tess's necklace.

"How…? It's not possible. Where did you get those?"

"Johnny gave them to my mother," Rowena said simply. "Can't you see? He must have bought the set and split them up. He gave these earrings to my mother, and that necklace to yours."

Tess shook her head, still disbelieving, despite the proof. She'd stopped wearing her necklace after the day Esther Fillmore had remarked so oddly about it. Something about the interaction had made Tess so uncomfortable she hadn't wanted to see it. She'd only put it on when she knew she was leaving. She'd put it on to go to the big house, thinking it might give her strength. But she'd never made it to the big house.

"When did you see my necklace? I don't wear it much…."

"I didn't see it, until last night, when I looked in on you, to be sure you were sleeping. I wish I had noticed it sooner. I would have known. Or at least I would have known there was something to know." She grimaced. "If that makes any sense."

Tess tried to smile. "I think I know what you mean. But I've never seen the earrings, either. Why—"

"I don't ever wear them." Ro dropped her hands,

letting her hair fall over her ears. "I mean *never*. My mom wore them all the time, so I just…couldn't. I put them on today so that I could show you. Kind of like…the sisterhood of the roses." She wiggled her eyebrows, probably trying to lighten the mood. "Flower power."

"It's amazing," Tess said. "He actually gave them both the same jewelry?"

"Yeah, it's exactly the kind of thing the old skinflint would have done." A trace of bitterness had crept into Rowena's voice. "He probably assumed that, since you lived so far away, there was little chance of anyone ever finding out. If you hadn't come here, deliberately seeking out your biological family, we never would have guessed. Never in a million years would anyone in California have rec ognized that necklace as part of my mother's set. Only here in Silverdell."

Yes. Only in Silverdell. Like Esther Fillmore, who had seen it, and had known it, and had, in a strange, disturbing way, disliked it.

Tess thought back to that moment, when Esther had stared so intently at the unassuming piece of jewelry. Even then, when Tess had no idea what the implications might be, she'd felt the ugliness of Esther's reaction. This necklace had meant something to the woman, something abnormal, and charged with poisonous emotion.

Tess had tried to dismiss it at the time. But now…

"Rowena," she said, closing her fist around her pendant as if the gem needed protection. "Esther Fillmore recognized it. One of the first days I was here. And the way she looked at it… I don't know how to describe it, but there was something terribly wrong about her reaction. If she knew it matched one your mother wore…"

She tried to find the right words. She didn't want to sound hysterical, or melodramatic. "Then I think…I think she had very bad feelings toward your mother."

Rowena frowned. "You mean something worse than jealousy, or prudish disapproval, or just an old lady's nasty ways. Right? Like she wrote the anonymous notes or wants to do us harm?"

"I don't know about the notes." Tess felt a chill. "But I think she hates you all. She hates Bell River. And, at that moment, she hated me because she thought the necklace meant I was somehow connected to Bell River."

"Yes. She does hate us. I've never been sure why…except that she's a judgmental old biddy, and we're a bunch of scandalous young upstarts."

Tess silently mulled over the possibilities. "You don't think that she and Johnny…? You don't think she has another piece of this set, do you? That would make her hate you, because she would have hated your mother for standing between her and the man she loved."

"You think Johnny took Esther as a lover?" Rowena laughed darkly. "He was crazy, but come on. Esther Fillmore?"

"Well, I didn't know her when she was younger. Maybe she wasn't quite so…"

"Yeah." Rowena nodded. "She was."

"I don't know why this sign of your mother's jewelry would upset her so much, then. And, now that I think about it, I wouldn't put it past her to have written those notes. She was there the day one was left behind the nameplate."

Rowena's eyes narrowed, her thoughts clearly racing. She took Tess's hand in hers. Her fingers, cool just moments ago, now burned with unnatural energy.

"Tess," she said, her voice thrumming with emotion, "let's say you're right. Let's say she did write the notes. Well…this may be crazy but…do you think that, if someone saw her leaving one of them—"

Rowena stopped herself, took another minute to gather her thoughts, then began again. "Do you think she might be capable of killing the man who caught her?"

SOMETIMES, JUDE THOUGHT as he smoothed his palm over a richly grained walnut plank, wood seemed to have a mind of its own. One minute he would be sanding the seat for a dining room chair, and then, out of nowhere, he'd realize the darn thing wanted to be an end table.

He couldn't say exactly when he'd realized that these lovely cuts of walnut, which he'd thought might work for a chest, were far better suited to be a swinging cradle.

He only knew that a couple of days ago he'd picked up a block and begun sketching the outlines of a swan's neck and head...and in his mind's eye he could picture the whole ornate, fairy-tale piece, with white muslin drapes rising from the swan's body like the sweep of wings.

It would be lovely. He could see the curves and scrolls, and the swan's elegantly arched neck, all simply from running his palm over the raw wood.

"Hey, is that going to be a cradle?" Mitch, suddenly appearing in the workshop doorway, tilted his head and tried to look upside down at the sketch. "What on earth is a cradle for?"

Jude kept sketching. "Babies sleep in them?"

Mitch, who had ostensibly come over to hang out with Jude, but had been in the kitchen eating cookies as fast as Molly could bake them, made a snorting sound.

"Yeah, smart-ass, I know what cradles *are*. What I don't know is why you're making one. Beeba's too big and wriggly for anything that small. And if you're thinking of Ro, she's bought so much baby furniture there's already nowhere for Dallas to sleep."

Jude glanced at his friend. He raised his eyebrows and blinked slowly, waiting for Mitch's brain to start working.

"Ohhhh." Mitch popped in the last bite of cookie and grinned. "I get it. *Tess.* The mystery woman you wanted to babysit the other night. Wonder what Haley is gonna think about that?"

"Haley?" Jude realized he'd spoken the name with a tone he usually reserved for profanity, and tried to lighten up a little. "What's Haley got to do with anything?"

"I dunno." Mitch sat in his usual chair, putting his feet up on the lower brace of a nearby sawhorse. "Don't blow a fuse, buddy. Molly said something about her, that's all."

Jude set down his pencil and paper. "What did she say?"

"I dunno," Mitch repeated, clearly uncomfortable. "Maybe she might have said something about Haley coming to Silverdell. Or maybe I imagined that. So, tell me about the cradle. Swan, right?"

"Don't try to change the subject." Jude was frustrated. Haley and Jude's sisters had been friends, and though Molly had been a little too young for true camaraderie, they had definitely become conspirators in the plot to return Jude to Hollywood. "Did Molly say Haley was coming home?"

Mitch screwed up his mouth, then nodded slowly. "Yeah. Didn't say exactly when, though. She didn't seem to know. In fact, she seemed to think it depended on you. She asked me to talk you into being nice, when Haley calls."

Jude glared, but Mitch held up his hands. "Hey, I was helpless. She bribed me with cookies."

Jude moved the walnut carving block to a safer spot, then picked up one of the turning blocks he'd ordered and studied the grain, trying to imagine how it would work for a leg.

"But between you and me, Jude, do you think it's a good idea to make her a cradle?" Mitch picked at an area of flaking paint on the chair. "I mean, Tess is nice and all. And she's definitely good-looking. But she seems a little hinky, maybe. Coming here without saying who she was? And her husband getting killed like that—"

"Ex-husband," Jude said, without looking up.

Mitch laughed softly. "Okay. But still…who's to say she's on the level? Even if she is the old man's secret kid, that's hardly something you'd put on a résumé, you know? He was a lunatic. And when she realizes that the inheritance is about ninety-nine-percent debt right now, and getting worse every minute, if bad press results in cancellations, who's to say how long she'll stick around?"

Jude stood, his chair scraping over the sawdust, releasing a clean, foresty smell. "Come on, Mitch.

She's not here for the money. If that was all it was, why take a job at the spa? She could have walked in and demanded to be cut in on the deal."

Mitch looked unconvinced. "So what is she here for, then? I'd say she was here to ruin the place. Because if this scandal escalates, that's exactly what'll happen. But there's not much advantage to her in that, is there? What does she lay claim to then? A quarter of nothing is nothing."

"It's not the money. And the idea that she'd lure her husband here and kill him just to cause a scandal that might turn her inheritance to a pile of dust…" Jude rubbed his chin and shook his head. "That's plain bonkers."

"So what does she want, then?"

Jude shook his head again. He didn't know, really. He had only his instincts, and the memory of the light in her face as she ran her hands over the soft, colorful quilt at the foot of her bed.

"I think she's looking for somewhere to belong," he said. "I think she might have been happy to be anonymous forever, as long as she could run the spa, do the work she loves and find a few friends."

"Maybe. But you can't get around the fact that *somebody* killed her husband." Mitch held up his palms. "*Ex*-husband. And since nobody around here ever met him except Tess…"

Jude looked intently at Mitch. "The state guy

wasn't dumb enough to arrest her, was he? I know they kept her downtown almost all day yesterday."

It had killed Jude to have to keep his distance and only guess at what was going on. Everyone was gossiping, but no one seemed to know what was happening inside the sheriff's department.

He even went to her cabin last night, to see if she needed company, to see if she wanted to talk. But Rowena's car was in the driveway, so he didn't go in. This morning, he heard that Ro had spent the whole night there. Again. Mother hen—a new role for Ro, but one she'd taken to like the proverbial duck.

"No. No arrests. I get the impression they're considering almost everyone a suspect," Mitch said. "Not that they tell me much. Which doesn't seem fair, since I'm the one who discovered the body in the first place."

"Yeah, because that matters."

"Maybe it's because you and I are friends. Maybe they think *you* killed the guy. You know, in a duel over the fair maiden."

Jude didn't laugh. Mitch made jokes about everything—it was his way. But Jude couldn't find anything humorous about the situation.

Tess must be terrified. He was unsettled, himself. He knew in his gut that she hadn't killed Craig Marsh, which meant a killer was walking around Silverdell right now.

Mitch's face sobered. "Seriously, Jude. Dallas doesn't ever gossip about his job. But I did hear they talked to Esther Fillmore. Farley Miller, too. And even Fanny Bronson, which is stupid, because if you ask me Fanny wants a man so bad she'd never reduce the available herd by even one head."

Finally, he shut up, clearly having run out of jokes. He tried to be silent, but it just wasn't in him.

"They'll find who did it, Jude. Tess'll be fine."

Jude nodded. "I know. She's a lot tougher than she looks." He set down the turning block and moved to his workbench, wondering whether he had the perfect bevel-edged chisel to carve the feathers on the swan's neck. He busied his hands, sifting through the tools.

He'd buy new ones, if he had to. He was going to make this the most beautiful hand-carved cradle ever, and he was going to give it to Tess, no matter what Haley, or Molly, or Mitch or anyone thought about it.

It was only a cradle, not a proposal of marriage. Why shouldn't Tess be given lovely things by her friends? Because she was an employee? Because she was an unwed mother? Because she was an illegitimate, unacknowledged by-blow of rotten Johnny Wright?

So what? Why shouldn't somebody make a happy fuss about this child? Why shouldn't Tess enjoy the fun of motherhood—as well as the fear, the labor? And why shouldn't her baby know, right from the start, that it was special, that the absence of a father didn't mean the absence of love and protection?

He wasn't going to treat Tess like a pariah or a suspect. He didn't give a damn what anyone thought.

"So," he said, not bothering to fake a casual tone. Mitch would know why Jude was asking, but he didn't care. "Is Rowena staying with Tess again tonight?"

Mitch didn't answer for a second or two, as if he were debating about whether to answer truthfully. "No, she insisted she was fine and actually needed to be alone. But, buddy, I've gotta tell you, I think your going over there would be really, really dumb."

Jude had to laugh. He turned, meeting Mitch's worried gaze with an honest, open grin. "Yeah? Well, I guess you'd know. If anyone is an expert on things that are really, really dumb, Mitch, it's you."

HOURS LATER, after Jude finally got rid of Mitch, and helped Molly put Beeba down for the night, he drove to Bell River. It had snowed all day, clearing only as darkness fell. Now, at about eight-thirty, the fields on either side of the road stretched out like melted marshmallow, fluffy and white under a full moon. Trees poked up like licorice sticks.

He'd missed nights like these, when he lived in

California. Sweet, peaceful. Hard to believe someone had been killed here. It was the first unnatural death in Silverdell in…well, since Moira Wright, almost seventeen years ago.

As he reached the edge of Bell River land, and their neat white paddocks began to border the snowy pastures, he belatedly asked himself whether Tess would be glad to see him. Maybe she'd meant it when she told Rowena she needed to be alone. He slowed for a second, thinking it through, his headlights shimmering on the black tarmac, diligently salted by the city.

It didn't take long to decide. He had to try. He wanted to be with her so badly it was as if someone had shoved an icicle between his ribs. If she really didn't want him there, he'd know it. He could read her. He'd be able to see it in her eyes.

But when he pulled around the curve that led to Little Bell Falls, he realized the decision was already made. She clearly had lost the argument about whether she should be left alone. Her cabin blazed with light, and in the square plot of front yard, several people were milling around.

Two women. Two children. A tall man stood on the porch, watching.

Even from this distance, Jude knew the man on the porch was Max. The children were Alec and Ellen, and they were arguing loudly as they bumped into each other, lifting their huge, paddled feet high with each awkward step.

They were practicing using snowshoes.

Jude couldn't take his eyes off the sight of the little family. Max clearly felt the same way, projecting a quiet contentment as he surveyed the innocent camaraderie. It had been choreographed, Jude could tell. Behind the scenes, Penny and Max, and maybe even Ellen and Alec, had conspired to create an evening that would banish any lingering ghosts for Tess.

The happiness campaign was working. The cabin lights pooled on the nearby snow while the moon lit the rest of the yard. The women tossed snowballs at the children, occasionally knocking themselves onto their own rumps with their ridiculous throwing motions.

They hadn't seemed to notice Jude's car, which he'd just pulled into the first few feet of the drive. He should have turned around. He should have left while he had a chance. But suddenly, Tess darted to the near side of the yard, dodging a snowball, and when she did, she spotted him.

Her expression grew tight, alert. Obviously a car appearing out of nowhere would be alarming, at a time like this. Then she recognized him. She smiled, waved and jogged toward him.

She called something over her shoulder to the others. They all paused in their pursuits, and watched Tess approach him. They didn't join her, which Jude found interesting. It was as if, without words, the family had begun to see them as…

As what? Not a couple, surely. They'd never dated, kissed only that one time.

But maybe the family saw him and Tess as something that could, with privacy and time, turn into a couple.

She reached him, her breath puffing out in little clouds. Jude rolled down the window and smiled.

"Hi," she said. "Everything okay? Want to come in?"

"Everything's fine, but I really should get back to Molly and Beeba. I wanted to be sure you were okay. That you weren't alone tonight."

She took in that comment, her eyes scanning his face as if searching for subtext. "I wanted to be, but frankly the Wright sisters aren't that easy to stonewall. They're taking turns keeping watch."

"Good for them." Jude had said he should leave, yet he couldn't bring himself to do so. "How are you? How was it at the station yesterday? They aren't giving you a hard time, are they?"

She shook her head. "I get the impression they're focused on other suspects. The state agent implied they think Craig's death probably wasn't premeditated, maybe the result of a tussle of some kind."

"A tussle with whom?" Jude frowned. *Tussle* wasn't the word they likely use to describe a fistfight between men. Tussle was lighter, more like the fussing and shoving a man might do with a woman.

"If they know, they're not saying. All they said is that, during a confrontation of some kind, he might have fallen and had the incredibly bad luck to hit his head the wrong way."

Jude wondered if that were true, or whether they were downplaying it, trying to lull her into confessing by implying she wouldn't be charged with murder. The idea angered him, but it didn't frighten him. He knew she hadn't killed Craig, so there was no danger of her confessing to anything.

"So they didn't keep you long?"

She smiled. "Oh, I didn't say that. I must have answered the exact same questions a hundred times. Yesterday, I was there all day. Today, though, all they said was that I shouldn't leave town. They might have more questions."

He reached over and touched her hand. "It'll be okay. I don't know how long it'll take them to figure it out, but they will."

"I know." She closed her fingers around his, as if grateful for the gesture.

"Are you doing okay, though, really? I mean… he was your husband, once, and—"

"I'm not grieving," she said, staring at their joined hands. "Not like that, anyway. Death is always tragic—especially one that feels so pointless.

He was only thirty, and that seems…" She looked up. "I'm not heartbroken, if that's what you're asking. I wasn't in love with him."

He nodded. He was glad. So ridiculously glad. He squeezed her hand, more tightly than he meant to. Glove-to-glove wasn't exactly intimate, but it was something. He tugged softly, bringing her hand into the car, up to the wrist. And then, because he couldn't stop himself, he bent and kissed her knuckles.

His nostrils filled with the scent of lavender and leather, and a tremor passed through her fingers, which felt very small in his.

"Thank you," she said. She'd bent toward the window slightly. Her voice was almost a whisper.

He lifted his gaze, though he moved her hand to his cheek, and pressed the smooth brown leather against his skin. "For what?"

"For believing in me, I guess."

Her fingers moved, making the tiniest, gentlest stroking motion over his cheekbone.

Oh, he was insane. When she touched his face, his body reacted wildly. He felt a swelling between his legs, an instant hardening that made his jeans seem rough and painful, three sizes too small.

Hopelessly insane. Just the back of one gloved finger, and he was physically on fire.

"And for coming here tonight. For wanting to be sure I was all right."

"Don't thank me," he said, his voice harsh. "I was being selfish, not kind. What I wanted…you know what I *really* wanted."

The others were moving toward them now. Alec and Ellen led the pack, their snowshoes off now and held high like torches. They ran in silly, serpentine tracks while Max and Penny strolled in a leisurely pace, arms linked. Alec was calling out Jude's name.

Just before they arrived, Tess leaned down, and whispered very close to his ear. "I think maybe I can keep them away on Saturday night."

Her breath was warm, and it moved into his ear and into his body, and he shivered, somewhere deep inside.

He glanced at her, hoping he'd heard her correctly. She was smiling. Then her hand twitched, and Jude released it. She straightened in time to catch the little boy missile launched at her.

"Max says enough of this dithering around." Alec wrapped his arms around Tess's waist, and he turned his freckled face toward Jude. "He says you need to either come or go, but for Pete's sake stop being such a moron."

Jude tried to give the boy a stern look, but being cross with Alec was practically impossible.

"Oh, he did, did he?"

"Yeah, he did." Max had reached them, and he winked at Jude. "We need Tess to take us inside and give us hot chocolate, and you're in the way. So come or go, but do it now."

Jude might have accepted the invitation, ungracious as it was, if he weren't wrestling with this fiery reaction to having kissed Tess's hand. No way he was getting out of this truck right now.

"That's okay. I was just leaving." He glanced at Tess. She wouldn't understand, but he couldn't help that. What he wanted...

Well, what he wanted didn't include sitting around drinking hot chocolate and making small talk with Tess's guard dogs, Max and Penny.

He had plenty of that kind of thing at the spa, or on the ranch, where they passed each other three or four times a day, and he was forced to smile and nod and pretend to be merely casual friends.

Of course, the fact that so far they really *were* just casual friends didn't help. In fact, at the moment, it only made Jude edgier.

"Okay, then, come on!" Alec tugged at Tess's coat. "Hot chocolate *now!*"

Tess caught Jude's eye and, smiling helplessly, allowed herself to be dragged toward the house.

Max lingered until the others were gone. Then he fixed Jude with a straight look. "She's *fine.*"

"Okay," Jude said. "I see that. But the thing is... you've got to read between the lines with Tess. She puts up a good front. She'd die before she admitted she needed anything. You know? That's why we didn't realize how sick and exhausted she was until everything hit the fan."

"I do know." Max smiled. "I've got one of those myself. Frankly, if anything proves she's one of the Wright gals, that's it."

True enough. And consoling, in a way. Now that they knew she was one of them, they'd understand much better how to handle her.

"Hey." Max nudged Jude's elbow. "If you absolutely must worry about something, worry about the ranch. It's early days, but several reporters have already called, and not just from the *Silverdell Sentinel*. If the story catches on, cancellations are sure to follow."

"I'm sorry." Jude frowned. "Maybe when the cops identify who did it…"

"Yeah. Maybe." Max sighed. "Anyhow, I guarantee you, Tess is okay tonight. Penny and I are staying over."

"Good." Jude glanced toward where Tess had slipped on the snowshoes and was galumphing merrily toward the cabin.

"Good," he said again.

And it was. She was getting to know her family. She was learning how to laugh, how to play. How to belong. He wouldn't interfere with that for anything. Not even to make this aching icicle between his ribs go away. Or the fire between his legs.

"Okay, then." Max touched his fingers to his cap, in a kind of sympathetic salute. "Later."

His tone was full of empathy, as if he understood how hard it was for Jude to leave. Jude was suddenly reminded that Max hadn't been married very long—and his own uncertain romance, the days when he didn't know whether he and Penny had a future, wasn't so long ago.

"Listen," Jude said abruptly. "I—" He shrugged. "Nothing. Just…thanks for looking after her."

It wasn't much, but it was man-talk for a million unsaid things. Max smiled, equally eloquent.

Jude put the truck in Reverse and headed home to spend another night alone. Halfway there, his cell phone rang, and he scrambled to pry it from his pocket before it stopped ringing. It might be Tess. She might have decided to send Penny away.…

He looked at the caller ID, as hopeful as a kid. But it wasn't Tess. It was Haley. As he processed his disappointment, the last buzz sounded, and then the screen changed. *Missed call.* He waited a few seconds, but the screen remained static. It never added the words *voice mail*.

Thank goodness. He already had six voice mails waiting to be played.

He was going to have to answer one of Haley's calls, sooner or later. She was the type who didn't take nonverbal hints, and she didn't take no for an answer. She kept coming back, eager to explain herself, defend herself, change his mind. She had gotten her way so often, that she never quite believed she wouldn't win.

He wondered whether that's why he avoided her calls. Was he afraid she was that good? Or that needy? Was he afraid that, if she cried, if she called up echoes of the early years, when her father had been so vicious, and Jude her only hope…

Was he afraid she might be able to talk him into returning to L.A.?

Surely not. He'd found a way to cut the dependence Molly had on him. She would be leaving for Chicago in early February, even though she was still sulking through the house like a thundercloud about it. Surely he could find a way to do the same with Haley.

He put the phone in his pocket. The moon had retreated behind a bank of snow clouds, and much of the milky glow had leeched out of the lovely night. He felt simultaneously edgy and exhausted.

He wondered if he'd be able to sleep tonight.

But maybe he wouldn't even try. Maybe he'd carve a cradle instead.

CHAPTER TWELVE

HAVING THREE SISTERS meant having a *lot* of guardians. Maybe too many. They seemed to have no intention of leaving Tess alone for a moment. Bree and Gray one night, Penny and Max the next.

That Friday night, it was Rowena's turn to babysit.

But this night was a little different. Dallas and Alec were sleeping up at Gray Stables because Alec's favorite mare, one he'd helped Gray pick out, was expected to foal. So Rowena, staying behind to be on hand for the guests, had invited Tess to have a sleepover at the ranch.

Though Tess was embarrassed to admit it, even to herself, the invitation thrilled her. She was as excited as if she were the poor servant girl getting the invitation to the castle ball.

Guess that inferiority complex was going to be a little harder to whip than she'd like. How ridiculous—when the "belonging" she'd always dreamed of seemed finally to be within her grasp.

The whole family had been so good to her, so supportive, since she'd told them who she was. No one had asked for a DNA test. No one had hinted, even for a second, that she might have been responsible for Craig's death—and would therefore, also be responsible for the cascade of cancellations they clearly feared might be the indirect result of the tragedy.

Instead, they'd welcomed her with open arms, more warmly than she deserved.

For the first hour or so of the evening, she missed her little cabin terribly. It had become such a safe place for her, and here at the ranch house everything was so grand and so unfamiliar. And crowded.

So far, there had been only one or two cancellations that could reasonably be traced to the news of Craig's death on the property. But Silverdell's weekly newspaper hadn't come out yet. Publication was an important event because, though everyone in Silverdell already knew, competitor papers in their part of Colorado would all read it in the *Sentinel* and if they jumped on it, too, that would be a bad sign.

But you'd never know Rowena was worried. She was the most relaxed hostess imaginable. She chattered and smiled, and introduced Tess to everyone as her sister, never acknowledging by so much as a blink that the situation was odd.

And she put Tess to work like a sister, too. Tess trotted extra blankets out to River Moon cottage, and loaned Cookie a bag of flour from Rowena's private pantry. She handled the phones for fifteen minutes while the college kid on duty took a break, and she looked up the tablature for a song about honky-tonk angels for Barton, who had a request from a guest.

Work. Actually, the strategy was perfect. Tess understood being busy. Whether Rowena had deliberately planned it or not, this type of work succeeded in banishing any of Tess's last vestiges of "employee" and turned her squarely into "family."

And she hadn't thought about Craig every minute, which was like a weight lifted from her brain.

Around seven-thirty, when the guests trooped out to the barn theater to watch an old cowboy movie, she and Rowena retired to the private Garwood quarters. In here, the scale was cozier. And the decor was so similar to her cabin.

Tess would be sleeping in Alec's room, which was quirky but shockingly tidy. Rowena's influence, no doubt. She set her small suitcase on the bed, grinning at the mason jar filled with Tootsie Rolls that dominated the dresser. Alec had attached strips of tape at intervals along the jar. *Monday*, the first one said in boyish block letters. Then, an inch down, *Tuesday*. Another inch…*Wednesday*.

"He's on a diet," Rowena explained, grinning. "Benny McAvee called him a lard-ass the other day, so he cut back to an inch a day. The Tootsie Roll diet. You think it'll catch on?"

Tess laughed. Alec was a wiry bundle of energy who would probably find it difficult to keep any meat on his bones at all when his growth spurt kicked in. "Benny McAvee must be blind."

They moved to the small living room, with a crackling fire beside them, and while they made salads for dinner they discussed the idea of outdoor spa treatments. Tess had worked up a proposal, and she'd brought the file with her. The plan was feasible, she knew—and the picture of the copper tubs in the moonlight, with Little Bell Falls cascading beside them, had captured her imagination.

It wouldn't be too expensive, either, except perhaps for the insurance—the quotes for that hadn't come in yet. Under normal circumstances, it should be within reach.

These weren't normal circumstances, though. They both knew that if the cancellations started, it wasn't likely that they would be adding any extra services for a while. In fact, if the press latched on to the story, dredging up all the "human interest" angles, like Isamar's staircase ghosts, they couldn't even guarantee there would be a spa at all.

Or, for that matter, a dude ranch.

Eventually, they'd talked over every detail of the plan. The fire dwindled low, and their conversation ranged all over the place, from silly to serious and back again.

They talked for hours, fighting sleep because

they were having too much fun. They changed to their pajamas, and made themselves slightly drunk with hot chocolate and laughter. Finally, the little mantel clock over the hearth struck midnight. The fire was so low it was merely three crisscrossed logs of mottled gold.

"You know, this is my first sleepover ever," Tess said. Then she yawned loudly and let her head fall against the back of the sofa. "I mean, the other nights this week don't count, do they? Because Dallas and Max and Gray were here, too."

"It never counts when the men are here," Rowena said emphatically. She lifted her mug and ran her tongue around the rim, trying to get the last sugary remnants. "Don't get me wrong. Nights with the men can be pretty amazing. But they definitely don't count as sleepovers." She wiggled her eyebrows. "If only because you don't get any sleep."

Tess laughed. "You're getting giddy. No more hot chocolate for you."

Rowena put down her mug, her face crumpled with pretend disappointment. Then she tucked her feet up on the sofa, and stared toward the embering hearth.

"Tess," she said finally. "I think I ought to tell you something."

Tess heard a new note in Rowena's voice. She put down her own mug and sat up a little straighter. "Sure. Shoot."

"Well, this is going to be a shock," Ro warned. "And Bree says it's too soon to tell you something we've kept such a closely guarded secret. But Bree never does anything dumb. She never takes chances. I'm the reckless one. Always have been."

"Ro, what is it?"

"Well, the thing is…" Rowena turned slowly and faced Tess. "I'm not your sister."

Tess tilted back, almost as if she'd been struck. *"What?"*

"Nope. I'm not." Rowena lifted one shoulder. "Bree is. Penny is. But I'm not."

"What are you *talking* about?"

"I'm not Johnny's daughter. Moira was my mother, so Bree and Penny are my half sisters. But you and me, Tess…we're not really related at all."

Tess dropped her hands to her lap. They felt oddly numb and heavy. She felt mentally fuzzy, too, as if this were a jigsaw puzzle, but she couldn't make the pieces fit.

"Are you sure?"

Rowena nodded grimly. She had her arms wrapped around her knees, as if she were trying to hold herself together. Maybe she, too, felt as if the pieces might fly away and be lost, if she weren't very, very careful.

"It isn't something I have told anyone outside the family," she said. "I had the DNA tests run last year. It's a hundred percent. I'm not his child."

"Oh, my God." Tess didn't know how to feel. Had that been a relief, maybe? Johnny Wright was hardly the man you'd choose for a father, if you could put in a custom order. On the other hand, Rowena had spent her entire life believing he was. "That must have been shattering."

"In some ways." Rowena nodded. "It was scary, but I can't say I was terribly shocked. He always resented me. There was always something wrong between us. And my mother..."

She seemed to hesitate, catching a little of Bree's caution for a moment. "Well, if you know the story of my mother's death, then you know it's not the only time my mother strayed. She was pregnant when she died, and the baby wasn't Johnny's, either. The prosecution believed Johnny had discovered it, and they suggested it was what caused the rage that led to her death. We'll never know that. Just as we never found out who the father was."

Tess nodded. That part she had known because it was part of the prosecution's case, and it had been in a lot of the coverage.

She touched Rowena's hand, overcome by a new awareness of how messy and painful life could be. For once, she realized how relatively straightforward her own sad story really was.

"I'm sorry," she said. That was inadequate, but it was all she could think of. "Did you ever find out who your biological father really is?"

"I did. Or rather, Bree did. His name is Rowan Atherton. I was named for him, obviously." She smiled. "He's a doctor. He seems like a good guy, but he has another family now. I keep meaning to write him. I keep *trying* to write him. But I haven't been able to find the words yet."

"You will."

Rowena nodded. "Maybe someday. I'd like him to know about the baby, anyhow. It might not matter to him, but it will be his grandchild, so…"

They sat in silence for a few minutes. And then Rowena finally let her feet drop to the floor.

"You see why I had to tell you, right?"

Tess tilted her head, trying to sort through the possibilities. "No. I don't think I do, exactly. It's all pretty mixed up, for all of us. But does it really matter? If we're going to be sisters, or friends, or…or whatever we're going to call it…it's going to have to be based on something more than DNA, in the end, anyhow. Isn't it?"

Rowena looked at her pensively, her eyes glowing like a forest creature, waiting, watching, catching the gold of the fire.

"You really don't get it," she said, finally. "Do you?"

Tess had a sick feeling stirring in her midsection. "I'm afraid I don't."

"Johnny left his land to his daughters. His will— well, it's all Latin and legalese, but the bottom line is that he didn't name us individually. He simply specified that Bell River should be divided equally among his offspring."

When Tess still didn't respond, Rowena raised her eyebrows. "His *offspring*. Of which, it turns out, I am not one."

Tess still felt incredibly stupid. "But surely that doesn't matter. If no one else knows about the DNA, who could possibly…"

And then she got it. She felt her blood chilling, as if the dying fire had allowed the snow to sneak into the room. She untangled her feet and stood clumsily.

"You mean me." She stepped back from the sofa. "You think I'm going to try to cut you out."

Humiliatingly, Tess felt as if she might cry. But she'd be darned if she'd show Rowena how much this hurt.

"This is why I was packed that night," Tess said hotly. "This is why I was going to leave. Because I knew that, if I stayed, if Craig went to you and told you the truth, this is what you'd think."

Damn it. Why did it hurt so much? Why had she let herself be lulled into thinking this was going to work? One sleepover didn't erase a lifetime of being strangers.

She turned toward the window. She wished she were at the cabin. She wished she were in L.A.

"I'd leave right now," she murmured softly, "if the police would let me."

"No, you wouldn't." The sofa rustled as Rowena stood, too. Then her arms slid around Tess's shoulders. "You wouldn't leave, because we wouldn't let you."

Tess waved a hand, dismissing the polite words. She didn't want platitudes. She didn't want consoling. She wanted to go home.

But where was that, now? Did she even have a home, anymore? She didn't turn, though, because the warmth of Rowena's hug was making the tears move closer to the surface. Her arms hung limp, denying the embrace.

"Tess, listen to me. Don't you see? That's why I told you now. I didn't ever want you to find out from someone else. I didn't want you to think I hid the truth because I didn't trust you."

Tess swallowed hard, her eyes burning. Rowena sounded sincere, but…

"I would never, *ever* take anything from you," Tess said thickly. "You'll never understand, because you've always had each other. But to me an inheritance is nothing. Money is nothing. But having sisters…having a family…that would be…"

Rowena exerted a little pressure with the heels of her hands, forcing Tess to turn around.

"You couldn't be more wrong," Rowena said, her voice husky. "We do know. For years, Bree and Penny and I lost each other completely. It was horrible. We were split up after our mother died, exiled from Bell River. And we were so confused, so angry, that we…"

Her eyes gleamed, as if they, too, brimmed with tears she was determined not to shed. "Anyhow, believe me, Tess. We know all about being alone."

And something in the way she held onto Tess, something in the wiry, hard-won courage that hummed through her body, convinced Tess as words never could. Tess knew touch. And this woman's touch was full of honesty and understanding, and the echoes of a terrible loneliness.

As her tears began to fall, Tess lifted her hands and hugged her sister back.

CHAPTER THIRTEEN

FINALLY, SATURDAY CAME. Jude had waited as long as he possibly could. Hour after hour. No matter what hard labor he involved himself in, the day had stretched out like sadistic taffy. When the spa's closing time arrived, he piled everything he needed in his truck and took off.

Getting up her porch steps was tricky. Then he had to wriggle things around a bit to get a hand free enough to knock on the door, but he managed to do it without dropping anything, thank goodness.

He didn't want her first clue that he'd arrived to be a clattering pratfall straight out of the Three Stooges.

She opened quickly, as if she had been waiting for him. Good. He'd been afraid he might have arrived too early, and she wouldn't be ready. If he'd tried to wait another second, he would have gone completely insane.

"Hi." She smiled, shyly but with feeling. That was good, too. He had wondered whether she might regret her impulsive invitation, and be sitting here secretly wishing he wouldn't show up.

"Hey," he said, as best he could around the sticks.

That made her finally notice the paraphernalia he held so clumsily in his arms, under his elbows, beneath his chin.

"What on earth?" She reached out, instinctively, wanting to help him but obviously not knowing where to begin without bringing the whole thing down like a house of cards. "What is all this?"

"It's our snowman," he said. "Or at least it's his accessories. The rest of him is lying around your yard, disguised as snow."

She squinted quizzically, as if this weren't at all what she expected, but then, as if she realized the benefits of getting outside and getting silly before...

Before whatever was to come.

She grinned. "I love it. Let me get my coat."

She wasn't gone long, not even long enough for him to get the pieces arranged on the sidewalk. But then, he had brought an absurd amount of junk.

An old top hat and a ski cap, a corncob pipe and a kazoo, a bag full of coal, carrots of all shapes and sizes, candy canes, several twigs and branches, a shovel, a broom, a pair of sunglasses, ski goggles and three pairs of colorful mittens. Oh, and a small wooden ramp.

As she skipped lightly down the steps, he stood back and surveyed the inventory. Then he glanced at her, smiling.

"I dunno. Overkill, maybe?"

She walked alongside the lineup, in her blue coat and blue beret, looking like a general reviewing the troops.

"Nope. Just perfect." She gave him a twinkling smile. "If we're making ten snowmen, that is."

He laughed. "Only one. I wanted you to have lots to choose from. This has to be the perfect snowman." He took her gloved hand. "Come on. It's getting dark. Let's start rolling."

But when he tugged, she resisted, her feet planted firmly on the ground, her pretty blue coat ruffling in the wind. He turned, and gave her a raised eyebrow. "What?"

"I haven't made a snowman before," she said, her face rosy in the last rays of daylight. "I haven't a clue how it's done."

"That's what I'm for, of course." He tugged one more time, and finally she danced along behind him. "What we are looking for is the fullest, deepest patch of snow we can find. And we don't want the fluffy stuff. We need some substance for our guy."

She probably didn't know how to tell good snow from powder, so he led her straight to the western edge of the yard, where snow had piled up against the wooden fence.

"Here," he said. "First we need a regular snowball." He bent over and scooped some snow between his hands. Instead of forming it, though, he held it out to her.

She accepted it as gingerly as if it had been an ostrich egg. Awkwardly, she began to pat it together. He got another handful and added it.

"You want to pack it tightly," he said. She nodded, and earnestly kept working the snow. Her gloved fingers pressed and molded, and she rolled the ball between her palms slowly and carefully, as if she might be graded on the perfection of its sphere.

Watching those graceful, knowing fingers, he found himself practically spellbound. When she held the snowball out and said, "What do you think?" he had to shake himself back to reality.

Good grief, Calhoun. He was probably the only man in history who got turned on watching a woman make a snowball.

Of course he'd discovered he could get turned on by almost anything this woman did.

"Okay, now this is the brawny-man part." He put the snowball on the ground and began rolling it across the snow, letting it pick up more bulk as he went. He made it big and fat, leaving trails of snowless earth crisscrossing the yard.

Finally it was big enough. "Where do you want the snowman to stand?"

She surveyed the yard thoughtfully. "Right near the door, I think. That way it's as if he's standing guard."

She probably hadn't meant to have subtext, but he knew the comment reflected a subconscious anxiety, and something inside him pinched. He made no mention of it, but rolled the first, biggest snowball to the spot she suggested. He ran his hands over it briefly, making sure it was steady on its base, and picking out the largest bits of dead grass that had been gathered up.

"Okay. Now a smaller one."

It took them longer than it should, because they kept being silly, and getting into impromptu snowball fights, and wrestling playfully until they fell over, squishing the ball they'd been trying to roll.

By the time they had the head on, they were sweaty and breathless, and the snowy man was bathed in moonlight.

Once the heavy work was done, and the finessing part started, her instincts were flawless. She brushed her fingers over the three mounds, smoothing and shaping, adding a little snow here for better balance, taking away a little there for clearer definition. She deftly picked twigs and blades of grass from the surface, until the whole man shone and sparkled.

She turned, her smile hopeful. "All good?"

"Perfect," he said, feeling breathless all over

again, but for a very different reason. He hadn't been able to stop thinking about how those nimble fingers had felt when they worked on him....

"Okay, then," he said, hoping he could cover his discomfort. "Now to give him a personality. If he's the guard, shall we give him a fierce scowl?"

"Oh, no," she said. "He has to be happy."

And so he was. Happy, in the dorkiest way possible. He wore a blue ski cap and yellow-and-blue checked mittens. His carrot nose was pointy and bent, ridiculous above his grinning-coal smile. In his hands he held not the broom or the shovel, which Tess nixed as too much like work, but the kazoo.

It would probably fall out of his twiggy fingers by dawn, but Jude didn't care. It pleased Tess to have a musical snowman.

"Oh, he needs a scarf, though, doesn't he?" She looked around, but that was the one thing Jude had forgotten. He'd practically emptied the junk box in the garage, but he hadn't brought a scarf.

"That's okay," Tess said. She unwound her own blue scarf. "This matches."

She circled the snowman's neck with the soft wool, then stepped back to admire the effect. "Perfect! Don't you think so, Jude?"

"No," he said, suddenly disturbed to see the snowman warm while she went cold. "*You* need that."

It was true. While they worked, the temperature

had dropped to a polar cold. Though they'd been too absorbed to notice, the wind had begun to bluster, making a frigid whistling sound through the eaves. Her beret had fallen off, somewhere during their silliness, and now her silky brown curls were twirling in the gusts.

The tip of her nose shone bright pink, as if it had been sunburned. Her cheeks had been scalded, too.

Suddenly the slim, bare column of her pale throat looked vulnerable, terribly exposed without her scarf. He removed the one he wore and, stepping very close, wound it slowly around her neck.

She looked up, her lips half-open, ready, anyone could see, to say a simple thank-you. But she didn't speak. Nothing escaped but warm, bewildered air.

Their gazes snagged, and he almost lost his balance, as if the ground beneath him had tilted.

One minute ago, they'd been playing. Now he was caught in a wicked thresher of desire. What had happened? Was it that she'd removed a piece of clothing, was it as simple as that?

Or was it the gradual building of tension as he watched her hands stroke and pluck and caress the mounds of snow? Was it the act of mutual creation, or the primitive bonding of braving the wind and snow together?

Whatever it was, it had him in a grip so fierce he felt it as a physical pain. He wanted her. And she wanted him. She didn't play coy. He loved that, loved that she was the kind of woman who didn't choose to misunderstand, or flutter like a caged bird confronting a cat.

He needed this…and there wasn't any time to wait. He needed to take her inside, and warm her body with his.

"Come," he said.

She nodded.

They didn't hold hands on the way in. He didn't touch her at all. He didn't dare, for fear he'd lose control and fling her onto the snow, and take her right there in the moonlight.

He didn't want it to be like that. He wanted their first time to be slow and tender…or wild, if that's what she needed. He would do anything. Be anything. He would make love to her hard, like summer thunder, or tenderly, like spring rain. Like animal or angel. Poetry, or music, or laughter, or love.

He was hers right now, laid out for her like the rows of mittens and coal, and all she had to do was tell him what she wanted him to be.

They started kissing as they reached the doorway. Her mouth was cold on the outside, but hot as flames between her lips. He explored the heat with his tongue, trying to claim that darkness so that it would forever belong to him.

While they kissed, she tugged at his coat, and felt blindly for the buttons. He fumbled for the doorknob, and prayed that she'd undress him before he died from the pain.

The bedroom was far, far away…and the sofa was so near. They stumbled toward it, peeling off gloves, thumbing free buckles and buttons, tugging at boots and struggling arms through tangled cloth.

She got him naked first, because he wore fewer layers. He managed her jeans, and the coat, and the sweater, but then he groaned with frustration as he encountered a silky white undershirt, too.

He couldn't get it off her, because she was reaching for him, skimming her fingertips down his bare stomach and finding the pulsing fire between his legs.

He groaned again, and pulled her hands away, raising them over her head, so that he could get rid of this maddening camisole. If there were a bra beneath that, he was going to have to tear the thing off…

But there wasn't. The silk whispered over her arms, and, as she reached down again, to take him between her hands, he made the white lace of her panties disappear, too.

What lies all those fancy promises had been! He wasn't laughter, or music, or rain. He was blind hunger and hot fire. He was pure need and raw passion. He slid back on the sofa, lifting her legs over his shoulders and dragging his lips down the long whiteness of her belly.

He didn't wait for a word. He felt a tiny extension of the muscles in her inner thighs, a shift of her heels on his back, as she opened for him, and that was enough. He buried his face against the moist, pulsing center between her legs, and took her into his hungry lips.

She moaned softly, and her hands dug into his hair, cupping his head as if she wanted to feel his movements that way, too. She was quiet and beautiful, and utterly honest. No theatrics or hysterics, and at the same time no hiding or holding back. Just a total surrender to every tiny sensation, and an open communication that made him imagine he could feel everything she felt.

When she twitched, his own groin pulsed. When she moaned, the sensation seeped into his blood and made it boil.

He had never encountered a woman so responsive—or so easy to read. After only a few minutes, he felt her swell and pulse under his tongue, and he knew she was ready. He rose up, and he entered her just as she exploded around him.

As she climaxed, her face was tilted back, catching a ray of moonlight that made her look as beautiful, as pure and perfect and wanton and sensual, as a woman from a dream.

His dream. The dream he'd never believed could be real.

He thrust once, twice…he tried to hold on, but

she was contracting around him with a fierce, erratic rhythm that was impossible to resist. He had no choice. One minute he was hard and driving, and the next he was collapsing over her, dissolving inside her, in a helpless, shooting fire.

TIME WAS IRRELEVANT, Tess thought, much later, as she floated in the warm darkness. They'd found where they belonged.

When they had muscles and minds that worked again, Tess had eased a few inches to the front of the sofa, giving Jude room to slide to the back. Their heartbeats slowed to normal. And they lay there still, feeling the lick and glow of the ebbing passion.

It was heaven. Naked, spooned and entwined. Arms and legs braided, her back against his chest, her feet against his shins, and his breath soft on her cheek.

She kept her eyes shut. *Forever,* she thought dreamily. She would like to stay right here, exactly like this, forever.

But she should have known better than to think the word. Fate was offended by greedy women who wanted forever when they should have been content with now.

When the room grew chilly, he got up and put a match to the logs. Almost instantly, the fire cooperated and began to blaze enthusiastically. She shut her eyes and smiled. Of course he was good at starting fires.

"What's that Cheshire-cat smile for?" He stretched out behind her again, and put his arms around her. He smelled of wood smoke, and his chest was warm.

"Nothing," she murmured sleepily. "I'm just happy."

Their bodies fit so perfectly, and the fire was mesmerizing. She shut her eyes, watching its light dance across her lids.... She lost track of time....

And then a crash exploded into the silence. The terrible, sharp shattering of glass. The chaotic clatter of things falling, hitting one another, dropping and thudding like maddened dominoes.

She jerked to a sitting position even as Jude did the same. Their eyes adjusted to the glare of the firelight slowly, so they were as blind as newborns for a few horrible seconds.

And then they smelled the burning. A log had rolled out of the fire, jarred by the collapsing end table and its contents, which had fallen into the chain-link fire screen. An edge of the beautiful quilt, lying too close, had started to burn.

"Get dressed," Jude said tightly. He had already found his jeans and started stepping into them. He put on a glove and tossed the log onto the fire. Then, picking up his shirt, he began using it to smother the quilt.

"Just put on what you absolutely need. Then call 911."

She was already fishing her phone out of her purse. Her nakedness seemed of secondary concern right now. She called 911 and gave them the basic details numbly while she stared, horrified, at the quilt.

"They're coming," she said. Then she grabbed her jeans and shoved her shaking legs into them, and buttoned them with trembling fingers. She pulled her sweater on over her bare skin, then slipped her feet, sockless, into her ankle boots. "Should we get out?"

"No." He shook his head firmly. "You don't know who's out there." Thankfully, the quilt seemed to have gone dark under his ministrations. He gathered it up and took it to the kitchen, where he dumped it in the sink and ran the faucet over it, full force.

She found his boots, and his coat, and laid them over the sofa, so that they'd be easy to slip on. Then she tried to figure out what had caused the crash.

The side window was broken into a million pieces, most of which lay on her pretty braided rug, winking evilly in the moonlight. But what had broken it? She poked carefully through the debris. Everything had fallen off the table below the window.

"Oh, no." She dropped to her knees.

Her mother's Christmas cactus had been shat-

tered. Potting soil and pieces of clay lay everywhere, half burying the broken pieces of plant.
She saw the one little red flower, and it looked so
tragic, lying there, that she felt a sudden burn behind her eyes.

Then her gaze shifted, drawn by something out
of place. Yes…that must have been what caused
the damage. With a sinking heart, she picked up a
very large, very dirty rock that couldn't possibly
have found its own way into her cabin.

Someone had thrown it through her window.
It was as big as a bowling ball, and every bit as
heavy. Whoever threw it must have been standing
on the porch. Must have been practically against
the window.

Looking in? For how long? Had they watched
while Jude and Tess made love? She felt all the
blood in her body swooping toward her stomach,
and she wondered if she might be sick. She looked
for a container, just in case. But everything close
enough to reach was broken.

Suddenly someone was pounding on the door.
"It's Deputy Bartlett. Is everyone okay in there?"

She tried to stand, but her legs wouldn't hold her.
Jude shrugged on his smoky shirt, but didn't take
time to button it. It dangled over his beautiful chest
as he walked quickly, on his bare feet, to the door.

Tess scanned the floor, irrationally worried that

he might step on glass—as if that were the most important thing to worry about right now.

And that's when she saw it.

A note, written in blood-red block letters. It was crumpled, almost domed, as if it had been wrapped around the mound of the rock. Somewhere, she thought numbly, they'd probably find a rubber band, or a piece of string, that had attached the paper to the rock.

With one half of her mind registering that Jude had opened the door and invited the deputy in, she reached out and picked up the note, trying not to think of the shadowy figure standing on the porch, watching, the rock and its message already in his hand...

She smoothed it out across her knee, and read it. It didn't take long. This time, it was only one word.

WHORE.

"I'M SORRY, DALLAS," Bartlett said. He sat on the piano stool in the parlor of Bell River, dangling his hands forlornly between his legs. "I was watching the Fillmore house. I'd been there since about four, long before dark. And I didn't see her leave. I honestly didn't see her leave."

Bartlett glanced at Tess, and she felt an ache of sympathy. He was clearly miserable. She tried to give him an encouraging smile, but wasn't sure it did much good.

"Don't worry about it, Chad," Dallas said. "Tess is okay, and they'll find Esther."

"Well, then. We obviously need something yummy to eat, right? I'm going to go raid Cookie's larder." Rowena stood, facing them with a jollying expression, as if she intended to raise their spirits by the force of sheer will. "Tess, you want to come?"

"Okay," Tess said, assuming it was what Ro wanted. They hadn't been alone yet, and Rowena undoubtedly was itching for some details about Jude.

When Dallas and the other deputies showed up at Tess's cabin, their first decision had been to move her to the ranch house. They gave her time to gather a few clothes, but that was all. She'd done whatever they asked, too poleaxed by the attack to want to stay there alone, anyhow.

Jude had gone home, to be with Molly in case the antagonism toward Tess spilled over to her illicit lover, or his family.

No one, official or otherwise, was pretending they didn't understand the "lovers" part. The scene Bartlett encountered, two half-naked people in a darkened cabin, surprised by a vandal while they were sleeping...

Didn't take Jude's rocket-scientist sister to figure that one out.

So maybe Rowena wanted to hear it straight

from Tess. Or maybe she wanted to make sure Tess was okay.

Maybe she even wanted to warn Tess about Haley Hawthorne. She might want to explain that Jude was probably still in love with the unparalleled Haley, that their estrangement was undoubtedly temporary.

At least Tess could set her sister's mind at ease there. Tess had been warned about that, long ago, by Molly.

But Dallas held out his hand. "No, Rowena. Take Penny or Bree. Heck, take Penny *and* Bree. I need to talk to Tess, and you ladies are worse than defense lawyers."

Rowena bristled, and Dallas sighed. "Ro, I'm not going to arrest anybody but Esther Fillmore. I just need enough information to nail her when we finally find her. Okay?"

Rowena made a face at her husband. "Okay, but stop bossing me around." She went over and kissed him, hard. "You're absolutely sure it's Esther, right?"

He nodded slowly. "We're sure the vandal is Esther, anyhow. She's the only suspect who can't be accounted for at home, the only one without an alibi. Her husband has no idea where she might be. Poor Alton. All these years of putting up with that mean old broad, and now this."

Tess didn't doubt Esther's guilt for a moment. She'd felt something wrong about the woman the minute she laid eyes on her, that very first day. But she noticed that Dallas was making a distinction, saying they suspected her only of the vandalism.

"What about Craig?" She didn't want to tell them how to do their work, but didn't it seem a stretch to think that there could be *two* unrelated bad guys running around Bell River in the darkness? Wasn't it almost inevitable that whoever committed one crime committed the other?

"You mean did Esther kill Marsh, too?" Dallas raised his shoulders. "Maybe. Probably. But her husband has given her an alibi for that night, so…"

"Oh, for heaven's sake!" Ro rolled her eyes. "You know what a spouse's alibi is worth!"

"Yeah?" Smiling, Dallas grabbed his wife around the waist and pulled her so close the baby belly rubbed his ear. "Would you lie to save my neck?"

"Of course not," Rowena said with fake earnestness. "But Penny would lie for Max, I bet. Wouldn't you, Penny? Of course, Max is nicer than you are. He never orders Penny out of the room when things are getting really interesting."

In spite of everything, Tess found herself smiling. The two of them were so cute—Ro with her irreverent, wild side, and Dallas so straitlaced and sensible, but so in love with his crazy wife.

Max laughed, then turned to his wife. "Penny, this is definitely not an order, but in the name of family harmony, why don't you go with Ro to find something to eat?"

Dallas shook his head and growled at Rowena. "First of all, you insufferable wench, getting food was your idea, not mine. Secondly, I'm not sure I would call having Tess's cabin vandalized and nearly set on fire 'interesting.'"

"Well, I would." Rowena's voice sounded naively innocent. "Look, we might as well see the bright side, right? Jude put the fire out, and rescued Tess, and no one was hurt. But it's very romantic, and we're about to catch the bad guy, and I find that *very* interesting."

Rowena sat on Dallas's knee and grinned at Tess. "Told you I was the reckless one."

Over on his forlorn perch on the piano stool, Bartlett didn't seem to be following the small talk. Obviously, Rowena was trying to keep the mood light until something was resolved, but he was too upset to be distracted.

"I let her get away," he said mournfully, staring at his fingers. "I thought I ought to check on Tess, but that was dumb. I knew Jude was there. I should have known he'd handle things at that end."

Rowena wiggled her eyebrows at Tess. "Nicely put, Chad."

Dallas growled again. "Hush."

"Ro, zip it." Bree shook her head. "You can't jolly us out of this yet. We have to catch the bad guy first. *Then* we make jokes and have pie."

Rowena wrinkled her nose. "Who says?"

Tossing up her hands, Bree turned to Tess with a wry smile. "Let it be noted that I tried."

From her pampered spot on the long sofa, Tess wondered if she were crazy to be a little bit happy right now. Sure, she had been the target of a vindictive, unbalanced woman who might be a killer, but she was, for the moment, cushioned in the laughing protection of her wacky, but extremely capable, family.

Family. Now that was a word she could get used to. It made even the worst things feel easier to bear. Amazing how strong you could feel when you weren't fighting alone.

And besides… She wriggled slightly on the sofa, flushing as her thoughts returned to her time with Jude. She'd had the most wonderful sex of her life.

The *only* wonderful sex of her life.

And—her temporary happiness bobbed down, like a deflating balloon—probably the *last* wonderful sex of her life.

"Don't blame yourself, Chad," Dallas said, still trying to buck up his deputy. "You didn't let her get away. She was long gone before you got the

911 call. Esther wouldn't have stuck around for a split second after she tossed the rock. She may be a lunatic, but she's not stupid."

Just then, his cell phone rang. It was like something out of a cartoon, the way everyone in the room froze in place and watched him answer.

"Garwood." He frowned. "Yes. Okay... Really." Another frown. "Well, that's all right, for now. Yes. I'll be there in ten."

The one-sided script was too cryptic to let anyone release the breath they were collectively holding. He clicked off the phone, slipped it into his jacket pocket and nudged Rowena off his knee gently.

"Gotta go," he said, putting his hands on her waist to help steady her to her feet.

"Dallas Garwood, if you leave this house without telling us what happened, I'll—" Rowena was so frustrated she couldn't even think of a good threat. "What happened? Did they find Esther?"

Dallas didn't offer his answer to Rowena. Instead he walked over and knelt down in front of Tess. Taking her hand, he gave her a bracing smile. "They found her, Tess. Eventually, she simply went home, if you can believe it. I guess she thought Alton would cover for her again. But this time, he wouldn't. They're taking her downtown, and I'm heading in to see what we can find out."

Relief washed through Tess. "I'm so glad. But did she…has she actually confessed?"

His eyes were somber. "I'm sorry, Tess. She's admitted to leaving the anonymous notes. But she absolutely swears she didn't kill anyone."

CHAPTER FOURTEEN

AT NOON THE next day, the Bell River sisters stormed downtown Silverdell.

When they reached the corner of Elk and Main, they split up into teams, Rowena with Tess, Bree with Penny. The plan was to shop at every store on the square, earning goodwill points by spending money while dropping off flyers promoting an ice-skating party tomorrow night.

Bree had complained about spending money when they clearly didn't have a nickel to spare. But Rowena had overruled the objection. With the story of Craig's as-yet-unsolved murder about to come to a head, and publicity about to rain on them like hail, it was time, she said, to present a confident, united front, so that everyone understood they had nothing to hide.

"We've hunkered down a full week now, in defensive mode. It's time to get out there and strut like winners. If we act guilty, they'll assume we are. If we act broke, they'll believe we're failing, and it will be self-fulfilling. You know how people are if they smell blood. So we strap on our armor, and fake it till we make it."

Bree had laughed, though she hadn't been immediately convinced. "But we have real issues here, Ro. Wouldn't it be better to keep a low profile until we—"

"Nonsense!" Rowena drew herself up like a queen, and stared down her nose at the very suggestion of lying low.

Tess smiled inwardly, watching them. Clearly *retreat* and *caution* were curse words in Rowena's personal dictionary.

"What issues? A secret sister is only a scandal if we act ashamed." Rowena's voice was emphatic as she laid down the law. "Even Craig Marsh's death… even that will be a lot less damaging if we make it clear we had nothing to do with it. If we hide, the grapevine goes crazy. If we come out with our heads held high, we can steer the conversation."

Finally, even the cautious Bree had been infected with Rowena's determination. "Oh, okay," she said, throwing her restraint to the wind. "You're right, darn it."

Penny and Rowena whooped out their approval, and Bree grinned. "We're sisters," she went on. "And together we're a force to be reckoned with. We're going to hold this ranch together, and if Esther Fillmore thinks she can close us down, she's got another think coming."

Penny's ordinarily gentle features were lit with the same passion. She was ready to go to war to save the ranch.

"Besides," Penny said, "you know we're not the only Dellians who dislike the irascible old bat. Let's give them a chance to line up on our side."

So here they were, launching the first skirmish of their Save Bell River campaign. Bree and Penny were to take the south side of the park—the art gallery, where Penny had plenty of friends already, as well as the coffee shop, the home-goods store, the travel agency, florist and newsstand.

Rowena and Tess took the north side—Bronson's Books, Donovan's Dream, the Grille, the Sweet Shoppe, Sterling's, the skiwear store, pet store, liquor store and tattoo parlor.

They decided to give the payday loan place a skip, because it might start rumors that they were hard up for cash. They'd cover as many businesses as they could, then meet at about one-thirty in the park.

For the finale, they'd join ranks and tackle Miller's Hardware at the eastern edge of the park. Ro practically licked her lips, eagerly anticipating that moment.

"Farley Miller is such a cowardly little creep— the sight of four ticked-off women bearing down on him will give him nightmares for years."

Though she still wrestled with guilt and anxiety,

and thoughts of Craig, lying dead behind her cabin while she packed, still haunted her too often, Tess was glad to have a mission.

Actually, she found the experience rather empowering. Her mother had been strong, in her way, but had always been more the stoic, endure-in-silence variety. She'd always been in retreat. Or maybe it was fairer to say she'd been in tread-water mode for most of her life. She'd worked ridiculously hard, but lived in fear of antagonizing anyone, of losing her job, of rocking the boat. She was eternally conciliatory, and consequently everyone had taken her for a doormat.

Tess knew her own nature was different. And here, where Rowena, Bree and Penny each brought their own unique brand of indomitable courage to the battle, she felt she could be at home.

She, too, would prefer to go down swinging—even though she'd never really understood that about herself before.

By the time they hit the pharmacy, Tess and Rowena were almost giddy with success. Predictably, word had swept through town when Esther was arrested, and Penny's calculation that the Bell River women weren't Esther's only enemies was proved one-hundred-percent true.

"I always knew Esther was jealous of your mother," the pharmacist, a late-middle-aged man with a shiny bald head and brown eyes, said conspiratorially. "You know, I wondered, sometimes, whether she had a crush on your dad."

Tess noticed a look of distaste pass fleetingly over Rowena's features, so she jumped in before Ro could lash out, ruining all their work so far.

"I'm sure it's more complicated than that," Tess said calmly. "I hope she gets the help she needs."

"Masterful," Rowena whispered appreciatively as they made their way out of the pharmacy. "You managed to point out that Esther is insane without sounding like a meanie. Well done, sis."

Tess felt happy warmth spread through her chest, even though the air was piercingly cold today. Of course, as Jude had warned her that first day, Ro was always hyperbolic, always expressing herself in extremes. Tess hadn't done anything masterful, or even particularly diplomatic.

Still, she would like to think that she had done a little something to help the situation.

"Besides, everyone automatically *likes* you." Rowena frankly scrutinized Tess from head to toe. "We should have trotted you around from the start. You make a great ambassador. You and Penny both have that adorable quality. You're like…like smart, sexy kittens. You don't prickle, the way Bree and I do."

Tess laughed with embarrassment. *Smart, sexy kittens?* Good grief!

"That's not true," she said. "You don't prickle—"

"Sure we do," Ro said, grinning. "The tiger and the ice maiden. Bree and I are definitely an acquired taste. Luckily, the right men acquired it."

Rowena tucked her arm under Tess's, as if she, too, had begun to feel the chill. They glanced across the park, trying to make out where Bree and Penny were. In summer the eye line would have been obscured by a leafy canopy, but now, with the tree limbs bare, except for the thin pines, they had a clear view.

The other women weren't immediately visible. "Well, we knew they might not keep up with us," Tess reminded Rowena. "They did expect to get delayed in the art gallery."

"Yeah. You can't pry Penny out of there with a bomb." Rowena seemed impatient, and Tess wondered whether she was getting tired. She was seven months pregnant, and though she was too feisty to admit it, she was going to hit her physical limit sooner than the rest of them.

She might have to forgo the pleasure of terrifying Farley Miller, after all.

Tess sharpened her search for the others. Surprisingly, there were a lot of people out today, given how cold it was. She kept her gaze alert for the bright pink winter coat Penny wore—it would stand out.

"Okay. Let's do one more while we wait. We can skip Donovan's, because Marianne's already playing on our team. But Bronson's Books is next, and Fanny's a big gossip, so it's important to nail her down."

"You sure you're up to it? You look tired."

"Feh. I'm a force of nature. Ask anybody." Rowena charged ahead, pushing open the bookstore door with a flourish.

Fanny, whom Tess had met casually several times in town, looked thrilled to see someone from Bell River Ranch. She hurried forward, the books she'd been shelving hugged against her chest like a child trying to contain some overwhelming emotion.

"Oh, Rowena! Tess! I'm so glad you came in. I've heard everything, of course. That terrible old woman."

Ro shrugged. "We're still waiting to hear all the facts. And while we do, we're trying to keep everyone's spirits up by having another ice-skating party. Any chance you could put a flyer in your window? Maybe leave some on the counter?"

"Of course." Fanny reached out to take the stack of flyers so eagerly Tess wondered what was behind all this chummy enthusiasm. The bookstore owner and Ro seemed on familiar terms, but not quite intimate, and yet Fanny seemed eager to pump them for details.

She sidled up to Rowena, her eyes intense and bright. "It's such perfect timing, having a community event right now. It'll be almost as if we're welcoming Haley Hawthorne home." Her gaze shifted to Tess subtly. "You knew Haley was back, didn't you? She came this morning."

Rowena's voice was studiously placid. "No, we hadn't heard. Weird. What did she come back for? Is she shooting something nearby?"

Fanny laughed. "Don't be silly. She came back for Jude!"

Tess willed her cheeks not to redden. She met Fanny's inquisitive gaze without blinking. So that part of the gossip was making the rounds, too. Fanny obviously knew that Jude had been with Tess, alone, when Esther had thrown the rock through the window.

"That's very exciting," she said with a smile, daring Fanny to contradict her. "I can't wait to meet her—she's one of my favorite actors. And I know Jude will be so glad to see her."

"He was," Fanny said, calling her bluff with those two simple words. "They were in Donovan's this morning. And he seemed very glad, indeed."

From there, as if she knew Tess's bravado had reached its limits, Ro took over the talking. Things were said, information was exchanged, but Tess didn't really hear any of it. The store felt claustrophobic, overcrowded and airless. All these millions of pages, all these biographies of dead people, horror stories, advice for the newly widowed and star-crossed lovers who ended badly…

She wasn't sure she could stay much longer. Her lungs felt clogged with dust and chemicals and ink and fear.

Finally, she felt Ro's hand under her elbow, guiding her out into the open air. She inhaled deeply, touching a lamppost, abruptly feeling the need of support.

"I need to go," she said. "I need to talk to him."

What a fool she'd been. She had told him with her body...told him how he made her feel...but she hadn't ever spoken the words. She hadn't ever said it, straight out, so that there would be no mistake.

She hadn't told him that she loved him.

Well, she'd do it now. As soon as she could find him, in front of Haley, if she had to. Maybe it was the adrenaline rush of spending the past hour as part of the Bell River army, but Tess simply could not—would not—let fear stop her.

She turned and met Rowena's somber eyes. "I have to go," she repeated.

"Why?"

Tess didn't have time to explain. Who knew what was happening right now, between Haley and Jude? She was probably trying to get him to agree to return to Hollywood.

He was free to leave if he wanted, of course. But how could he make a decision if he didn't know all the facts?

She didn't intend to beg, or apply pressure, or manipulate through guilt. Their lovemaking had been between two consenting, fully aware adults. He had made no promises, and she'd stipulated no conditions.

He might find Tess's declaration absurd. He might not even come close to feeling the same way. Haley might snicker, or worse, pity the plain young yokel who thought she had a chance against the Hollywood goddess.

But let her snicker. Tess didn't care. How much more absurd would it be to let him go off with someone else, never realizing there was even a choice to be made?

But where were they right now? Surely not the airport, not this soon.

Her hotel, maybe? Or his house? Haley and Molly were friends…maybe she'd want to say hi and see the baby.

Somehow, Tess would find him.

"Hey." Rowena jiggled her elbow, which Tess belatedly realized was still gripped by Ro's fingers. "You okay?"

"Yes," Tess said. "But I have to talk to him."

"I'm sorry." Rowena glanced at Bronson's, where Fanny's pale, round face could be seen at the window. "Haley is his… Was his… Look, no one wanted to say anything, because, well, it's none of our business. And besides, we were hoping it was over. He never speaks of her, and we thought maybe—"

"It's okay," Tess said. "I knew. I've known all along."

Rowena closed her lips, nodding soberly. She put her other hand into one of Tess's. Through their gloves, the warmth of her tight grip was kind.

"Maybe we should go home," she said.

"Yes, you should. I know you're tired. But I need to find him. There's something I need to tell him."

Rowena hesitated a moment. "Do you?" Her eyes were sad. "Don't you think he already knows?"

That stung. But Tess lifted her chin. "I hope he does, but I can't be sure. And I don't plan to just sit by meekly and hope for the best. I love him. And I'm not ashamed to tell him so, in front of anyone."

Rowena took a deep breath. "Tess…"

Tess met her gaze squarely. "Isn't that what you would do?"

After a slight pause, Rowena laughed. "Apparently you don't know about the fifteen years I lost—fifteen years I could have spent with Dallas—because I wasn't as smart as you are."

She shook her head, obviously more at herself than at Tess. Then she sighed, lifted her chin and smiled.

"Okay, then, I'll ride in Bree's car, and you take mine. Go." Rowena winked in the way Tess had come to love. "Don't let that silicone harpy take your man."

Tess wrapped her arms around Rowena and hugged as hard as she could. "Thank you."

Letting go, she whipped around, trying to remember where they'd left the cars—and instantly bumped into a small, stopped man. A stranger who stood far too close for comfort.

"Oh," she said, recoiling with an instinctive alarm. The events of the past week were still too fresh.

"I'm sorry," he said. His voice was deeper than his wizened form prepared her for. It was well modulated, educated, and, looking more closely, she realized she'd seen him before.

He was the self-effacing little man who had followed Esther Fillmore into Donovan's Dream when Tess was there with Craig.

"Mr. Fillmore?" She breathed the name tightly.

He nodded. "I didn't mean to alarm you, Miss Spencer, but I need to talk to you." His gaze moved to a spot over Tess's shoulder. "Alone."

"No way," Rowena declared. "She's with me."

"It's all right," Tess said. "Whatever you have to say to me, you can say in front of Rowena. I haven't got any secrets from her."

He smiled wanly, but it was enough to hint that once he might have been a handsome man. Tidy. Dapper. Perhaps a man of wit and humor.

"Fair enough. I don't suppose that, in a very short while, I will have any secrets, either." He inhaled raggedly, keeping his eyes on Tess. "I'm heading to the sheriff's department now, but I wanted to tell you first, because…"

Tess felt such pain radiating from him that she impulsively put her hand on his arm.

"What is it?" She tried to sound kind. He wasn't responsible for Esther's hateful actions, and she suspected that in the past twenty-four hours he'd been made a pariah along with his wife. "Whatever it is, you can tell me."

"Yes. Well. I wanted to let you know how sorry I am, Miss Spencer. My wife…she's filled with hatred and spite toward your family. But she's telling the truth when she says she didn't kill your husband."

He took a breath. "I did."

HOURS LATER—it almost felt like days—everyone had gathered in the Garwoods' warm kitchen at Bell River, where Dallas filled them in on the details of Alton Fillmore's story. Although the room was almost too small to hold them all, it was the best place to get both privacy from the staff and guests, who were all deeply curious.

Tess thought it was inspired of Rowena to have slipped an apple pie into the oven. No one was hungry, of course, but it filled the room with homey scents, a subtle reminder that not everything in their lives was darkness and death.

"Okay. So Alton tells it pretty much the way we thought," Dallas began. He sat next to Rowena, holding her hand. "He followed Esther that night, trying to make sure she didn't do anything crazy. Apparently she'd taken to spying on you, Tess, and then leaving her little notes behind. He says she didn't know he followed her. He knew he couldn't stop her obsession with the ranch, but he hoped he could keep her from going over the edge."

"Ha." Rowena's syllable held a note of quavering bravado. "Too late."

Penny and Bree nodded. Mitch had thoughtfully taken up a post next to Tess, so that she wouldn't be the only one sitting alone. It was a kind gesture, but in a strange way it only made her feel more isolated.

There was someone whose hand could give her comfort. But Jude was...somewhere else. No one seemed to be sure where.

After Fillmore's confession, when Tess realized she couldn't get free, probably for hours, she had telephoned Jude. She got the voice mail. She didn't leave a message. Declaring love face-to-face was one thing. She'd be able to read his eyes, his body language...and she'd know whether the news was welcome or not.

In a voice message, though—that felt pathetic and pointless, accomplishing nothing. He might not even listen to it, and she would never know. The brave knowledge that she loved him, the assurance that had inspired her to seek him out this afternoon, seemed to have abandoned her. Now, she was no longer sure she would tell him. And maybe she would never have the chance to even see him to decide. What if Haley had won him over and whisked him to L.A. immediately?

Tess picked up a violet polka-dotted kitchen towel and held it against her chest. Her heart ached, but with even this much cover she at least no longer felt her pain might be visible to everyone in the room.

"Anyhow, that night Marsh was out there, too," Dallas said, "and apparently he spotted Esther. What Marsh was doing out there behind the cabins, we can only speculate."

Tess shuddered, her focus intently on Dallas's story now. She could easily imagine. Craig had been creeping around in the darkness, because, like Esther, he was filled with nastiness. Hers was envy, Tess supposed, and Craig's were jealousy and greed. But all those dark emotions came from the same evil center.

"Anyhow, when Esther was gone, Fillmore says he confronted Marsh, and it got nasty. He says Marsh threatened to tell everyone Esther was leaving anonymous notes at the ranch, and Fillmore lost his temper. He says Marsh shoved him first, and he merely retaliated. He says he just wanted the man to back off."

Mitch twitched in surprise. "Alton got violent with someone half his age?"

"And twice his size." Dallas shook his head, equally incredulous. "If it really happened that way, there must have been a lot of adrenaline involved. He says Marsh lost his balance—he wasn't used to this terrain, I suppose—and fell against the rock."

"Dear God." Bree grabbed Gray's hand. "Just think how much he must love Esther, to try to defend her like that. And why? I don't get it. I mean, she's so—"

"You never know what draws people to each other," Tess said softly, thinking of the sad echoes of a younger, more confident Alton Fillmore she'd seen. "She may have been very different, once."

Rowena made a rude sound. "Sorry, Tess. I know you're a sweetheart, but I'm not going to wax sentimental about Esther Fillmore. I've known her too long. She's a nasty piece of work, and she always was."

Bree nodded, but Tess noticed that Penny, like Tess, seemed more sad than angry. She leaned her head against Max's shoulder and stared pensively at the floor.

Both the Fillmores had confessed to crimes that would make the town hate them. Even if it hadn't been murder, manslaughter would still undoubtedly mean prison.

What would become of Esther now?

"There is one more thing," Dallas said. He bent toward Rowena. "Alton told us what made Esther feel so much hatred toward your mother, and by extension, all of you. He thinks it's his fault, and I suspect it's that guilt that's made him put up with her all these years."

Rowena's eyes were very wide, the green depths reflecting the light from the chandelier overhead. She didn't speak, but those eyes were enough of a question.

"Apparently, a long time ago, Alton and your mother…" He paused, giving all of them time to understand where this was leading. "He says they were lovers."

The kitchen was as hushed as a cathedral. Suddenly Tess was intensely aware that this room was an exterior one. She imagined she could hear the wind, fretting at the door, the windows. The whole ranch house felt suddenly alive with whispers, none of them human.

"Impossible," Rowena finally said, her back very straight.

And on the surface, it seemed so. But, again, Tess remembered glimpsing the trace of a different man. A gentle man, bookish, soft-spoken and kind.

Kind enough, perhaps, to be powerfully appealing to a woman who was married to a brute.

Dallas shook his head. "If you'd been there, I think you'd believe him, Ro. When he talked about Moira, he broke down. He is mourning her still, I think."

"When was this?" Rowena turned, as if uncomfortable, and fiddled with the stove, though she merely turned the temperature up, then dialed it down again. Her energy and indignation obviously needed some outlet. "When does he say this happened?"

"Not long before she died." He took Rowena's hand and placed it against his cheek, as if he wanted to warm her fingers. "Honey, it's been killing him, all these years. He's a broken man, and not just because he lost your mother. He says the baby was his."

"Oh, my God," Bree breathed.

Tess was lost for a moment, but then she remembered what Rowena had confided the other night. Moira had been pregnant when she died, and Johnny was not the baby's father. But they had never known who was.

Until now.

For the first time since she'd met her sister, Tess saw tears on Rowena's cheeks. It was clearly too much. The years had held so many secrets, so many questions…and such an endless well of pain.

For a moment, Tess felt once again like a stranger to this group. They shared things she could barely imagine. She had known poverty, yes, and she'd lived with an aching hole where the image of "father" should have been. But tough as it was, it had been easier than this.

She sent a prayer of thanks to her mother. Her wise, gentle mother, who had recognized the poison of Johnny Wright and spared her daughter from it.

Abruptly, Rowena stood. Without explanation, she began unloading the dishwasher.

She worked quickly, bending over, straightening, sliding forks and knives into slots in nearby drawers. She used sharp, focused movements, as if getting this room tidied were the most important thing in the world. And through it all her tears continued to fall.

She held half a dozen plates against her chest when Dallas rose, and took her in his arms.

If he murmured something against her ear, it was too soft for anyone else to hear. They all sat in silence, as the ripples of grief moved through the room. For a minute, Tess thought she ought to leave. It seemed so private...so deeply personal to these women who were suffering anew the loss of their mother.

Their mother. A woman who had been wronged by Tess's mother. Tess shouldn't be here.

She stood. "I'll—I'll be back in a minute," she

said. No one seemed to notice. She turned, reaching for the door.

She pulled open the door as Jude was about to knock. Her mouth dropped open in surprise, as she saw him standing there, backlit by the moonlight, his knuckles poised to rap.

"Tess." He smiled.

She would have smiled, just to show she could, just to show there were no hard feelings and her heart wasn't broken... But she couldn't. She was still in a strange state of half shock, with the echoes of that sad, sweet voice in her ears.

His smile faded. "Tess? Is everything okay?"

"Hey, cowboy, it's cold out here." Over Jude's shoulder, a beautiful, pale oval of a face appeared. "Let's get inside and thaw out!"

Tess looked at the beautiful, impatient woman. It was Haley Hawthorne. He'd brought Haley here, to Bell River.

She stepped aside, and Haley rustled in, red lips, glowing eyes, golden hair. She trailed perfume and expensive scarves and glamor. She waved her hand at the group. "Hi, everybody! I'm back!"

Jude entered more slowly, his gaze on Tess. "Is everything all right?" he asked again. But she shook her head. What words could adequately answer that question?

"Jude!" Haley turned, both teasing and accusing. "The least you can do is introduce me."

Giving Tess one last, sober glance, Jude moved in to oblige. He went around the room, reminding Haley who everyone was. Dallas, Mitch and Gray seemed to be the ones she remembered best. That made sense, of course, as the Wright sisters had left Silverdell when their mother died, and hadn't returned until a couple of years ago, when Haley was in L.A.

Finally, Jude came around to Tess, the only one standing outside the circle.

"And this is Tess Spencer," he said. "Tess, I'd like you to meet Haley Hawthorne."

Haley's eyes lit up, as if she could turn on an internal glamour glow at will. "This is *Tess?*"

Jude nodded.

Haley smiled, and for the first time a little of her blinding wattage dimmed. She held out her hand, rather than enveloping Tess in a big Hollywood hug, as she'd done with the others.

"I'm glad to meet you, Tess," she said. "You're a very lucky woman."

I am? Tess almost said the words out loud, but she stopped herself in time. Instead she mouthed the commonplace phrases. *Good to meet you, too. I've admired your work.*

Haley nodded, as if they'd actually had a serious conversation instead of a collection of disjointed, awkward platitudes. Then she turned to Rowena, the Hollywood glow once again in place.

"So Jude tells me that all the stuff that's happened around here lately might cause some problems at the ranch."

Rowena glanced at Jude.

"Yes," she said, frankly. Rowena was always frank, Tess knew, even in front of glamorous strangers. "We thought we'd managed to shed the past, but all this has raked it up again. But that's okay. We'll figure it out. We rose above it once, and we can do it again."

"Of course you can," Haley said blithely, waving a beautifully manicured hand. "It's a magnificent ranch, and Jude tells me you run a tight ship. I thought maybe you could use a little help."

Rowena was openly bristling now. "If you mean money, we're not—"

"Oh, God, not money," Haley said, laughing. "I'm talking about something much better than money. I'm talking about *buzz.*"

Rowena frowned. "I think buzz is what we have too much of, Haley."

The starlet trilled with amusement. "There's no such thing as too much buzz. You just need the right kind. I was thinking I might stay in Silverdell for a few days, and I'd like to bring some friends. Would you have room to put us up, do you think?"

So she was staying....

Tess looked away, toward the door, as if she'd like to escape. But she couldn't. She couldn't bring herself to leave. And so she returned her gaze to Haley and Rowena.

Rowena narrowed her eyes. "How many friends?"

"Maybe…" Haley pretended to count on her fingers, then gave up, laughing again. "Maybe exactly however many rooms you need to fill. And these are people who talk. I mean, you know, talk to the press, talk on social media. A lot. They'll all go home excited, spreading the word about the amazing Bell River Ranch."

Rowena shook her head slowly. "Why would you do this for us?"

"Well…" Haley rested her hand on Jude's arm.

Tess had to look away, because the intimate gesture sent a tiny dagger of hot pain through her chest.

"You see," Haley explained, "I thought I might be taking Jude with me to California, but apparently that's not going to happen."

The two of them exchanged a look that Tess couldn't quite interpret. But he wasn't going to California. That, at least, was good. That was something.

Or was it? Maybe it would be easier to make a happy life in Silverdell if he weren't always around to remind her.

"So I figure I might as well do something good, as long as I'm here, right?" Haley beamed. "Redeem myself a little bit?"

Jude frowned, and she patted his arm, laughing. "Don't worry. I'm not dreaming that I can fix things between us that easily." She gave Tess a sly, teasing glance. "*Or ever*. As they say, I'm pretty sure that ship has sailed."

Tess looked at Jude. What ship? What did Haley mean?

Tess felt an almost sickening lurch of hope but she tried to smother it before it could take hold. It would be harder to hope and be wrong than never to hope at all.

"Rowena," Jude said, without taking his eyes off Tess. "You think you and Haley might be able to work out some of the details while I talk to Tess? You don't need us for this part, do you?"

Rowena glanced at Tess. "It's okay with me if it's okay with Tess."

Jude moved away from Haley and stood inches from Tess. She couldn't help noticing that Haley followed him with eyes that held a shadow of sadness.

"Is it okay with you, Tess? It's cold, but will you come outside with me?"

She nodded. "All right," she said, though her heart was beating so high in her throat she could hardly form words.

He grabbed her coat, then took her hand and led her out of the house into the night. And suddenly it was as if they were the only human beings in the whole world. An utter silence descended.

The night twinkled with starlight and with glinting snow, and he was right. It was very, very cold.

He took off his scarf and draped it over her hair, knotting it loosely at her throat. He let his hands drop to her shoulders, and gazed into her eyes. He was so beautiful, she thought, aching from the memory of that face above hers, that naked body covering her with its hard, velvet warmth.

Beside him, even Haley looked ordinary.

"I thought you were going back to her," she said. "I thought you were leaving."

"No." He didn't smile. Whatever had happened, it had caused him pain. Tess could feel it in his hands, and the gentle way they cupped her shoulders, as if he couldn't bear to cause any more pain to anyone tonight.

"In her heart, she knew I wouldn't," he said. "I'd told her so a hundred times, but she couldn't quite let go. I don't think she believed me, even now. Not until I told her about you."

She swallowed, and the motion hurt, because something jagged was lodged in her throat. "What about me?"

"That I love you."

She made a strange sound, partway between a gasp and a cry. After that, she didn't trust herself with words.

"I know it's happened fast," he said. "Too fast, given what you've been through. I know you're still confused, about Craig, about the baby. About your father, also, I guess. I don't expect you to be ready to say you love me, too."

She gazed at him. She heard the words, but she couldn't quite believe this wasn't a dream.

"I don't mind waiting," he went on. "We'll take it slow. I know you have to think about what's best for the baby. I understand that, but I know—" his voice carried a husky undercurrent of emotion "—I know that it's me. I'm what's best for you, and for the baby, and I hope someday you'll see that, too. I don't care how long it takes. I'll make the baby mine, if you'll let me. I'll make you happy, both of you, if you'll let me. Your child will never know a day without a father's love."

"But..." She struggled to understand. "What happened? I mean, to you and Haley? Molly said... everyone said...that you two have loved each other since you were children."

"It's over." His eyes grew dark. "But I'll tell you, if you really want to know."

"I do," she said. "It's so hard to believe that she... that I—"

He put his fingers over her lips. "I understand."

She nodded. She would let him tell it his way, at his own pace.

He took a minute to start, as if organizing his

thoughts. "I don't know if I loved her," he said finally. "But I certainly wanted to protect her. Her father was a drug addict, and he did unspeakable things. I was her bodyguard, her confidant, her chauffeur, her paycheck… I was whatever she needed. I guess it felt normal, because after my father died I was more or less all that for my sisters, too."

He smiled ruefully. "Mitch says I have a white-knight complex. I think he may be right. I wanted to help her because she was broken. I went to Los Angeles, although I knew I belonged here, because it was her dream, and she was afraid to go alone."

Tess tried to imagine that glittering beauty she'd met being afraid of anything. It wasn't easy. "What happened in L.A.?"

"The usual story. She was ecstatic, and she was a big hit. It was obvious she'd make it, and it went to her head. Success brought out all kinds of…aspects of her personality that I'd never known were there. Parts of her I simply couldn't understand… much less love."

"How? Was she unfaithful?"

"I don't know." Shockingly, he didn't seem concerned, as if that part were a technicality. "What I do know is that, about a year ago, she found out she was pregnant, and she was absolutely horrified. She nearly had a breakdown, she was so undone by the thought of being tied down, of giving up all the opportunities that were starting to come her way."

Tess opened her mouth, but she didn't know what to say. She thought of the small, invisible life she held inside, and wondered how anyone could not welcome such a miracle. On a very deep level, she had rejoiced in her pregnancy, even while it terrified her. Even while she despised the baby's father.

But if her child's father had been Jude...

"What did she do?"

"She wanted to get rid of it. When I told her I'd leave her if she did, she—" He smiled, a twisted, unhappy thing. "She went wild. Wild enough to leave her marks on my back. I think it's possible that she would have liked to kill me."

Tess's fingertips tingled, remembering the shape and path of those scars, as she clutched his back and cried out in her moment of blissful, physical release. How could anyone have inflicted those wounds on him in anger?

"And the baby? Did she—"

"No. She miscarried a week later. I don't blame her for that. It happens. But she was so relieved to see our child disappear like that...."

He shut his eyes briefly. When he opened them, Tess saw the pain and reached up her hand, as if she could take the hurt away.

"Whatever I'd felt for her, or tried to feel for her, whatever I'd been hanging onto—whether it was

love, or a white-knight pathology, or just infatua-
tion—it was over."

She felt an ache inside that was a reflection of
his. It was as if they shared whatever organ this
agony resided in.

"You never told anyone, though. No one knows
what happened."

"Why would I tell? I don't want to hurt her. I
would like to think she's learned from what happened, that someday she'll find a relationship that's
not quite as unhealthy as ours was."

He glanced toward the house. "I suspect that,
much as I did with Molly, I let her use me as a
crutch too long. It would have been better for us
both if I'd pulled away years ago. She'll grow up
now, because she's ready—and because she'll have
to. I'd even like to think that her gesture in there,
trying to help the ranch, is one way of showing
she's ready to change."

How could he be so forgiving? And yet…wasn't
it one of the things she loved most about him? He
was a protector, a guardian.

A good guy.

"Jude," she said softly, though it made her heart
burn to speak these words, "have you considered
the possibility that maybe I'm just another broken
thing you want to fix? Maybe this isn't love, either.
You saw me sick. You saw me afraid. Maybe the
healer in you simply—"

"No." He spoke the word with passion. "I told myself that, at first. I warned myself that was all it was. I think the power of my feelings—and how fast they overpowered me—scared me, a little. I was determined not to make the same mistake again."

"Of course," she said gently. She had been afraid of it, too. After Craig....

"But you're not broken," he said vehemently. "I don't heal you, Tess. You heal me."

"Heal you?" She shook her head. "If you mean just your leg, your back...anyone could—"

He laughed, lifting her in a sudden, swirling embrace. Overhead, the stars swam dizzingly.

"No, my love, I'm not in the habit of marrying women to get a free massage. I get my massages free anyhow, remember?"

She smiled. *My love,* he'd said. *My love.* The stars above them seemed to multiply, and glow brighter, as the words floated up and mingled there.

"Oh, that's right," she said solemnly. "Perks of the job. I must have forgotten that."

He eased her slowly to the ground, but kept her tight against his chest.

"I mean you *heal* me. You complete me. We speak the same language, Tess. We see the world the same way. But it's so much more, too. You heal my heart, and you heal my soul. I take strength from your smiles and your kindness, and solace from your body. I believe in love, because of you. I believe in life, because of you."

Amazingly, she knew he was telling the truth. She knew, because if she'd been asked to describe what finding him had done for her, she would have said exactly that.

In that instant, she took the stars into her heart, and felt their light fill her with joy.

"So will you give me a chance? I'm just a carpenter, and I don't ever want to be anything more than that. But will you take me, for all that? Will you let me show you, day by day, just how much I love you, Tess?"

"I will," she said softly. "With all my heart, I will. And if you'll hurry up and fix that window on my cabin, my beautiful carpenter, I'll let you start showing me tonight."

CHAPTER FIFTEEN

One month later
Valentine's Day

"Hurry. Get that door." Dallas, dressed in his sheriff's uniform, looked pretty impressive as he shoved his way through the emergency room of Silverdell Memorial Hospital, his arm wrapped around his wife.

Impressive, that is, until you looked in his eyes and saw the naked panic there.

Tess, who was carrying the Lamaze bag, glanced at Rowena.

Her sister was grinning.

"Men," Ro said, rolling her eyes.

And Tess smiled, too.

"Yep," she agreed, but in her heart she hoped that Jude would be every bit as precious and panicked, when her time came. She twisted the small, sparkling diamond she wore on her left hand, knowing she'd have to set a date soon. She was four months pregnant now, and she wanted Jude to attend the birth in his official, legally sanctioned role as Daddy.

Two weeks ago, Molly and Beeba had moved to Chicago, where they seemed to be loving Flora's cushy, well-heeled life, though they were already holding their collective breath, waiting to hear a wedding date so they could fly to Silverdell.

Jude missed them, but Tess knew he was happy that Molly felt strong enough to start building her own life. And happy that she was a thousand miles from her abusive ex.

Jude had already begun work on their nursery. And, in his workshop stood an exquisite walnut cradle, with a curved swan's head, waiting for the child that someday would sleep in its sheltering basket.

But first they had to see Rowena's baby safely into the world.

The others were on their way to the hospital, having been called from their various posts around the ranch. Tess had driven with Ro and Dallas, because she'd been first on the scene.

She and Rowena had been together, cleaning up the remnants of Bell River's first annual Valentine's Day party, when Ro had plopped onto a dining room chair, and emitted a low, moaning sound.

"What?" Tess had abandoned two half-empty

flutes of pink champagne and bent over her sister, worried. "What?"

"I think it's time." Rowena had looked at Tess sheepishly. "I've been having contractions for about four hours. I was determined to get through the party first."

While Tess recovered from the shock, Ro took a deep breath and rubbed her belly. "The party was such a success, wasn't it?" She brushed a sprinkle of pink-and-red confetti from her skirt. "It was so worth it. Of course, Dallas is going to kill me."

Now the contractions were only a minute apart— and Dallas was far too busy having his own nervous breakdown to take time to scold his wife. He was arguing with the receptionist in the E.R., a middle-aged bottled blonde who apparently had seen too many women in labor to think she had to jump up and stop the presses.

Her phlegmatic insistence on spelling Rowena's name correctly was apparently driving Dallas mad.

Rowena listened patiently for a few minutes, then apparently got bored. "Tess, if I forget, please remember to tell Bree about the interview for the new head wrangler. It's Tuesday—"

Rowena widened her eyes as a new contraction started. She started to pant slightly, which actually made Tess feel a little panicky, too. Pant-blow wasn't supposed to start till much, much later.

Rowena screwed up her face, still trying to track down her mental notes about the interview. "I can't remember. Is it Tuesday at three o'clock?"

"Ro, forget the wrangler. Breathe."

The doors swished open behind them, letting in a spiral of cool air. Bree, Gray, Penny, Max, Ellen, Alec and Jude all swept in, dominating the little emergency room like the official Rowena Garwood Army.

"How is she?"

"How close are the contractions?"

"Ro, are you okay? What on earth is wrong with you, waiting all through that stupid party?"

"It wasn't a stupid party," Rowena insisted with vigor. She glared at Bree. "It was fabulous, and a reporter from Crested Butte was there, and he's going to write about it, so we'll get all kinds of publicity."

"We don't need publicity," Bree declared irritably. "We've got more guests than we can handle already." She glanced toward Jude, a one-sided smile on her lips. "When Haley sets out to make amends, she doesn't fool around."

Jude hooked Tess's thickening waist with one arm, and scooped her in for a kiss.

"Hi, good-looking," he said with that sexy grin that always made her knees go weak. "Taking notes?"

Tess laughed. "Yes. My first note is when I go

into labor, plan on getting someone else to finish the stupid party."

Rowena growled. "You guys are such sissies." Then she grimaced and began panting once again. She raised her voice slightly. "Dallas, tell them it doesn't matter how they spell my name. I'm pretty sure it's show time."

That was all he needed. Dallas stalked to the receptionist and leaned over the counter as if he'd like to grab her shirt and shake her. No one heard his words, but the body language said that if she didn't get the doctor on the phone, and put Rowena into a bed in the next thirty seconds, he'd jump behind the counter and do it himself.

Bree, Penny and Tess all exchanged smiles. Alec laughed and pointed. "Dad's about to blow a fuse, for sure," he said. "Ellen, look. I told you he'd go nuts."

Behind her, Tess heard the electronic doors rustle open one more time. She turned, stupidly surprised. She'd almost forgotten they weren't the only patients in the world tonight. Well, at least this newcomer would get prompt attention. Dallas had scared all the jaded apathy out of that woman behind the counter.

A man in a wheelchair rolled into the room. Handsome, and surprisingly imposing, given the wheelchair, he was probably just this side of sixty, dark-haired, with blazing green eyes. In fact, except for the chair, he looked like one of the healthiest, most athletic people Tess had ever seen.

"I'm looking for Rowena Garwood," he said. Oddly, he said it to Tess, as if he already knew she was part of Rowena's entourage.

Tess instinctively moved in front of him to muffle his words. Though she sensed movement behind her, as orderlies settled Rowena in a wheelchair and scooted her to maternity, she didn't turn around.

Dallas was busy. So Tess was the guard dog now. She had no idea who this guy was, and she had no intention of letting anyone upset Rowena tonight.

"She's a little busy," she said politely. "In fact, she's just been taken to a room."

"Oh." He looked disappointed, his raven-black, dramatically arched eyebrows diving together over an aquiline nose. "I had hoped I'd get here in time. Do you think someone could get a message to her? I'll wait, however long it takes. But I'd like her to know I'm here."

His confident, authoritative tone was curious. Tess studied the man more carefully. He looked familiar, in some mildly disconcerting way. She knew she'd never met him before. But those green eyes, that forceful, elegant bone structure, that air of natural command and impressive, barely contained energy…

"I'll let her know," she said slowly. "And who shall I tell her—"

"I'm Dr. Rowan Atherton," he said. He drew himself up straighter in his chair, and Tess thought maybe she recognized a hint of nervousness in his eyes. It didn't seem to belong there, as if very few things ever left this man ill at ease.

"Atherton," Tess repeated, to be sure she had it right.

"Yes." Finally, he smiled.

And in a lightning flash of recognition, Tess knew why he seemed so familiar. *Oh. Ro,* she thought, her heart almost bursting with joy. *Oh, Ro. You sent the letter, didn't you? And he's here. He's here.*

"Atherton," she said again, grinning.

"Yes. Atherton," he repeated with another of those charismatic, indescribably sweet and dynamic smiles, as if he found her confusion amusing.

"I'm her father."

* * * * *

LARGER-PRINT BOOKS!
GET 2 FREE LARGER-PRINT NOVELS PLUS
2 FREE GIFTS!

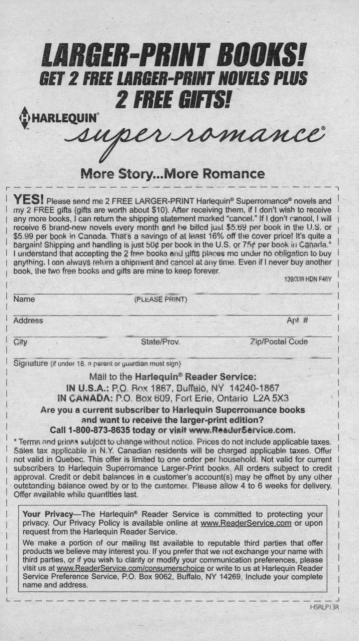

HARLEQUIN®

super romance®

More Story...More Romance

LARGER-PRINT BOOKS!

HARLEQUIN *Presents*

PASSION GUARANTEED SEDUCTION

GET 2 FREE LARGER-PRINT NOVELS PLUS 2 FREE GIFTS!

YES! Please send me 2 FREE LARGER-PRINT Harlequin Presents® novels and my 2 FREE gifts (gifts are worth about $10). After receiving them, if I don't wish to receive any more books, I can return the shipping statement marked "cancel." If I don't cancel, I will receive 6 brand-new novels every month and be billed just $5.05 per book in the U.S. or $5.49 per book in Canada. That's a saving of at least 16% off the cover price! It's quite a bargain! Shipping and handling is just 50¢ per book in the U.S. and 75¢ per book in Canada.* I understand that accepting the 2 free books and gifts places me under no obligation to buy anything. I can always return a shipment and cancel at any time. Even if I never buy another book, the two free books and gifts are mine to keep forever.

176/376 HDN F43N

Name	(PLEASE PRINT)	
Address		Apt. #
City	State/Prov.	Zip/Postal Code

Signature (if under 18, a parent or guardian must sign)

Mail to the Harlequin® Reader Service:
IN U.S.A.: P.O. Box 1867, Buffalo, NY 14240-1867
IN CANADA: P.O. Box 609, Fort Erie, Ontario L2A 5X3

**Are you a subscriber to Harlequin Presents books
and want to receive the larger-print edition?
Call 1-800-873-8635 today or visit us at www.ReaderService.com.**

* Terms and prices subject to change without notice. Prices do not include applicable taxes. Sales tax applicable in N.Y. Canadian residents will be charged applicable taxes. Offer not valid in Quebec. This offer is limited to one order per household. Not valid for current subscribers to Harlequin Presents Larger-Print books. All orders subject to credit approval. Credit or debit balances in a customer's account(s) may be offset by any other outstanding balance owed by or to the customer. Please allow 4 to 6 weeks for delivery. Offer available while quantities last.

Your Privacy—The Harlequin® Reader Service is committed to protecting your privacy. Our Privacy Policy is available online at www.ReaderService.com or upon request from the Harlequin Reader Service.

We make a portion of our mailing list available to reputable third parties that offer products we believe may interest you. If you prefer that we not exchange your name with third parties, or if you wish to clarify or modify your communication preferences, please visit us at www.ReaderService.com/consumerschoice or write to us at Harlequin Reader Service Preference Service, P.O. Box 9062, Buffalo, NY 14269. Include your complete name and address.

HPLP13R

Reader Service.com

Manage your account online!

- Review your order history
- Manage your payments
- Update your address

*We've designed
the Harlequin® Reader Service
website just for you.*

Enjoy all the features!

- Reader excerpts from any series
- Respond to mailings and special monthly offers
- Discover new series available to you
- Browse the Bonus Bucks catalog
- Share your feedback

**Visit us at:
ReaderService.com**

RS13